Elle Klass
Scarlett
Evan's Girls
Book 1

I0586525

Copyright © 2017 by Elle Klass
Published by Books By Elle, Inc.
All rights reserved
ISBN: 978-0-9992504-2-6
Cover art created by TL Katt
Editor Dawn Lewis Bookmarks
Editing

Author's Disclaimer

Dedication

I dedicate this series to all the readers of the Ruthless Storm Trilogy. It was their inquiry of the girls that made this series possible. I enjoyed writing Scarlett and discovered so much about her while doing it. Thank you!

Books to look forward to in the Evan's Girls series

Emily

Debbie

Chelsea

Felicia

Chrissy

Eden

Erica

I was Evan O'Conner's first victim. Nov. 5, 1954, at 7:01 p.m. I entered the world, unwanted and uncherished. My mother was raped at 15 by Evan's grandfather. Distraught and full of hate. A hate I now understand. She gave me up and I spent my tender years in foster care.

At age 17, I met my biological sister, Philmonia, born from the same father. Young and naïve I thought I'd finally found family. She was married to a wealthy man, Evan O'Conner Sr. They promised me a fairy tale life. I swooned and fell into their trap. My princess life was stopped short and became my prison.

They perpetrated unspeakable crimes against me. The worst was inseminating me with the sperm that gave life to a monster that grew inside me. I tried to abort the fetus but he clung to my uterus like a leech. The demonic seed grew and grew inside my womb for nine months. The monster's fingers clawed against my insides. His feet kicked against my bladder and his soul ate at my heart, turning it black with hate. The little demon ball of cells clung inside me, refusing my wishes until he was ready. He was in control even then. My hate deepened each day for the devil inside me.

A child created by lust and scientific experimentation developed into a monster so cruel, so vile he'll never be forgotten.

When my contractions started I pushed with everything I had to force him out of me. Finally I shed the little beast. My sister and her husband took the screaming, bald creature and held him with amazement while I shivered in relief. The little beast became the most renowned serial killer in history – The Hurricane Killer.

My name is Scarlett Jones and this is my story.

Part 1
The Purple Mask

Chapter 1
Pseudo

April 1959 5 years old

The sunny day in April carried a light breeze as I jumped off the last step on the bus. No sign that the hot summer was approaching quickly. My blue apron skirt bounced with the spring in my step and my saddle shoes beat against the pavement as I ran towards my mommy waiting at the front door.

She leaned down, her skirt brushing the cement walkway and wrapped her arms around me. "Hi, baby."

"Hi, Mommy. Look what I made today," I said with pride as I lifted a large purple paper butterfly from my backpack.

"Oh, isn't that beautiful," she said with surprise in her voice. "Let's hang that in your room, shall we?"

"Yes, yes," I agreed and rushed toward my room. The white walls garnered many butterflies of every color and size. My twin bed had a lavender comforter covered with purple and white butterflies and lavender curtains hung across the windows. My room was a haven made of my favorite color – purple. I stood by the spot where I wanted Mommy to hang my new butterfly.

She entered the room, her yellow skirt flounced at her knees with each step she took. Her dark hair tied up in a ponytail and her bright brown eyes smiled at me. "This is where you want it?"

"Uh huh."

She took a thumbtack and pinned the butterfly to the spot I pointed at. "There you are. We'll show Daddy when he gets home." Her smile large and full of love.

"OK," I said, bouncing into the kitchen for my after school snack.

The sun lowered in the sky and Daddy came home. As soon as I heard the door open I rushed toward him and he scooped me into his thick arms filled with tickling hair. "How was your day?" he asked, his hazel eyes beamed with joy and sparkled in the setting light of the sun. His blond hair slicked back against his oval head.

"Good. I want to show you what I made."

"I must see it," he said in mock surprise.

"Mommy hung it in my room."

He hoisted me over his head and sat me square on his shoulders as we headed down the hallway. He entered the room.

"Do you see it, Daddy?" I asked.

"No," he said spinning around and making me dizzy. "Is it here?" he asked, stopping and pointing to an old butterfly.

I giggled. This was our routine. "No, Daddy."

He spun again, then asked again before he settled on the new one.

"It's just gorgeous, almost as pretty as you – my little butterfly." He lowered me.

I smiled a partially toothless smile. "I love you, Daddy."

"I love you. Hmm… where is my other love?" he said, asking about Mommy.

"I think she's finishing dinner."

He widened his eyes. "Oh, let's sneak up on her," he said, tiptoeing down the hallway and placing a finger over his mouth.

I stifled a chuckle and followed on my tiptoes. We peeked around the corner and Mommy gazed our way. "Oh, what do we have here?" she said, her eyes wide as if in surprise.

I giggled and Daddy wrapped his arms around her, planting a kiss on her lips.

It was a Friday and Genevieve, our elderly neighbor, came over about seven p.m. as always so my parents could enjoy date night. I couldn't pronounce her name so I called her

Gen. She wore her white hair in a bun and had kind blue eyes.

When the bell rang I rushed toward it and flung the door wide open. "Don't you look pretty," she said.

"Thank you," I answered, spinning in my purple nightgown.

"Genevieve, come in," voiced my daddy.

She stepped inside and took a seat with me at the kitchen table. I had the cards already out and waiting. I so enjoyed Friday nights and our card games, which she usually let me win.

My parents kissed my head and walked out the door.

Gen's blue eyes gazed into mine. "One day you will do something great. Very few people have eyes like yours and they give you a special oomph that others don't have."

I smiled. Gen loved my eyes. One was green and the other amber. She and my parents agreed that I was something superior like a fairy. They insisted my eyes gave me special powers.

After an hour of cards Gen tucked me into bed. "Goodnight, Scarlett," she whispered, planting a gentle kiss on my cheek.

I woke up hours later to a large commotion in the house and the sound of Gen crying. Scared and worried, thinking Gen was hurt, I jumped out of bed and scurried down the hallway, halting at the end of it. A police officer dressed in uniform sat beside Gen on the couch. She was OK but where were my parents?

My heart thumped against my ribcage. Another officer walked into the house, his eyes rested on me.

"How are you?" asked the officer. His mustache moved up and down with the motions of his mouth. He steadily walked towards me as I backed down the hallway. Flashes of fear and unidentifiable blood-smeared images rattled my mind.

"I need you to come with me," he said, getting closer with his hand out. I gazed into his dark eyes. There was no sparkle inside them. My heart beat faster when he took another step. Remembering the games I played with Daddy, I side-stepped him. His hand grabbed for mine when I slid underneath his legs, ran as fast as my two small feet carried me and jumped onto Gen's lap. Wrapping my arms around her neck, I clung for my life.

I don't know what scared me so much, but an ominous sensation entered my gut and I knew my life was about to change for the worse. I should have woken up to Mommy and Daddy giggling not Gen's sobs and two unknown people in my house. They wore badges but to me they were strangers.

"Shhh… Scarlett," Gen soothed as I scrambled to plaster myself against her.

"She has to come with us," said the officer in a deep voice.

"She's a little girl and confused. I will go with her," Gen said, her arms wrapped around my trembling body.

"Suit yourself," the deep-voiced officer huffed.

"Where's Mommy and Daddy," I whispered in Gen's ear.

"Oh, Scarlett. You sweet baby. Your mommy and daddy…" she choked back a sob, "they aren't coming home."

I traced the flowered pattern on the couch with my finger as her words sunk in. "Why not?" I asked, my brows furrowed.

"They've gone to heaven," Gen responded in a gentle voice as she caressed the back of my head.

I didn't really understand. "Without me?"

Gen took a deep breath. "Yes but it wasn't their choice. Their time on Earth has passed but you still have a job to do." She lifted the hair above my ear and whispered, "Remember, one day you will do something magnificent."

I leaned back, still planted on her lap and looked into her blue eyes. "Because my eyes give me special powers."

"Yes," she chuckled, "because of your eyes."

Hand in hand with Gen I walked out of my home, never to return, and climbed into the back of the police car.

There were many things that happened within those few moments that I wouldn't understand until a few years later.

Chapter 2
Eye Opener

Two years later

I was placed into a home for abandoned and orphaned children. Gen visited every so often for two years than never returned. My heart broke; she was the light in my life, my reason for living. Every day my heart ached for my parents. They loved me and my memories of them are burned into my heart with love.

"Hey, funk eyes," quipped Michelle, "no one will ever want you with those funky eyes. You'll be an orphan forever." She stood in front of me with her legs forming a wide V, preventing me from swinging. Her brown hair hung like limp spaghetti. She was my age, but much larger than me.

I stared at her, trying to tap into the special powers that existed in my eyes. I imagined telekinetically flinging her backwards into the concrete school. Her broken body sliding against it and puddling on the cement playground. I understood full well my eyes didn't really have any special powers but I enjoyed pretending they did.

"You're in my way," I said.

"Make me move," she grunted.

I would if I could. A kickball rolled beside us and she left her stance long enough to lean down and grab the ball. I pushed hard and forced the swing as high as I could make it go in the few seconds I had. It whooshed past her, knocking her to the ground.

"Funk eyes," she sneered, dusting the dirt from her dress.

Ignoring her comment, I continued pumping the swing for the rest of recess. Michelle wasn't the worst. I only had to see her at school. At the home, Dana made it her life's purpose to destroy me. Within the week the home had taken in a few more children, placing Dana and I in the same room. It was small, with barely enough room for the two beds and one tall dresser.

"Catch," shouted Dana as she threw her backpack at me and slid onto the bench school bus seat beside me. The heavy bag felt as though it was loaded with bricks. I pushed it toward her. Since I had to share a room I had to put up with being her mental punching bag. But I had a plan to at least keep my peace with her. She deplored kitchen duty so I volunteered to take her share of kitchen chores.

I loved the kitchen but was sure not to tell her that. It was far better for her to think she had me under her thumb.

Dana's hefty bag took up the space between us on the bus and she sat with her legs in the aisle so she could talk with the other students. Everyone knew we were the orphan kids but she played like she was something more and vied for popularity. She was pretty, with her long, straight, dirty-blonde hair, oval face, and deep blue almond-shaped eyes.

The bus rolled to a stop and Dana stood. "Can you get that?" she asked, pointing to her brick-laden backpack.

I smiled, stood and hefted the bag over my shoulders. The bag hit her in the side, knocking her into the seat on the other side of the aisle.

Her blue eyes glared at me and shot bullets into mine. "Watch it!" she screamed.

I didn't say a word, certainly not an apology; after all, I meant to do it. She thought much of herself and I was a couple years younger and only weighed forty-five pounds but I was smarter than her. I marched off the bus, one step behind her. She stopped abruptly and I almost fell backwards from the weight of her bag but the boy behind me caught the bag, evenly distributing the weight so I caught my balance.

I went straight to the room and dropped her weapon of a backpack onto her bed then jaunted straight to the kitchen. I loved it there as we were the first to taste any treats. I wrapped the smallest apron around myself. It was a couple sizes too big so I had to wrap the strings all the way around and tie it in the front and the bottom hung just above my ankles.

Today's treat was homemade brownies and milk. I piled them onto a plate while Mario, another orphan, grabbed the milk and a stack of cups. I left the innermost brownies in the pan and winked at him. He winked in response as we carried the snack to the others in the dining hall.

Once we dropped it off and served the others we ran-walked back to the kitchen for our brownies, the moistest in the pan.

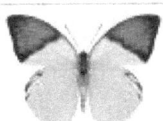

Later that night, after dinner and clean up, I sat with the others as we watched The Andy Griffith Show and took turns bathing. We didn't get baths nightly since there were only two bathrooms and a limited amount of hot water. The ladies put us on a schedule according to room assignment. Tonight was mine and Dana's night as well as a couple other kids.

Dana strolled out of the bathroom after her fifteen minutes was up with a brush in her hand. She slicked down her wet hair as she took a seat beside me. "Your turn," she smirked.

"Dana, no brushing in the family room," scolded Moira, one of the ladies who ran the place.

"Yes ma'am," she said, seething under her breath and following behind me as I entered the bedroom to grab my bundle of night clothes.

She dropped her brush onto the dresser which she'd taken over. I had nothing on top of it and one drawer at the bottom to put my clothes in. I didn't have many materialistic items anyways, mostly I had memories of the butterflies on my wall and my two beautiful parents.

Not wanting to miss anymore TV Dana scurried out the door without saying a word. I headed towards the bathroom.

By the time I was finished it was bedtime and the ladies scuttled us into our rooms. They were always in such a rush for us to get into bed. It was a routine they never deviated from. Moira poked her head into the room, seeing us both in bed she closed the door and went onto the next room.

Dana turned towards me, I never slept with my back to her as I wanted to see the attack head-on. She folded her pillow and curled her fingers around the edges of it. "I overheard the ladies talking and they said your parents hated you," she whispered.

I knew better. "Why would they say that?"

"Because it's true, dummy. All our parents hated us, except mine. They loved me," she said with a taut smile on her face.

"How do you know? You're here too."

She ignored my question. "Your daddy is in jail and your mommy gave you up."

That's ridiculous, my parents died, I thought but didn't say it. Instead I asked the question again that she'd side-stepped. "What about your parents?"

Still ignoring my question she rolled her eyes. "Your daddy hurt your mommy." She emphasized *hurt* and it stung deep in my soul.

I didn't know at seven what she meant and was tired. She was mean and ugly inside so I shut my eyes.

"Your daddy hurt her and a bunch of other women, that's why he's in jail," the words rolled off her tongue with stingers attached.

I ignored her words and kept my eyes closed. That was the first I learned of my biological parents.

The following day was Saturday and I waited for Cat, the lady who worked in the kitchen directing and teaching us, to disappear for her afternoon walk. I gulped down a little lemonade to wet my throat that was parched from the anticipation of what I was about to do, then left the kitchen and padded down the hall. Making sure no one was around, I peeked my head around the corner of the door to their small office.

The kids were all outside playing a game and Cat was on her walk, easy peasy. I slid into the room and headed straight to the file cabinet. The ladies made sure we understood this room was off-limits but since nobody ever attempted to get inside they'd grown lackadaisical about locking it.

I stood on my tiptoes and thumbed through the folders. Finding mine, I opened it. What I read brought tears to my eyes. Everything Dana said was true. A church lady dropped me off at the orphanage when I was a newborn. It said in bold letters she was a rape victim and wanted nothing to do with the child. My birth certificate was inside the file; Melissa Jones was listed as my mother. The family I'd always thought were my parents took me in at three months old. They filed for adoption when I was five but the papers were never finalized because of their early deaths.

Tears dropped from my eyes and my nose grew hot and leaked. I swiped my face with the apron and stuck my folder into its rightful slot. Rape -- that word didn't exist in my vocabulary. Edging close to the door I leaned in and hearing nothing but the vacant house I went back to the files and found Dana's.

It turns out her mother had her out of wedlock and was forced by her family to give her up. I thumbed through until I found her birth certificate and it listed Sam Courier as her father. I knew that name, I'd heard it somewhere before.

A door slammed and brought my mind to the present so I shoved her folder back into the cabinet and closed it. Female voices and clicking on the floors moved closer to the office. Panicking, I slid underneath the large wooden desk and curled into a tiny ball.

"See you at dinner, Cat," said Moira as she pushed open the office door and took a seat at the desk. Luckily I was small and scrunched into the darkest corner. All I saw was her black heels as they tapped the floor to Chubby Checker on the radio.

What felt like hours went by and my bladder was near bursting. Clutching against myself I fought the urge to pee all over. The glass of lemonade I stole before sneaking into the office was my penance for the wrongs I just committed. A drizzle of pee trickled over my fingers and I knew I couldn't hold it anymore. I looked around and spotted a vent on the other side of Moira's legs but didn't know how to get there without bumping into at least her feet.

Over the sound of the radio, I heard Cat call, "Moira."

Moira scooted her chair back and stood, offering me the opening I was waiting for. With one hand squeezing my crotch and my bladder muscles tensed to keep it in I scooted with my

back against the desk and wall to the
vent then pushed aside my soaked
panties. The pee burned as it streamed
into the floor vent, a little splashing
against my legs and the floor. I guessed
the vent was for heat but that wouldn't
be used in Albuquerque, New Mexico
until sometime in the winter. My flood
of urine would be dry by then, although
it would probably cast an awful odor
once used. I shrugged, unconcerned as
I felt so much better.

Moira left the office with Cat and I
climbed out from under the desk. My
wet panties felt cold and gross against
my crotch. Scurrying to the door I
peeked out. Moira and Cat went
around the corner toward the front
door. I heard it creak open then closed
and seized the opportunity to sneak to
my room, hoping Dana wasn't there.

My lucky day, the room was vacant,
then I heard voices calling for me. My
panties uncomfortable against me I
walked bowlegged and wanted to
change but thought to wait. I figured
they were looking for me since I'd been

gone so long. Scooting into the tiny area between my bed and the wall I grabbed a Nancy Drew novel, The Secret of the Old Clock, and began reading. At seven I read better than any of the students in my class.

The door opened and Moira walked in. "Scarlett."

I cringed. "I'm here," I replied, waving my hand in the air.

"What are you doing? We've been calling you for several minutes now," she said with concern in her voice.

I stood, a dribble of pee from my panties ran down my left leg. "I'm sorry," I said, hanging my head, "I was really into my book and didn't hear." I placed the book atop my bed.

She sighed. "Scarlett, I should have known." She moved to the front of my bed where I was now in full view. "Did you have an accident?"

I peered down my apron, a large wet spot was at the end of it. I must have accidentally peed more than a trickle when I soaked my hands. I shook my head no and responded, "I snuck a glass of lemonade earlier and I must have spilled some on my dress." I didn't want her to know, worried that at some point when they turned on the heat and the smell took over the house that they'd know I was the culprit, meaning I'd been in the office.

"Well come on, let's get that off you."

"OK, Miss Moira." I walked closer to her and she moved back, allowing me the room.

Her eyebrows made a V while her forehead wrinkled. "You don't need to lie."

What? How did she know? Then I saw the wet bubbles shining on the linoleum right below where my butt had been. I thought back and assumed the splashes were more than I thought too.

"Turn around?" she asked.

I did, reluctantly.

"The back of your dress has a wet spot too."

I gulped. "I'm sorry. I guess it happened while I was reading. I didn't

27

even know." I rested my face in my hands and cried.

"It's OK, honey, you're still a young girl and accidents happen. Right now we need to get these clothes off you and get you into something dry. And you need a bath."

After my bath I washed my clothes and hung them to dry. I'd be the laughing stock as everyone would know I peed myself. It was embarrassing, but at least no one knew the reason.

In bed that night Dana teased, "Do you need diapers like a baby? Do you need a bottle too?"

I tried to ignore her but then she said, "The little bastard baby nobody wants is retarded and still pees herself. Wa Wa." Her mocking tone made all the anger inside me rise to the surface.

"I'm not a bastard baby! My parents adored me."

Her eyes widened. "What a big vocabulary you have. Tch," then she turned over and went to sleep.

That night I waited for her to start snoring then left the room and grabbed a small disposable cup from the bathroom. I filled it with cold water and went back to my room and held the cup below her fingertips slowly bringing it as far over her hand as I could and waited a few minutes.

She moved in her sleep so I quickly drank the water as I'd made no plans on how to get rid of it and jumped onto my bed, stuffing the cup into my pillow case.

Dana continued to wiggle in her sleep then jumped out of bed. I kept my head buried in my pillow to stifle my laughter.

"What did you do?!" she shouted.

I turned and jumped in mock surprise. My eyes wide and mouth forming an O.

Within seconds Cat was at the door. "What's going on in here?" she demanded.

Dana looked at her then me and her face grew red. "I… my bed."

Cat's eyes moved across Dana's nightgown. "Dana, you are eleven years old!" she scolded, her hands on her hips.

"I didn't, it was Scarlett," she said, tears in her eyes.

"Scarlett did not pee your bed. Grab those sheets and get a clean nightgown. You will take a bath and make your bed with new sheets. First thing in the morning you'll wash them."

Dana harrumphed, "But..." Cat gave her the stink eye with one eyebrow raised and Dana shut her mouth and did as she was asked.

I curled back onto my side and didn't hide my smile as they headed out the door.

Chapter 3
Boiling Point

*T*he next morning I woke early when Cat entered the room and woke Dana to wash her sheets. My head buried in the pillow, I didn't see her but felt knives stabbing my back from the insidious stare I'm sure she passed my way.

Once she left the room I dressed and went to the library. There was a thick dictionary in the center of it and I wanted to know what the word rape meant. It said: unlawful sexual penetration of the vaginal area, anus, mouth, or sexual organ. I spent time looking up all those words and was still lost as I was only seven. My best guess was it meant an act of violence.

My mind rolling with new vocabulary I sauntered to the kitchen. My face must have worn a curious look as Cat asked when I entered, "What's on your mind?"

"Nothing," I responded and skipped to the stool I used while working and jumped on. "What are we making for breakfast?" I had the menu memorized and knew every third Sunday of the month we had waffles, scrambled eggs, and sausage.

She smiled and slid over a dozen fresh eggs, milk, a large bowl, and a whisk. "Go ahead and get started on the eggs," she said, pouring a cup of waffle mix onto the griddle and pressing down the top. Within thirty minutes Mario joined us and we were serving breakfast.

Dana stared at me, hate filling her eyes. I smiled as I walked past her and skirted towards the kitchen to eat the special waffles Cat made for Mario and I that had extra fresh strawberries cut on top.

Dana's behavior and torture grew worse over the next few months. I did my best to ignore her until she went too far. It was my birthday and Cat knew how much I loved butterflies and purple. I'd grown to like her and we had many kitchen conversations in which I'd told her about my parents. Her smile always kind.

For our birthdays we always got something from the ladies and cupcakes. The evening of my eighth birthday -- Tuesday November 5th -- all the children and ladies gathered around. Cat made me special cupcakes with purple frosting and a piece of Dubble Bubble gum on top. As the ritual demanded I sat at the head of the table for dinner and cupcakes. Dana sat at the end. She didn't look my way until I received my gift.

Carefully, I unwrapped the curly purple bow and laid the thin gift, a square lump on top upside down and slid my finger under the tape and peeled back the paper. My eyes widened when I saw the glittery purple butterflies. In excitement I forgot my manners and snatched the gift out of the paper. A notebook and crayons.

"So you can draw and write your own stories," said Cat, smiling.

I jumped off the chair and ran to her side. "Thank you," I beamed, hugging her then Moira.

That day I forgot all about Dana and drew the night away, creating a story about magical butterflies. In bed that night I felt Dana's eyes on me. When I glanced her way, they were filled with hate. It was my day so I ignored her and went to sleep.

Two days later I woke up to my notebook ripped into three chunks and my story ripped from the notebook and lying in pieces by my head. Tears burned in my eyes. I understand now that Dana was jealous. The ladies loved me and did something special but at the time anger brew inside me. Dana wasn't in the room but my shock and scream that I don't remember making alerted Moira.

She flew into the room and clutched me in her arms. "What's wron..." she began, then noticed the balled up papers and chunks of notebook. "I'm so sorry, honey."

Moira walked me to the kitchen. She glanced at Cat. "It looks like someone destroyed her gift and I have a good idea who. Please stay with her until I sort this out."

Cat nodded then looked at me. "How about we deviate from the menu and have crepes for breakfast?" She ran her palms across her apron.

I knew she offered since that was my favorite with blueberries. I shuddered, sniffed back my tears and said, "OK."

It didn't take Cat long to find Dana. She appeared at the doorway to kitchen. "Scarlett, honey, please come with me."

By this time Cat had me in a good mood and full of fresh fruit. I nodded and hopped off my stool.

Dana sat at the dining room table hanging her head.

"Dana, look at me," ordered Moira, folding her arms. Dana peered upward through her hair. "Sit up straight and look at me." Dana did as asked, her face now visibly red from crying. I hoped she'd gotten a good whipping from Moira but knew she didn't as the ladies didn't believe in physical harm. Instead they used their eyes and guilt.

"What you did was wrong. You owe Scarlett an apology." Her eyes bore into Dana's.

Dana turned, swallowed hard, then glared at me. There was no apology or sadness for me in her eyes. "I'm sorry," she said in a quiet voice.

"Scarlett, you may go back to the kitchen," said Moira.

"Thank you, Dana," I said, taking another glance at her before I scurried back to the kitchen.

All day Dana glared at me; a look of hate painted on her face. Luckily she was older and we didn't see each other much in school but on the bus and after school she stuck virtual blades into my soul over and over. I don't know what else Moira told her but knew it would mean more torture.

That afternoon, while I was reading another Nancy Drew novel in the library Jenny, one of the older girls, entered and cleaned the windows with a new cleaner. She placed it on the table and left the room for a minute. I took a sip of my water then got an idea. I chugged my water then set it beside the cleaner, unscrewed the top and poured a little inside my glass which I then took to the kitchen. Cat's back turned, I shoved it to the back underneath my station and scurried out of the room before Cat noticed I was there.

I showed at the kitchen to do my chores. While prepping foods I caught sight of an empty spice bottle in the trash. It was the right size to hold the window cleaner sample. With everyone preoccupied I grabbed the empty spice bottle, poured the cleaner into it, then closed the top and stuck it in the pocket of my oversized apron. I couldn't pour it into dinner because everyone might get sick or it would be too diluted to have much effect. So I waited for the opportunity.

It happened Saturday. I kept the cleaner with me at all times because I didn't want to miss the one opportunity I'd have. Dana brought a glass of milk to the living area with her then left. A few other children were in the room but playing a game so they didn't notice when I dumped the entire sample of cleaner into Dana's milk. I left the room before Dana returned and rinsed the small bottle then buried it in the kitchen trash. Nobody was in the kitchen, so that part was easy.

I walked through the living room to get to the library and Dana was drinking the milk. I felt a tinge of success. But real happiness came a couple hours later when she was doubled over in pain and threw up. Immediately she was taken to the infirmary where doctors and nurses who donated their time determined she had a virus since no one else was ill.

That night, and the next few while she was in the infirmary, I went to

sleep with a huge smile on my face
until I was given devastating news.

Chapter 4
Big Changes

*M*oira pulled me aside before Dana returned. Her face glum and her words making my heart drop. "Scarlett. You are such a wonderful and helpful young lady. We love having you here but feel you'd be happier in the community and with a family."

Tears stung the backs of my eyelids as I absorbed what she was saying. She took my hands. "We're going to miss you." Doom hung on each of her words and I couldn't help but wonder if they suspected I'd poisoned Dana. "You're leaving us to live with the Campbell family. They are wonderful people, upstanding members of the church, and have a girl your age and a son a couple years older." Her voice quivered and her eyes moistened.

"I'm leav-ing?" I asked.

She nodded and pulled me towards her belly, holding me tight. "I know you and Dana don't get along. This family is so happy to have another girl their daughter's age. It'll be wonderful, you'll see."

I couldn't swallow and lost my breath. "I'm leaving." The tears burst from my eyes.

She bent to meet me at eye level. "Oh sweetie, we'll miss you, but Lindsey is a wonderful girl who I think you'll make quick friends with."

I looked towards the floor, tears streaming down my cheeks. I'd miss Cat, Mario, and all the wonderful books in the library. But I wouldn't miss Dana or Michelle or school. My life was changing.

The Campbell family picked me up on a Saturday. All my belongings fit into two boxes. Mr. Campbell was tall and thick. He had short, thinning brown hair and a mustache. His brown eyes didn't smile. Mrs. Campbell was thin with straight, light brown hair and brilliant hazel eyes void of a twinkle.

My insides roiled as my instincts told me something wasn't right about the situation.

Nonetheless, I smiled and went with them, slipping Moira and Cat an expression of morbid fear as I slid onto the car seat. Cat's face returned my expression. She didn't want to see me go and I didn't get why they didn't make Dana leave. After all, she was the bad one, but I sucked it up and chose under duress to give the family a chance.

Their house was an average home. It was long and appeared made of concrete. The roof was nearly flat with a tiny peak in the middle and they had a two car garage. Bushy, neatly manicured shrubs stopped short just beneath the windows. Inside, the entrance opened into a large living room with a split level that went down to the kitchen, bathrooms, and bedrooms.

"Wait here, Scarlett," Mr. Campbell instructed, pointing towards an olive green vinyl chair at the kitchen table. I sat. Within a few minutes two children appeared, a young girl about my age. I assumed Lindsey and a young boy a few years older. Both had straight brown hair like their mother, Lindsey had her father's eyes and the boy had green eyes like his mother.

"Lindsey, Luke, this is Scarlett," said Mr. Campbell in a firm tone.

Obediently they replied, "Hello Scarlett."

A chill filled with horror rippled through my body. Children don't act that way naturally. *Would they expect me to act the same way?*

Mr. Campbell stared hard at me. "Hello," I responded. It was already starting.

He gave a thin, straight smile then turned to Mrs. Campbell who hadn't said a word. "You'll take care of getting her set up," he ordered, waving his hand towards me and left the room.

"Lindsey, Luke, Scarlett, follow me," she said in a flat tone.

We followed behind her like a train. "That's yours and Lindsey's bathroom," she pointed towards a room on the left, further down the hall she pointed to another door, "that's Luke's bathroom. You are never to enter it."

The chills returned. *Why?* I thought but didn't ask.

We doubled back and she pointed to a room across the hall between the bathrooms. "This is yours and Lindsey's room." She glanced to Lindsey, "Why don't you help her get settled in? "Luke," she ordered, "bring her bags into the hall and drop them beside the door, then you need to complete your chores."

He nodded and left us. Lindsey opened the door. "This is my bed and that one is yours. I cleared half the closet for you and we made room in the dresser by donating my old clothes that didn't fit anymore to charity," she said, pointing towards everything.

A shelf on the wall held a small collection of books and my eyes and body immediately went to it. "Are all these yours?"

"Yes. We have to read for an hour every night before bed," she said as if it was a chore.

Every one of them was in hardback. I grabbed one off the shelf and ran my hand over the cover. Lindsey snatched it out of my hand and snapped, "It's not bedtime yet."

Books that could only be read before bed? What kind of demonic family had I been sent to live with? I sighed. A small knock at the door frame and Luke's voice alerted us.

"You can start unpacking. You have twenty minutes, then go to the parlor for a family meeting." His voice void of emotion and his eyes glued to the ground as if looking at us was a mortal sin.

It didn't take twenty minutes to unpack my sparse belongings. In that time Lindsey filled me in on the dos and don'ts of the house. "We do all our chores daily as soon as we get home from school. They have to be done by the time father gets home for him to inspect." She shot a glance at me, her eyes filled with a warning I didn't quite get at the time. "We have an hour to complete our homework which is to be done by dinner time. Mother checks the accuracy of our work. We never go into any other bathroom or bedroom than this one. You can't even glance inside. If they catch you," she visibly shuddered, "well, just don't."

What would happen if I caught a glimpse into another bedroom or bathroom? Would I melt?

She continued, "After dinner we shower then watch TV for one hour. After that we go to bed and read for an hour. Mother listens to us while father listens to Luke." I guessed that was since we couldn't go into each other's rooms. *Mother* being a female was OK to be with us and *father* being a male was OK to be with Luke? "Always call them Mr. and Mrs. Campbell. Always, " she warned.

I nodded. Everything was very routine and I was sure I'd catch on quickly. We padded into the parlor, joining the rest of the family. Mr.

Campbell cleared his throat. "I assume Lindsey has told you the house rules," he said more as a question.

I nodded confirmation.

"Nodding is not an acceptable response. 'Yes, Mr. Campbell' is," he said with a steady, concise tone.

I responded, "Yes, Mr. Campbell."

He continued while we all sat, intently listening to him as if he was a god. "Chores are as important as rules. A house has to be maintained and orderly. Rules can't be broken. Everything must be done as required. There's no room for any mistakes." His eyes bore into mine. "I have redone the list. I have divided the list into thirds. Lindsey and Luke, because Scarlett is here you will have fewer chores." He narrowed his eyes at them.

Mrs. Campbell stood still and straight as an arrow. Her expression flat, eyes on the floor and hands rested on her legs as she sat on the chair across from us. Mr. Campbell stood next to her chair as he continued his speech. "Lindsey, you and Scarlett will swap chores each week. This week you and Scarlett will complete this list together so she knows exactly what I expect. The following week Scarlett will clean your bathroom and dust the main living areas; the parlor, living room, and hallway. I expect no dust on any furniture or fixture." Lindsey, who was sitting next to me, shifted her elbow, gently hitting my side as if in warning when Mr. Campbell shifted his gaze for a millisecond.

Mr. Campbell didn't appear to notice and Mrs. Campbell noticed nothing as her eyes were still planted on the floor. He continued, "Lindsey, you will make sure yours and Scarlett's bedroom is spotless and mop all the floors in the common areas. Is that clear?" His rectangle face grim and his brown eyes glowering at us.

He went through Luke's list which included taking out the trash, mowing the lawn, trimming the bushes and wiping the outdoor furniture. In the event of rain Luke was to assist us in cleaning the inside. It was no wonder the front yard and house looked as though they belonged in a magazine. Everything was kept perfect daily. I wasn't sure about the family's reactions but was fully accustomed to chores.

Before he called the meeting to an end he said, "Scarlett, those clothes of yours are hideous. No child living under my roof will wear such rags of filth." He pointed to the corner of the room at a couple large store bags. "Those are yours. Put them away and place the clothes you bought here in the bags. Leave them outside your door and Luke will collect them. Don't attempt to keep a single shred of your clothing. Is that understood?"

"Yes, Mr. Campbell." I didn't know what was wrong with my current clothing. The dress I wore was my best with its flouncy lavender apron skirt. There was a tiny hole by the apron pocket but it was barely noticeable.

Falling in step and following Luke and Lindsey's leads we left the room.

"How about weekends?" I asked as Lindsey and I marched to our room.

"The same; except Sunday we don't have any regular chores. Sundays are special," she answered with an edge to her voice I didn't quite understand.

In the bedroom I grabbed all my clothes, not that I was attached to them in any way but thought it was a waste to get rid of them. In the bags were flouncy apron and jumper dresses along with tights, new underwear, sleepwear, and a couple pairs of tapered pants with matching blouses and two pairs of shoes and socks. "What do we wear to clean the house?"

"Whatever you are wearing for that day. Don't get it dirty. Father doesn't like dirty clothes," she warned.

Chapter 5
Heed the Warning

That evening I learned why Lindsey hated reading so much as she struggled through her chapter in the bible. After listening to her floundering and stuttering long enough I whispered a word she struggled with. My hand was met with a sharp ruler slap and Mrs. Campbell's words, "We don't cheat here and give each other the answer. She must figure it out on her own or she'll never learn. Is that understood?"

The cold plastic stung my hand and heart. I was only trying to help. "Yes, Mrs. Campbell." *Who were these people I was stuck living with?*

The next day I learned what made Sundays special. Mr. Campbell was a pastor at a local church, thousands in the congregation. As children, we were carted off to Sunday school as soon as the stiff, unemotional hymns were sung.

Luke, being older and male, went to a different room than Lindsey and I. The classroom was dressed in pictures of heaven and biblical characters. Our teacher had kind eyes that reminded me of Cat. We read verses from the bible, mostly related to why sexual relations before marriage were frowned on. We should always keep our eyes free from lust. I wasn't sure what she meant but over time grew to understand.

The first week with the Campbells went smoothly as Lindsey taught me how to clean. Every item was taken off the tables and shelves for dusting then replaced exactly as it was. The windows and mirrors were cleaned. The bathroom was sprayed in bleach and wiped down to destroy germs and the floor was mopped, moving all furniture out of the way. When Mr. Campbell came home he took a white glove and fitted it over his hand as he inspected every inch of the house. Since he found not a speck I wondered what would happen when he found one. I cringed at the thought, imagining a dungeon below the house he'd place us in, giving us scraps left after dinner.

By the eighth day I couldn't take it anymore. Lindsey struggled with each word out of her mouth and glanced at Mrs. Campbell in fear when she couldn't get a word and got a ruler lick to her arm. That night I pretended to sleep listening to the sounds in the house until none existed then got out of my bed and padded to Lindsey's.

I gently pushed her until she peered at me with sleepy eyes that quickly widened in fear as she sprung awake. "Go back to bed," she said in a whisper.

"No." I shook my head and crawled into her bed. She quivered beneath the covers as if my proximity would boil her from the inside out. "I can teach you to read."

Her brows furrowed, she pushed me to the edge of her bed. "Get out."

"Everyone is asleep. I can teach you at night like this and during recess at school. They'll never know," I insisted, planting one foot on the ground to keep myself on the edge of her bed.

She let out an exasperated sigh. "You're not leaving until I agree and if they wake up we'll both be in trouble."

"Yes and probably." The dungeon picture shot through my mind but I ignored it. The Campbells were strict; Mr. Campbell liked everything a specific way and treated us as slaves and the family was weird, but my stay wasn't entirely unpleasant. She needed to learn to read. I surmised her tallest hurdle to jump wasn't reading but her tenseness while doing it.

"Fine," she said. "We can start tomorrow. Now go to bed."

"Pinky promise." I held my little finger out for her to wrap hers around. She eyed me curiously then wrapped her pinky around mine.

The next day at school I took her to the library with me during lunch instead of eating. She grumbled over her empty stomach but I insisted, pulling her along. I grabbed *The Snowy Day* by Ezra Jack Keats. It was one of my favorites and easy reading. We spent the next thirty minutes reading it again and again. When she stumbled over a word I corrected her, sounding it out using phonics. She relaxed when I didn't slap her hand and by the end of our session she was able to read it without stumbling.

The bell rang and she got up from her seat at the table we were sitting at. "We can't be late. Let's go," she urged, pulling me along.

"I have to put the book up. You go back to class. I'll be there in a minute."

"Hurry," she said with a worried frown, and she ran off.

I placed *The Snowy Day* on the shelf where we got it and grabbed *Stone Soup* by Ann McGovern. It was a trickier read and offered a wonderful message in which an entire village is tricked into making a tasty soup by a group of cunning strangers.

"You're going to be late," warned the librarian as I placed the book on the counter.

I glanced at the clock. I still had two minutes. If I ran I could make it. "I'll hurry."

A warm smile spread over her round face. "Here," she handed the book to me. "Don't dilly dally, run to class."

"I will," I promised and scampered out of the library not stopping until I reached the classroom. The bell rang as I entered, holding the book firm against my chest. Everyone was settling into their seats so I quietly scuttled to mine, hoping to go unnoticed by Mrs. Perkins, our teacher. Lindsey eyed me with a look of horror when she spotted me slipping through the door. I slid the book into the open side of my desk and took out my journal.

The first thirty minutes after lunch we spent writing. I created stories in which I was a super hero. My two-colored eyes able to see inside the soul of others and turn a soured heart into a loving one. In my adventure that day I rescued a dog from the vicious hands of his owner who treated him with disdain every time he was bad; forgot to fetch the paper or didn't obey an order immediately. Now he gave him hugs every time he obeyed and gently reminded him the times he didn't.

I always drew a picture to go with each story. My outfit was a purple cape that looked like butterfly wings and I wore a matching purple butterfly wing mask over my eyes, one amber eye in the middle of a wing and a green eye in the middle of the other wing.

As the day neared an end and everybody was packing up their belongings Mrs. Perkins called me to her desk. My heart beat against my chest cavity and blood rushed through my veins. I was sure she caught me and I'd get a scolding. With my hands to my sides and my eyes wide I stood at her desk.

"Scarlett," she started. *Oh no!* I felt it coming, then she pulled out my journal. "I've been reading your stories. They're very creative."

I gulped and my fear washed away. "Thank you, Mrs. Perkins."

"I don't often see this much talent in an eight-year-old but you have a vivid imagination and a vocabulary much higher than the average student." She pointed out a couple words, *catapult* and *revolting*, from today's story.

"I enjoy reading and writing."

"I see and you spelled each word correctly," she pointed out. "We have a spelling bee every year. Each grade level competes within that grade for a winner. When a winner for each grade level is chosen there's a school-wide competition. The winner of the school competition goes to the county and so on. At each level the winner gets a prize. I think you should seriously consider this competition because you could win." She relaxed into her chair and took in my shocked expression.

"I've never done anything like that," I said, flabbergasted.

"The grade level competitions take place next week," she slipped me a small packet, "study these words." She leaned in. "I think you can win."

I shifted while I grabbed the packet from her. "Thank you, Mrs. Perkins." I skipped to my desk. If I was good enough at something, I could win a prize. It excited me. I stuffed the packet into my backpack.

Lindsey strode up beside me. "What did she want?"

"The spelling bee. She thinks I can win," I said with wide eyes, then grabbed *Stone Soup* from my desk.

"Really? That's exciting." Her eyes shot a quick glance at the book as I stuffed it into my backpack. "What are you doing?"

Alarmed at the sudden sharp tone in her voice I replied, "Taking it home. We'll read tonight."

She grabbed the book. "You can't do that. You'll get us both into trouble."

I snatched it back, sliding it into my backpack and zipping it. "Yes I can and no we won't."

She huffed away and stayed silent during the bus ride. I slipped the book out of the backpack and inside my shirt, tucking it partially into my pants as the bus came to a halt at the end of our street. Mrs. Campbell always inspected our backpacks as we did chores.

When we reached the house I went first to the bathroom I shared with Lindsey and pushed the book in the space behind the toilet and wall, tucking it tight against the top where the tank met the wall. I flushed the toilet and ran the water, so Mrs. Campbell would think I used it, then went into the kitchen and grabbed the appropriate cleaning supplies to complete my chores.

The tub of cleaners on the floor, I glanced over my shoulder and not seeing anyone sifted through a couple drawers searching for a flashlight. I didn't find one but found something else. Several candles and matchbooks. I grabbed one of each, stuffing the long candle into my right sock and shoving it down as far as it would go and crammed the matchbook into the left sock. The loose legged pants covered the bulges.

That night, when the house was quiet and everyone was asleep, I tiptoed to the bathroom and pulled the book from its hiding spot and tiptoed back to our room. I lit the candle, held it in my hand, and nudged Lindsey awake.

Her eyes large she gasped, "Where did you get that candle?"

"From the kitchen."

"My dad counts everything. He'll know. You need to put it back," she urged.

"It'll be fine. He'll never know. We have reading to do."

Reluctantly, she sat up. I laid the book in her lap. She opened the cover and began reading. We worked through the book and when we'd read it cover to cover I hid it beneath my mattress. Mrs. Campbell washed sheets every

Wednesday. That day I'd find a different place to stash it. I stuffed the matches under the mattress with it and blew out the candle, propping it inside a shoe in the closet.

For the next week we read every lunch and every night. I switched out books and kept the candle and matches hidden. Slowly Lindsey was improving and Mrs. Campbell noticed and ruler-slapped her less.

The day of the class spelling bee I sat on the cafeteria stage at school. My nerves fluttered as I nervously walked to the front for my first word. I'd studied all the words Mrs. Perkins gave me. They were easy, yet I was filled with anxiety.

"Trust," I repeated. "T-R-U-S-T, trust."

"That is correct," said the teacher in charge.

I scurried to my seat, less nervous, and when it was over I was handed a blue ribbon. I hadn't missed one word.

That evening, during TV time, lightning lit up the darkening sky followed by roars of thunder. The lights flickered and the power went out. Mr. Campbell rose from his seat and barked orders. "Mrs. Campbell grab the candles, Luke get the candelabra and bring them to me."

I heard Mrs. Campbell rifling through the drawers and sat very still. Lindsey grabbed my hand and we sat tight and stiff. I felt the fear rising inside Lindsey as she clutched my hand, her body shaking.

Mr. Campbell roared, "What's taking so long?!"

Luke rushed into the room with the candelabra and placed in on the living room table. Rain pattered against the windows and roof and lightning shot through the air, illuminating Mrs. Campbell in the doorway with a cluster of candles in her hand and a matchbook in the other. Terror painted on her face as she shuffled into the room.

She placed them into the slots until each candle had a home and one slot was left vacant.

"Where's the other candle?!" Mr. Campbell roared.

"I uh… I… it wasn't in the drawer," stuttered Mrs. Campbell.

"Explain this!" he shouted as thunder bellowed through the air, accentuating his voice.

I knew exactly where the candle was but didn't have a way of grabbing it, so I watched in horror as Mr. Campbell grabbed his wife's arm and tossed her across the living room. She hit the wall with a thud and dropped to the floor.

I watched his form march towards her sunken body. "I said, where is it?!" He kicked her stomach. She whimpered and sobbed.

Lindsey latched onto my arm, tears flowing from her eyes.

"I--"

The word hung off my tongue as Luke interrupted me, "I have it!"

Mr. Campbell turned his eyes from his wife to son and he stomped towards him and buckled his fist, thrusting into his abdomen. Luke doubled over but didn't fight back.

I didn't know what to do as this man knocked the breath out of his only son over a candle. My heart collapsed and I ran from the room into my bedroom. I searched everywhere in the dark, using lightning to guide my way. The violence in the other room growing louder as my heart beat faster. It was gone!

I slipped back into the living room, my head hung low in shame. I caused this. It was my fault. The beating was mine to tolerate. "I took it," I confessed.

Mr. Campbell stopped, his hand fisted and ready to punch his son again when he shot a gaze towards me and seethed, "Don't lie for him. He already confessed and gave me the candle. Use this as a lesson to never disobey me."

I glanced at the candle set inside its holder, every one present and accounted for, waiting to be lit. Rewinding my mind I remembered the length of time it took for Luke to get the candelabra. He snuck into our room and grabbed it. *How did he know?*

I sucked in a deep breath and watched in horror with Lindsey as he lit each candle. The reflection of the flames bouncing against the walls and gleaming in Mr. Campbell's brown eyes as he grabbed his son by the ear and pulled him. His body thumping hard as it went over the steps of the split-level to the kitchen below.

Lindsey watched in dread and tears as he dragged Luke through the kitchen. Mrs. Campbell whimpered in a puddle on the floor. A door creaked open, Luke's body slid along the floor, small groans emanating from his lips. Another door opened, shuffling, then the door slammed shut. He'd locked him in the garage. A room I hadn't yet been inside.

Chapter 6
The Dungeon

After the event, Mr. Campbell went back to normal as if his acts of violence and rage hadn't existed. Never in my life had I witnessed such brutality. In my wildest nightmares I wouldn't have ever imagined such a thing. My mind recalled what Dana said about my parents and the information I learned about Melissa Jones and the definition of the word *rape*. *Had my true father done something to my true mother as horrible as what Mr. Campbell did to his family?*

Tremors filled my body as I thought about it and what I did to Dana. *Did she deserve it? Was I like Mr. Campbell?* Snuggled into a ball with the covers over my entire body, I wept. When the tears dried up and my sniffles stopped, I listened. The house was entirely quiet.

I crawled out of bed and down the hall. Every door was closed since it was *immoral* to see the opposite sex in bed. On my tiptoes I coasted through the kitchen to the garage and tried the knob. It was locked, so I turned the lock and tried again and it opened. I felt against the wall and found the light switch. When I flipped it nothing happened. The power hadn't returned yet so I felt along the wall as my eyes adjusted to the darkness.

Careful not to knock anything over, I slowly walked the length of the wall. My eyes made out shadows and forms. In the middle of the garage was the car. I felt for its sleek edge and, finding it, followed it until I was on the opposite side of the garage. Taking a step towards the wall, which didn't appear to have anything dangling from it or shelves, I pressed my hand against it. Luke was in here somewhere.

I coasted towards the door; my hands feeling along the wall, somewhere there had to be a knob. I'd distinctly heard two house doors open and close. My left hand hit something. A small square area indented in the middle. It was metal by its cold feel and inside the square was a rough area like something a key would fit into. It was a pocket door. I tucked my fingers against the side of the indented lock and pulled but it didn't budge. I wasn't surprised. He'd locked him inside it.

"Luke," I called a notch above a whisper. "Luke," I repeated.

"Scarlett," he responded and shuffling on the other side meant he was there.

"Are you OK?" I asked.

"I'll be fine. I've taken worse from the man," he responded in a husky voice, obvious his mid-area was sore and he was short of breath when speaking.

"I'm sorry, so sorry. Why did you do that? I would have taken the beating over you. It was my fault." My eyes teared up again.

"I'm larger, and all the yard work toughens my chest and abs. That's where he hits so nobody sees the bruises. I can take the beating. You, he might have killed you."

Killed me? Then it hit me, maybe the monster had done this before. "Has he brought in other kids like me?" I closed my eyes, dreading his response.

After a few seconds he responded, "Yes, once." I could hear the cringe in his pained voice.

"And he killed her?" I squeezed my eyes tighter, terrified of the answer.

"Yes. He reported her missing and dumped her body somewhere. I... I don't know where." His voice shaky.

I let out a deep breath I realized I was holding. That's why they were all scared. I swallowed hard. "How did you know?"

"I see flames in your eyes. When he barks orders your green eye becomes amber, matching the other. You have free will and defiance and Lindsey is my sister. I know everything she does and will never allow him to harm her," he said, more as a warning than heroic.

It wasn't me he was trying to protect but Lindsey. "I'm sorry I put her in a position where he'd have beaten us both. I didn't know. I wish you'd told me. I wouldn't have taken the candle. I was just try… ing to help her read." My throat choked and tears poured over my cheeks.

"You need to get back and act normal. Don't fall out of line at all. I can't protect her while I'm in here but should be out in a couple days."

"OK, I won't let anything happen to her." I dropped my hands from the wall and slipped back inside the house, locking the door behind me. Poking my head around the hall corner, all the doors were still locked so I scurried on tiptoe back to our room and slipped into bed.

The next day at school Lindsey avoided me; she wouldn't even make eye contact. I squeezed to get behind her in the lunch line and seated myself next to her at the table. "I'm sorry."

"No you're not. I warned you," she said, anger and sadness smoldering in every word.

"I didn't know anything could be that bad." Guilt ate at me inside and I couldn't eat a bite.

"Now you do," she smarted, then shoveled a bite of applesauce into her mouth clueing me the conversation was over.

At home we acted normal and completed all our chores. Mrs. Campbell strode towards us, wincing in pain with each step. Daggers struck me in the heart as I was the cause of all her and Luke's pain. I had to make it right.

"You will have to pick up Luke's chores for the week. Lindsey knows where the weed can is," she stated, then turned on her heel and walked towards the kitchen where she was starting dinner.

I volunteered to get the trash while Lindsey started the weeding. I figured it was the hardest of the jobs since there weren't any weeds in the perfect lawn. I emptied every trash can in the common areas and stuffed them into the main trash in the kitchen. Mrs. Campbell eyed me but didn't say a word. I lifted the bag but it was so heavy I had trouble getting it out. She strode towards me and helped me lift it. "Thank you, Mrs. Campbell."

Her always straight expressionless lips turned upward in a smile. I considered dragging the bag but it might have opened and the contents littered over the clean floor so I grabbed it between both arms, dropping it gently to the floor and re-hefting it to carry it into the garage. I then dropped it again and re-lifted it, carrying it in a hug. The pungent aroma of its contents wafted up my nose making it flinch.

After heaving it into the large trashcan I glanced towards the wall and thought of Luke trapped in the tiny room. I didn't stop to say anything, fearing Mrs. Campbell would hear me. When I reentered the kitchen I padded towards the back door to help Lindsey but Mrs. Campbell stopped me.

"You need to spray the can with bleach. When it dries you have to put in a new bag," her eyes drifted over my dress, "and change your dress, now, bring that one to me."

I glanced downward and caught a small dark stain from the trash. It almost blended with the flower pattern and was barely visible but her hawk eyes caught it. "Yes, Mrs. Campbell."

I scuttled to my room and changed then rushed back and handed her my dress. She nodded and I bolted outside to help Lindsey. I knew Mrs. Campbell wasn't trying to save my hide but hers and Lindsey's.

I caught Lindsey standing still, staring at something on the ground. When I approached I looked down and saw a dragonfly resting on a blade of grass. It flapped a wing but the other didn't move. "It's hurt," I said, leaning down, placing my finger beneath it and lifted it up. Its wing moving but only serving the purpose of knocking itself off balance and falling off my finger. I caught it with my other hand.

"Maybe we can save it," she said.

"Where should we put it?" I asked.

She pointed to a tree in the corner of the yard. "There."

Lindsey picked up a few blades of grass and placed them in a nook where the thick branches started. I carefully placed the dragonfly over them.

"We'll check him every day after school," she said with purpose in her voice.

The rest of the evening went like normal. We finished our homework, ate dinner and watched TV, then read for an hour and went to bed. After dinner Mr. Campbell went into the garage with a plate of food. I heard the door open and close, keys jingled and he returned. I didn't acknowledge with my eyes or behavior but listened so I didn't cause alarm.

That night in bed I didn't wait up to help Lindsey read or sneak into the garage. My dreams visions of the nightmare I witnessed. I was alone in a meadow filled with colorful flowers, butterflies and bees bounced from petal to petal when suddenly night fell and drops of blood replaced the bees and butterflies. I ran through the meadow towards the woods, heavy footsteps following me. I hid inside a hollowed out log and spotted a pair of dress shoes -- Mr. Campbell's -- halting near the log. I sat still and they left. Scratching and growling from the other end of the log forced me to turn my head in the small space. His face grossly misshapen with large teeth gnashed at me. My heart beat and sobs choked me when the alarm buzzed, spitting me out of dream world.

We lined up for lunch and recess. Lindsey fell in line behind me. "Let's go to the library."

I furrowed my brows. "I don't think it's a good idea until... you know."

Her brown eyes sunk. "We have to. I'm finally getting it."

I smiled and we ran off to the library. I decided to start her on chapter books because she was reading really well, so we chose *Pippi Longstocking.* At the home, where pleasure reading was encouraged, I'd read it a couple times.

Pippi was a girl our age with red hair and pigtails. She doesn't understand normal acceptable behavior and does all sorts of eccentric things. In our half hour lunch Lindsey made it through the first two chapters, giggling between words.

Instead of checking the book out, since night time reading was out of the question, I took it to the librarian. "Can you hold this book for us?"

Her round face held a warm, curious smile. "You can check it out."

"No, since Luke is sick," I'd overheard Mrs. Campbell's conversation on the phone about his absence from school, "we have a lot of chores and have to help take care of him so we'll be reading it here."

She smashed her eyebrows and her words lingered, "I'll place it behind the counter for you."

"Thank you," we said and skipped off to class.

After our chores we rushed outside to the dragonfly and found him lying still. I touched his wing. He didn't respond.

"He's dead," said Lindsey in a melancholy tone.

I nodded.

"We have to bury him."

"Where?" I asked, my eyes roving for a place in the yard that Mr. Campbell wouldn't notice if it wasn't perfect.

Lindsey twisted her lips. "Behind the tree. There isn't much grass there, so Father won't notice."

We used our fingers to dig a little hole in the ground behind the tree, near the flowers by the fence, and placed the dragonfly inside then covered the dirt back over him. "Now he can rest in peace by the flowers." I was happy about our little burial and it was the perfect spot.

She smiled and grabbed my hand as we skipped towards the shed to collect the tools we needed to complete Luke's chores. I'd never had a friend like Lindsey. I was in kindergarten when my parents died and at the home Cat became my best friend but now I had a friend my own age.

When Mr. Campbell came home he took out his white glove and scoured the surfaces as was his daily routine. Then he went outside to inspect the yard. Lindsey and I held pinkies under the table and held our breath as we peered at our homework, pretending to finish. Both of us were too nervous to focus.

The sliding door slid open and closed, signaling his return. "Girls, join me."

I squeezed my eyes and Lindsey squeezed my hand as we rose and joined him at the door, fully expecting a fist to our stomachs and the breath knocked out of us. I waited, breathless and silent.

"You see that yard?" He pointed towards the tree. I sucked in my lips and prepared for the blow. "It looks beautiful."

I let my breath out and heard Lindsey do the same.

"Girls can be as competent as men when they need to be," he said, glancing at us. "Back to your homework."

Lindsey and I flashed a quick smile of satisfaction to each other then scampered back to our work. The rest of the evening and the weekend went smoothly. Saturday he let Luke out of the room.

My heart skipped a beat when I saw him. His skin and eyes were pale but he was free. Nobody said anything and life in the Campbell home was *normal* as we passed by each other like ghost slaves for the devil.

The school and bus were our only freedoms. Monday I slipped beside Luke on the school bus. He shifted a sideways glance at me. "How are you feeling?"

"I'm fine," his response was quick. I nodded and we rode in silence the rest of the way to school.

Chapter 7
The Purple Mask

*T*he next several months went by without incident. I won the school spelling bee and a trophy. Mr. Campbell signed permission for me to go on a field trip and attend the county spelling bee. I won an award and another trophy. He agreed to let me go to the state spelling bee so long as I kept up on my homework. At school I continued writing my stories during journal time. The Purple Mask saving everyone from harm and brutality and spreading love.

A warm day in April Mrs. Perkins called me aside, my journal open and resting on her desk. She looked me in the eye. "Scarlett, how are things with the Campbells?"

That was a weird question. I was sure I hadn't said anything at school to her or anyone else about our lives as slaves and Mr. Campbell's outburst the day of the storm. "Fine."

She sucked her lips in and out. "They treat you well?"

"Yes."

She grabbed my journal off her desk. "I like reading your episodes about The Purple Mask saving people and animals from harm and changing everyone's heart to good. Your drawings are excellent too and I like how her eyes are like yours. Are you The Purple Mask?"

I nodded, unsure where she was going but thrilled she enjoyed my stories.

"Hmm... She started saving butterflies and animals now she saves people and I see a villain who keeps returning that she can't seem to catch and turn good."

"Every super hero needs a villain," I responded. She should know that.

"Yes they do." She smiled but it quickly dropped. "Are you sure everything is good with the Campbells?"

"Yes, and me and Lindsey are good friends." I finally started to understand what she was getting at and wanted her to know to leave it alone. I didn't want Lindsey harmed because of me.

Two nights later there was a knock at the door as we were sitting down to eat. Mr. Campbell's eyes shot us all a warning as he ordered Mrs. Campbell to answer the door and tell the salesman to go away.

I heard Mrs. Campbell's voice in the living room and that of another woman but couldn't quite hear what was said. A few minutes later Mrs. Campbell returned to the dining room. "It is someone with the foster agency," she said, barely making eye contact with Mr. Campbell.

When they left, me first, followed by Luke and Lindsey got out of our seats and scooted towards the kitchen to eavesdrop.

"I'm sorry to drop in unannounced but that's part of the requirements for allowing you a foster child. I haven't been in a hurry since you're such upstanding pillars of the community and I'm sure Scarlett is in the best hands, but protocol requires me to talk with you, Scarlett, your other children and tour the house." Her voice was kind and dripping in honey.

I swallowed hard, remembering Mrs. Perkins questioning me. Lindsey, Luke, and I met glances as we stood nervously listening at the open doorway.

"We were just sitting down to eat, may we do this another day?" asked Mr. Campbell.

"I'll be quick but I must have this report in. I've let it go too long," she answered.

We listened to the conversation as she asked them questions about my adjustment, school, any illnesses. It sounded routine and she didn't bring up anything about The Purple Mask.

We scurried back to our seats when she asked to meet us and sat straight as arrows, smiling like cherubs when they entered. We decided our only plan of action was to be angelic and perfect, that way she'd leave and no one would be in trouble. "Good evening," we said in unison.

She placed her hand over her heart. "Oh my, I rarely get such a polite greeting from children. Good evening."

She talked with us as a group while Mr. and Mrs. Campbell were asked to wait in the living room. I felt Mr. Campbell's fiery anger, imagining rage building inside him.

After several minutes and a few nonsense questions she asked me to join her outside in the back yard. I did as I was asked.

Once we were outside she took my hand. "It appears you're well taken care of by the Campbells but I still have to ask you questions."

"I understand," I answered but I wasn't prepared for the questions.

"Luke missed a week of school a few months ago because he was ill. Do you remember that?"

"Yes." *Why was she asking questions about him?*

"But he was never taken to the doctor."

"I don't think so but I was in school all day." It was a safe answer.

She grabbed my other hand. "Look into my eyes. He wasn't really sick was he?"

I used the super power in my eyes to stare into hers and drew on its strength to form my lie. "He was. I think it was the flu."

She sighed. "This isn't the first time he's missed a considerable amount of school and never has a doctor's note. I don't think you're being honest."

"He was sick, he was, and Lindsey is my first, best and only friend." The words poured from my mouth.

"How about you? I read your stories. The ones written when Luke was sick were the most disturbing." She dropped to one knee and, her eyes in line with mine, she asked, "Are you sure you have nothing to tell me?"

"The Campbells are nice people and I'm happy," I persisted with my charade as I didn't want any harm to come to Lindsey or Luke.

She slipped a hand in her pocket and stuffed a card into my hand. "Call me if you ever need to."

"Thank you," I answered as we walked back to the house.

She inspected each room by walking into it and sweeping her eyes over it then bade us goodnight and left.

Mr. Campbell ushered us into the kitchen as Mrs. Campbell was working to reheat everything. "Sit and let's eat." He said his usual prayer and Mrs. Campbell filled his plate first as always then she took a seat.

Mr. Campbell raised his first bite to his lips and shoveled the spoon of mashed potatoes and gravy into his mouth then he spit it out. "It's cold!" He swung his plate at Mrs. Campbell. It hit her in the collarbone, she squawked in pain and it sent her flying backwards. She and the chair crashed to the floor, her head bounced and blood dribbled over her yellow dress.

He stood. "Which one of you sent her here?!" His voice echoed off the walls and through my head.

Mr. Campbell stepped over his wife who lay motionless, knocked out or dead on the floor. I kept my eyes down as did Lindsey and Luke. He walked behind Luke and from the corner of my eye I watched him brush a finger against Luke's neck then force his thumb against it. "Was it you? You're always the one in trouble." Rage burned in Luke's eyes.

Removing his thumb, he walked behind me and pulled my ponytail back until my eyes faced his. The back of my head stung as each hair was lifted from its comfortable spot on my scalp. "Or was it you? She was checking on you." Fury framed the edges of his face and he shifted his jawbone then dropped my head.

He took a step behind Lindsey. "Surely it wasn't Lindsey. She never gets into trouble. She always obeys. My golden child." Then in a quick movement from the corner of my eye he shoved his elbow into the crook of his arm and downward onto Lindsey's head. She dropped from the chair and, without thinking, having no control over my body as if motivated by an external force, I was clinging to his back, digging my fingers into his face in search of his eyes.

We swung in circles and he attempted to throw me off. There was commotion but all I saw, all I was aware of was the hate inside me and gouging out his eyes. I wanted him to feel the pain he inflicted on his family.

Soon we were thrust forward and I felt someone beneath me. Heat rose against my face as I fell forward with Mr. Campbell onto something hot. Arms pulled me from behind and a voice brought me back.

"Scarlett, Scarlett," it called until the fuzz cleared and Lindsey stood above me, one hand clutching her head. I blinked in clarity and saw her worried face. "We have to get out of here!"

I gasped at the flames rising above the stove, licking at a facedown Mr. Campbell and the curtains. Luke plowed his hands beneath his mother. I grasped hold of Lindsey's hand and she helped me up, then I let go and grabbed Mr. Campbell around the middle and pulled him, flames and all, to the ground. His face was on fire.

"What are you doing? Let's go," shouted Lindsey.

I gasped, took her hand, and we jumped up the stairs and through the living room, flying out the open front door.

Neighbors rushed to our yard and watched the flames rise on the backside of the house. Smoke filled the air and within minutes a fire truck appeared.

Chapter 8
Saying Goodbye

Mr. Campbell was dead but Mrs. Campbell survived and was loaded into an ambulance. I hugged Lindsey and Luke before I settled into the social worker's car. The ride was quiet until she pulled the car up in front of a large house. "What happened?"

"I wasn't in the room. I don't know. By the time we saw the fire it was too late. Luke managed to get his mother but Mr. Campbell was in flames. I don't want to talk about it," I said in a remorseful, sappy voice. Inside I cheered that Mr. Campbell was gone forever. I'd miss Lindsey and Luke but now their life could be better.

She nodded then smiled. "We'll find you a new home soon."

"Why can't I stay at the other home with Cat?" I asked.

"They're full and this one is closer. You'll go to the same school and will see Lindsey and Luke every day."

With only the clothes on my back we walked up the steps of the large house. It stood three stories high, each level growing smaller and a circular turret that started ground level and stood higher than the rest of the house and pointed into the clouds. It had windows and awnings as if each level of it was a separate room. The house was painted in dark grey with cream trim and fluffy bushes with tiny purple flowers surrounded it. The wooden steps creaked as we climbed them. The door opened and we were greeted by an old woman. Wrinkles webbed across her face and her neck and blue hair covered her head.

The social worker soon left and the lady guided me down a long corridor, the wood floor creaking beneath our feet, and pushed a door open. "This will be your room, Scarlett."

I gasped at the old fashioned furniture that rested on curved legs with balls on the end. Worn filigree covered every curve and the bed matched and was set against a large window. The olive green curtains behind the bedframe touched the floor with tattered ends. A matching olive green bed covering was tucked beneath cream pillows adorned with gold tassels. I spun, taking it all in. A large full body mirror was positioned in the corner near the closet.

"Who is my roommate?" I asked. This room was far too large for a single occupant.

"Just you."

I hadn't had my own room since I lived with my parents and it wasn't near this large. "Is there anyone else here?"

"Yes, Penelope is in the room next to yours. We passed it, and the twins, Vince and Jeffrey, are across the hall."

"Do I have chores and things I need to do? Rules I need to know and follow?"

She chuckled. "Tonight. why don't you take a bath and I'll make you a little something to eat? I'm sure I have clothes around here that will fit you. I'll have Penelope find some."

I followed her into the bathroom. It was all tile. Tiny little white squares of tile with four blue squares -- one on each corner. The tub was raised on legs like the furniture in my room. She turned the faucet and let it run, testing its heat with her finger.

"Do you like bubbles?" she asked with a small jug in her hand.

Bubbles. I hadn't taken a bubble bath in years. I nodded my head with excitement and she tilted the jug into the running water, bubbles filling the tub.

"Take your time. I'll have Penelope put clean clothes outside the door for you." She turned on her heel and left, closing the door behind her. I listened to her footsteps and heard voices in the hall.

After several minutes there was a knock on the door. "I found you a nightgown. I'm leaving it here. I left a few other things on your bed." The voice sounded older, a teenager maybe, and sweet.

I soaked in the bubbles until they all popped, I pruned and the water turned cold. I wrapped a towel folded on the rack around me and creaked open the door. A pink nightgown lay on the floor. I slipped it on and left. The door next to mine was open a peep. I knocked on the frame.

"Yeah," called the same voice that brought my nightgown.

"Penelope?" I asked as the door opened. In front of me stood a girl with her long red hair in a braid that hung over her shoulder. Her brown eyes were warm.

"You must be Scarlett. I think Sara is making you something to eat. You want a tour?"

"Yes, please."

She giggled. "This place isn't like others. We don't have to be formal and don't have a list of chores. Sara gives us a verbal list every week and I think half the time she forgets. She forgets a lot. That's the twins' room." She pointed towards a room across the hall from hers. "They aren't home much because they have jobs after school and the weekends. You can watch TV almost anytime you want. I read with my free time--"

"You read," my face lit up.

"Yeah, all the time. I have a bunch of books that are young for me that I can give you."

"I love to read. Thank you!" I squealed.

"OK," she chuckled.

We passed a great grandfather clock I hadn't noticed earlier. It jutted from the floor and was surrounded by glass encased in dark, rich-colored wood. "The second floor is Sara's area. Her room is there and don't play with her chair," she said pointing to what looked like a wheelchair attached to the banister.

"Through there is the kitchen. Oh, and every other day Selma cleans the house and cooks us meals. She makes enough to last until her next visit, and once a week Freddy comes by and mows the lawn," she winked and left.

I walked into the kitchen and was greeted by Sara, "I hope grilled cheese and tomato soup is OK?"

"Yes, thank you!" I took a seat at the butcher block style table. The wood worn and the shine gone. I hadn't been asked what I wanted to eat since I lived in the home and Cat made me a little something special.

The soup was delicious and Sara was kind. Servants did chores, all we had to do was be kids. I couldn't believe I'd fallen into something so good. That night in bed, I snuggled into the thick mattress and pulled the fluffy comforter up to my chin and within seconds fell into a dreamless sleep.

Chapter 9
Kitty Kitty

*S*oft tickling against my nose woke me in the morning. I brushed my hand to my face and felt a soft lump on the pillow next to my head. When I opened my eyes, a fluffy silver cat lay on the pillow next to me. "Hi, Kitty." I stroked its soft, puffy fur and it shifted its head against my hand and rubbed. I sat up in bed and grabbed the cat, laying it on my lap while I petted and caressed it.

The house was silent. I creeped out of bed, the cat at my heels, and coasted into the hallway and into the large living room. Humming filled my ears and I followed it into the kitchen where a short, squat lady with copper hair wrapped in a bun was chopping vegetables.

"Are you Selma?"

Her eyes shot towards me and with a smile on her round face said, "I am and who might you be?"

"Scarlett," I said as I stepped into the kitchen. "I can help you."

"Good morning, Scarlett, delighted to meet you. I could use a little help. On the shelf above the stove are spices, can you take these down for me." She handed me a list. "There's a stool in the pantry."

I glanced around the room, pots and pans hung from above our heads and cupboards filled the walls, a curio in the corner contained a set of shiny cream dishes with gold trim. Past the curio was a door. I opened it and there were shelves of dried and canned foods. Leaned against the shelves was a small ladder.

I dragged it to the stove with the list in hand and took down all the spices on the list, that's when I noticed the cat was gone. I spun around but he'd vanished.

"Did you lose something?" Selma asked.

"No, well kind of. There was a cat and now he's gone."

She chuckled. "A cat huh. There's no cat here, anymore."

I know I'd seen a cat; a fluffy silver one. "Do you need help with anything else?"

She stopped and looked at me. "What different eyes. Very pretty. It's said that a person with different colored eyes can see into the spiritual realm."

I took a seat and scooted towards the table. "What does that mean?"

"People with heterochromia, or ghost eyes, can see and sometimes interact with spirits of the dead."

I didn't remember ever seeing a ghost. "If I can see ghosts how will I know them from other people?"

She gathered the vegetables into her hands. "That I don't know. Are you hungry?"

"Yes, please."

She winked. "We have Frosted Flakes and Raisin Bran. Which will it be?"

I didn't like raisins. They were soft and squishy and looked like little bugs so I chose Frosted Flakes.

She placed the bowl of vegetables in the refrigerator and wiped her hands. "When you're finished put your bowl in the sink." She strolled towards the doorway then stopped and turned. "Why is it you're not in school today?"

I shrugged. I had no answer. I'd overslept and nobody woke me up except the cat.

After breakfast, I dressed and went on an adventure. I searched the downstairs of the house high and low but didn't find the cat. I did find another room, it was like a sitting room encased in glass with doors that opened up to a garden filled with all types of cactus walled in by various large bushes with yellow, purple, and orange flowers.

"Kitty, kitty," I called, following a worn path between the cacti. It led to a stone bench beneath a large tree that offered shade from the already blazing sun.

The branches wiggled above my head and a small meow resounded in my brain. I glanced into the tree to see the cat. His paws poised on a large branch. "Are you stuck?" I asked and stood on the bench then curled my hands around a large branch and lifted. Using my feet to scale the trunk, I managed to sit upright on the branch and grab the cat from the branch above me. He purred in my arms.

From the tree I had a view of the city. Its many houses and buildings spread out, appearing as Lego homes, and further down the path was an adobe building that didn't match the house but looked more a part of New Mexico than the construction of the house. I put the cat over my shoulder, his fur tickling my face, and climbed down. He jumped off my shoulder and rubbed against my legs.

Curious, I followed the path to the strange little building. It had tall points at each of the four corners and open windows with bars on each side. I pushed the door but it didn't budge, on tiptoes I reached for one of the windows, gripping the ledge tight, and pulled but my fingers slipped and I fell. The next time I gripped the ledge and scaled the wall with my legs then grabbed hold of the bars. It was empty, except for a small brass loop embedded in the floor.

"Scarlett," carried a gentle voice through the still air. It sounded like Sara.

I dropped and, with the cat on my heels, ran towards the voice. Once I got to the tree I slowed and followed the path towards the house.

"Scarlett," it called again, only closer.

I continued down the path and spotted Sara by the house. She spotted me. "What are you doing out here?"

I glanced down and the cat was gone again. "I thought I saw a cat."

"Oh, well. why don't you come in and have some lemonade? I wouldn't want you to get heat stroke." She placed her arm around my shoulders as I neared her and we went to the house.

"I took care of all the paperwork at the school today, so tomorrow you'll go back," she said, spreading peanut butter on a slice of bread. The aromas of whatever Selma had in the oven made my mouth water.

"Will I be in the same class?" I liked Mrs. Perkins even if she was nosey.

"Yes, and will see Lindsey and Luke every day." She laid the knife down after spreading jelly on the other slice of bread and smashed them together, cut through the middle of the sandwich, and slid it towards me.

"Thank you." I grabbed it and took a bite. Peanut butter and jelly, cereal and grilled cheese, and I didn't get yelled at for exploring. I liked this place better every minute.

Footfalls and voices drifted closer to the kitchen until I saw Penelope followed by two boys. I guessed they were the twins since they looked alike, with wavy dish water blond hair that hung to their shoulders and deep blue eyes like the depths of the ocean and matching dimples.

"I'm Vince and this is Jeff," said one of them, pulling open the refrigerator and taking out a carton of orange juice. Jeffrey took glasses out of the cabinet and placed them on the counter.

"I told them about you on the morning bus," Penelope said, joining me at the table.

"Peanut butter and jelly for everyone?" asked Sara.

"We can get it ourselves. Go on, I know you're missing your shows," said Jeffrey.

Once she was gone Vince turned to me, "It's her routine; every weekday she watches her soaps. I'm surprised she made you a sandwich, but there aren't any house rules so you can fix something to eat whenever you want."

"She has one rule--" Penelope was cut off by Jeffrey.

"She's too young to worry about it," he said with a mouthful of PB and J.

"What did you do all day?" asked Vince. "Did you explore the house?"

"A little," I answered.

"Enough," said Penelope, a warning painted in her brown eyes. "I have books for you. Come on."

I scooted off the stool then glimpsed Jeffrey and Vince one more time. They'd already forgotten about me and were using salt and pepper shakers, the peanut butter and jelly jars to plan something out.

"Never mind them. They're cool cats but also full of shit." The sunlight blazed through the large windows, making her hair shine red as a fire engine.

She slid her closet open and the top shelf was lined with books. Maybe I died in the fire and this was Heaven. Her arms full, she dumped stacks of books onto her bed.

"Join me," she said, patting the mattress.

Several Nancy drew books, a couple Beverly Cleary, Where the Red Fern Grows, Old Yeller and Charlotte's

Web, Little House on the Prairie, and a few others. "These are all yours?" I asked in amazement.

"Now they're yours. I'm more into Hitchcock and Ray Bradbury."

"We're heading to the field to play ball," called one of the boys as he poked his head between the frame and door. "Wanna come? Kevin will be there," his voice warbled in a sing song tone.

"I'll catch up later," she tossed a pillow at the door but he pulled his head out before it hit him.

Despite what Mr. Campbell and the church preached, there didn't seem to be anything evil about viewing the opposite sex's room. They did it here like it was nothing.

"Suit yourself," he called from an unknown location in the hall.

"Boys. They can be so irritating!" She pulled her knees to her chest. "Those two care more about making money and buying a car when they turn sixteen this summer and girls than school," she said with an exasperated sigh.

"What about you?"

"I care about getting into college. Without anyone to pay for it I'm working towards a scholarship."

I picked up a Little House on the Prairie book and ran my fingers over the soft, worn cover. "What grade are you in?"

"Eleventh. I have one more year."

"Is Kevin your boyfriend?"

She twitched her mouth. "No, not really. We kissed once, but a boyfriend would ruin my plans to become a lawyer."

I knew lawyers were the ones responsible for dilly dallying about my adoption and so when my parents died I ended up an orphan with no family. That didn't make me like them much. "What happened to your family?"

"My mom died when I was born so I never knew her and my father when I was about your age. He had a heart attack. What about yours?"

That was a tricky question. The parents I thought of as my parents or the woman who gave birth to me and the man who raped her? "They died three years ago in a car wreck."

"So what did you do today?" she asked, changing the morbid subject.

"I went outside looking for the cat."

"Cat. Sara had a cat but he died last month. There is no cat anymore."

"I found him and picked him up," I insisted, remembering him clearly. He wasn't my imagination.

"Probably a stray. Why don't I help you carry those books into your room? I have a lot of homework I need to get started on." She gathered a load of books into her arms.

I nodded and we moved the collection to my room. I spent the rest of the afternoon until dinner and into the wee hours of the night reading Little House on the Prairie. There was nobody to stop me; no one screamed that my light was on, so I devoured the book, barely able to take my eyes off the pages until I heard voices in the hall.

I glanced at the large golden clock hanging on my wall, eleven forty-five. I set the book down and peeked into the hall, the boys and Penelope were giggling as they walked to their rooms.

Vince caught a glimpse of my face. "What are you doing still awake?"

"Reading."

"Uh oh, another bookworm," laughed Jeffrey.

Penelope winked at me and disappeared into her room. At midnight the grandfather clock struck midnight with twelve gongs.

I went back to school the following day. I didn't see Luke but since Lindsey and I were in the same class we shared glances until recess and lunch. It felt like a million years ago that I lived with them in Mr. Campbell's house of horrors.

"Where did they take you?" she asked as we sat down with our trays.

Her eyes were bright and her smile wider than I'd ever seen. "To an old house a mile or so from yours. It's up the hill and I can see the entire city from the back."

"Sounds nice. We're living with a couple from the church while Mother is in the hospital. They're nice, and we don't have any chores to do and they let me read," her voice vibrated with excitement.

I told her all about Penelope and the many books she gave me, offering that she could read any she wanted. My heart was filled with joy that she learned to read and loved it. Books were filled with wonderful places and characters who did marvelous things. I hoped to travel the world one day; not just in a book, but for real.

That evening I was lying on my bed reading Nancy Drew. I admired her more than any other character because she always solved the most intriguing mysteries and she was a girl like me only a little bit older. Something scratched at the window behind me, so I pushed the cover over and saw the puffy cat.

111

I pushed the locks that were glued with dust and dirt after a struggle and lifted the window but it didn't budge. Blowing out a breath, I slipped my shoes on and trudged to the glass room. Flashes of light from upstairs where Sara was watching TV lit my way. In the dark, chilly night air I walked around the house until I found my bedroom, but the cat was gone again.

I called and called until I found him on the bench by the tree. He rubbed against my legs then rubbed against a small clump of flowers near the base of the tree. The moon's light shone on an object beneath the flowers. I pushed the flowers aside. It was a rhinestone collar with the name *Salem* embedded on it. "Is this yours? Are you Salem?" I asked the cat. He responded by rubbing against my legs again.

"Well, Salem, I'm taking you to bed with me." I grabbed him up and we returned to my room where he lay on the edge of my bed, kneading at the covers.

Chapter 10
Ghost Town

The following week I went to the state spelling bee in Santa Fe. It was the first time in my life I'd been anywhere but Albuquerque and it took an hour or so to get there. The colorful, reddish-hued desert structures, occasional small clumps of shrubbery and miles between areas of civilization made for a boring drive. I dreamed of leaving the desert for a place lush with flora.

Once there, I was registered and ushered to a table with other children. We all sat quiet as all our faces were foreign to each other and ate the lunch they provided -- a ham and cheese sandwich and apple wedges.

After lunch they steered us to the stage and called us by name alphabetically to a seat. My last name Jones, I was always in the middle. The rules were gone over and adults were filed into the room. All adults, I assumed the children's parents. For me there was no one.

Into the third round the large door creaked open and a familiar redheaded Penelope, followed by a boy I didn't recognize, quietly walked up to a row in the back and dropped into the hard red plastic seats everyone else sat on. Her eyes scanned the stage and when she saw me she waved.

I watched her cling to my every letter as I spelled out word after word until there were three of us then two of us. I was given the word *prospicience*. I'd never heard or read the word before. I gave it a try and missed, but second was better than I'd ever dreamed when Mrs. Perkins first told me about it.

When it was over Penelope ran up to me and wrapped her arms around me. "You were so good!" She pulled away. "This is Kevin. He drove me here. You wanna come back with us? We'll stop for ice cream."

"Yeah, can I?"

"We'll find out." We scoured the area for the volunteer who drove me, and Penelope, with all her worldly wisdom, talked him into allowing me to ride back with them.

I licked the top scoop of my Neapolitan ice cream in a cone, catching a smooth glop of chocolate when Kevin spoke, "Want to see a real live ghost town?"

"She's eight." Penelope glowered at him and punched his arm.

"I want to see it. I'm not scared," I begged until Penelope gave in.

We drove through Santa Fe, leaving the tall stretch of mountains behind and surrounded by much smaller ones. The car rumbled over the road and bumped over the potholes in the packed dirt. Without the light from street lamps the night was almost black, the distant stars shedding a glow that caught the top of a cross as he stopped the car.

Long adobe structures spanned the shabby dirt street.

"Come on," he said. "Hide and seek?"

"Noo!" she punched him again.

He grabbed the scarf from her hair and ran. "Kevin!" she screamed after him. My eyes wandered the street and buildings. I pushed on a door that creaked open. Dim light from the moon bathed the inside and I was able to make out a counter and shelves as if this place had been a general store.

Giggles and tussling caught my attention. Out the window I saw Penelope tugging at her scarf, her long red braid now loose in waves that covered her back. I went behind the counter into a room with many shelves, I imagined were for storage. There was another door that led to the outside. I pushed it open and wandered behind the structures until I came to another door. It was heavy and didn't want to budge.

"I'll get that," said Kevin as he pushed hard against the door and it creaked open. We all went inside. There were a couple broken tables and chairs, a long bar with shelves behind it and a long spiral staircase.

Kevin slipped behind the bar. "I could be the saloon bartender and you'll be my barmaid," he said, taking a broken glass in his hand and a dusty bottle, pretending to pour when something dropped from the bottle into the glass. "Holy shit, we got a doobee," he said, rubbing his fingers over the object that looked like a cigarette.

He jumped over the bar. "Woohoo." Once on the other side he pulled out a match and lit it. "Here," he choked out between coughs handing it to Penelope. It stunk like rotten trash.

Penelope took it from him. "I can't believe I'm doing this. We don't even know who left this. What happens when they come back?"

I followed the staircase, their voices quieter as I went allowing the moon's light through the windows to guide my way. There were several rooms upstairs, some still had doors intact and others were falling off their hinges. The loose floorboards squeaked beneath each step until I hit one that gave and my foot went through.

I screamed from the surprise and pulled my leg out. My ankle was scratched and bleeding. I coddled it for a minute then placed my hands on the floor and pushed up but the floor gave and I went down. "Penelope!" I shrieked in horror.

My body thumped against something soft and I rolled off to the floor, tufts of dust filling the surrounding air. Footfalls pounded the floor. "Scarlett, where are you?"

"I fell into a room. I think it's behind the bar," I noted the location before falling and that seemed right.

"There's no door," she answered with a strained voice. I heard their hands against the wall then something clicked and the wall moved slowly outward and halted. "Scarlett, are you in there?"

"Yeah," I answered. Penelope's head peeked around the corner as she tried to slide her body through the small opening. "I can't fit but I know you can."

I stood, luckily I wasn't hurt except my ankle. With a slight limp I walked towards Penelope's voice and form. Taking one more glance at the room, I noted I'd fallen on top of a rolled sleeping bag. That didn't fit. It didn't make sense.

I slipped through the door and Penelope pressed me against her. "Are you OK?"

"Mostly, except the scratch on my ankle."

She leaned down and rubbed her finger over the small trail of blood. "Grab onto my neck. I'll carry you."

"Let's get out of here," suggested Kevin.

We made it out into the summer night air. Its familiar chill clung to me as we walked to the car and settled inside. With the windows down, Kevin turned the car around and slowly coasted up the road. I turned around in the back seat and spotted the form of a man silhouetted against the church.

I squeezed my eyes shut and reopened them and the man was still there. I tugged Penelope's arm propped on the arm rest. "There's someone else. Look." I pointed.

"I don't see anyone."

How couldn't she see him? "There, in front of the church."

"I don't see anything either. It's your imagination," Kevin added.

"Kevin!" shouted Penelope in anguish.

He swerved the car and I was forced against the steel door but clearly saw the coyote. His eyes glowing in the dark as he ran directly in front of the car.

"You scared the shit out of me. Watch the road!" Penelope scolded. "And step on it. It's ten o'clock. I have to be back by midnight."

We made it home with ten minutes to spare. That night was the most fun and adventure I'd ever had, but only a snapshot of what was to come.

Chapter 11
Chimera

*I*t was the last day of school when, with tears in her eyes, Lindsey told me they were moving. They were going to live with their grandmother in California. I was devastated as I'd hoped we could play that summer and everything would be better now that Mr. Campbell was gone. She was my best friend and I'd lost her.

I stepped off the bus and dragged home, dropping onto my bed and crying into my pillow. Penelope and the twins went out and Sara retired as always to the second floor. I wandered into the glass room and took out a Nancy Drew story. I wasn't into the fourth chapter when a shadow passed by the window.

It caught my attention and I watched and jumped off the couch, skipping to the window. It was a boy

121

with a baseball hat propped on his head. I grabbed the flashlight by the door and walked outside barefoot in my nighty and followed the boy along the cacti path, staying several feet behind him. When he got to the tree, he stopped and shifted his head my direction. My heart skipped and I dropped behind a cactus. After several minutes he moved on.

I continued on the path and stopped when I got to the tree. He walked downhill past the little adobe building. When I couldn't see him anymore I jogged to it. He disappeared and my heart dropped. *Where did he go?*

A familiar soft fluff rubbed against my leg. "Hi, Salem," I whispered, shoving the flashlight beneath my arm and picking him up and padded downhill, the dry, cracked ground firm against my feet. Once I got to the bottom of the hill I expected to see the boy but it was an empty meadow of sparse wildflowers. Salem meowed and wiggled so I put him down.

He traipsed through the flowers and sat then meowed at me. "What are you doing, silly cat?" His response was given in meows. Beneath him was a plank of metal, moving him aside there was a handle. I took a deep breath and lifted.

"What are you doing out here?" shot a voice through the darkness.

A shadow form moved closer to me and I soon recognized the ball cap of the boy I followed.

I halted with the door in my hand. "I'm exploring," I stated confidently but inside my nerves were tied in a knot.

When he got close enough I made out his features, a pointy nose, oval face, and thinnish lips. Blond curls popped out from under his cap and bright green eyes twinkled under the starry night. His pant legs were tattered on the ends and his feet were as bare as mine.

"Exploring at night?"

"Yes." I continued lifting until the door stopped.

"What do you think is down there?" he asked, gazing into the blackness of the hole.

"I don't know but I'm going to figure it out," I declared and Salem stared into the hole with us.

"We can't go in there without any light."

I clicked the flashlight on, pointing it into his face. Icy green eyes framed in a pale, almost translucent, face stared at me. He knocked my arm and guided it downward. "Don't point it at me but in the hole."

The beam lit up a staircase. I gasped and placed a foot onto the first cold step then the next.

"We shouldn't go down there," he warned and stepped away.

"And why not?" I smarted, taking another step. I was daring him because I wasn't really brave enough to go alone. Salem stepped behind me as if he was my little protector.

"Fine!" He stepped onto the stairs and followed Salem and I into a long room with a door at the other end.

Along the walls of the room were drawers, rows and rows of them.

A string of lights came to life and buzzed from the ceiling. "There's a light switch," he smirked, leaning against the wall.

"What is this place?"

"It looks like a crypt." He pushed off the wall. "Inside all those drawers are dead people."

Tobias Beloved Husband 1833 - 1893
Gwendolyn 1863 -- 1865

My eyes scanned them all until I came to blank ones. "What about these?"

He pulled the drawer. "Let's see."

"No, you can't do that." I pushed it back. "You'll disturb them."

"Don't you think we already are?"

I hadn't thought of that. "I guess so, but we can't open the drawers -- that's disrespectful."

He nodded. "My guess, no one's in them yet. The blank ones are for those still alive."

Still alive? Sara lived here alone. I shrugged. The earliest drawers dated back to the early 1800s. The latest dates were more recent.

Sharon 1930 -- 1945

Jonathan 1899 -- 1965

Sharon was only fifteen; how did she die? "Scarlett," voices in the night reverberated against the walls of the crypt interrupting my thoughts.

"Hey we should..." my words hung in the air. I stood alone in the crypt. I didn't know where he'd gone, or Salem. He'd vanished too. I scurried up the steps and peered over the edge. Three flashlights shone and waved in various directions over the hill. I climbed out and dropped the lid then scurried towards the lights. "Here, I'm here."

Penelope's eyes, bronze beneath the light of the moon, scowled at me. "What are you doing out here? It's almost midnight."

I swallowed and she grasped my hand and dragged me along. "I found her," she called and we were soon joined by Vince and Jeff.

I stumbled to keep up with Penelope's swift, long stride, my little hand firm inside her solid grasp so much it burned. Past the tree and through the cactus jungle we rushed until we reached the glass room. Vince swung the door open and we rushed inside. The large grandfather clock rang as the door fell into place. Bolts clicking rumbled through the house, followed by a rolling scrape as long shutters fell against the glass panes of the room.

Vince dropped onto the couch. "We made it."

Penelope let go of my hand and scolded me, "Don't ever go wandering out there at night again. Sara's only rule is to be home by midnight. Once the doors lock you can't get in until morning."

A tear rolled down my cheek. I'd disappointed her and she'd always been good to me, even gave me a wonderful collection of books.

She knelt down, fear and sadness in her eyes. "I'm sorry. I'm not mad. I was worried for you and didn't want you stuck out there all night. You understand?" She wiped the tears that were now streaming down my face.

I sniffled. "I'm sorry, Penelope." She held me to her and I asked, "Why?" Our rooms in the back of the house muffled the noises and my stubborn window made sense. It must be glued or nailed shut.

"We don't know," Jeff shrugged, "it's the way it is and we follow the rule."

The scent of bacon wafted into my room and teased my nose until I opened my eyes. I loved crispy bacon and followed my nose to the kitchen. Sara, Selma, Penelope, and the twins were already seated around the large block table, piling bacon, eggs, and waffles onto their plates.

"The Chimera's awake," said Jeff holding a fork loaded with three layers of waffles and dripping with syrup to his mouth.

"What's a Chimera?" I slid into an empty chair across from him.

He swallowed after a couple chews. "It's a mythical animal made of two types of animals."

"So my eyes make me one?" I grabbed three slices of bacon.

"It's a good nickname for you. I've never met anyone with different colored eyes."

I liked the sound of it and repeated it in my head *Chimera, Chimera* as I scooped a load of scrambled eggs and dumped them on my plate then buttered a waffle and drizzled syrup over it until it ran over the sides. According to Selma, my eyes gave me the ability to see and interact with spirits, and now I was a combination of two different animals. Gen always told me my eyes gave me special powers and it was all coming together. I needed to rethink The Purple Mask and write new stories where she discovers she's a fairy-human Chimera and learns she has the power to speak with the dead.

Sara pushed her chair out and stood. "We don't all sit down for breakfast together often but today is a special day." I noted smiles erupting on the twins' faces. "Happy birthday, Vince and Jeff!"

Penelope started, "Happy birthday to you..." and the rest of us chimed in. A birthday breakfast was so thoughtful and made me wonder if they'd get a special dinner too. What a great present. I won two hundred and fifty dollars from the spelling bee and hadn't spent a dime, which gave me a really great idea.

After breakfast I stopped by Penelope's room and stuck my head in. "Can you and Kevin take me to town? I want to buy the twins a present and a new journal for myself and colored pencils."

The sun against her hair always made it shine bright red. Maybe she'd be a new character in my stories and help The Purple Mask fight evil. "I'll call him. What are you going to buy them?"

I shrugged. "I'll know when I see it."

Her eyes lit up. "Come in and close the door."

From under her bed she pulled out two '33 size LPs, Peter, Paul and Mary and Chubby Checker's latest. My eyes widened. "They'll love those!"

She giggled. "I know and Sara got them a new record player."

When home, it was common to hear music coming from their room, but the player they had didn't always work right. Vince said he had the magic touch and had fewer problems with it then his brother who was less patient. I could get them another record but wanted to get something different, something unique they'd always remember me by.

Two hours later Kevin pulled his green Impala in front of the house and Penelope and I rushed outside and jumped in, leaving the mouth-watering aromas of their birthday dinner. The mall was filled with so many stores. It was like walking into a bakery and having to decide between chocolate or maple glazed, or maybe lemon-filled. I gawked at the stores; everything anybody could ever want was inside the magical palace of stores.

They first brought me to the bookstore. My eyes marveled at the shelves of books and their shiny covers. In the back corner of the store I found journals in every color. I chose one with a plain cover so I could draw my own and a new pack of twenty-four different colored pencils. As we left the store I spotted something else, *A Wrinkle in Time* by Madeleine L'Engel. I so wanted it, the story intrigued me. Then another book caught my eye, *We Have Always Lived in the Castle* by Shirley Jackson. I considered buying both, but remembered I still needed to get the twins something.

"I'll get it, gotta feed the book worms' minds," said Kevin, squeezing the top of my head. It was as if he read my mind.

"You'd do that, for me? It's not a special day for me or anything."

"Gifts don't have to come only on special days but to special people any day," he smiled and grabbed one of the books, tucking it under his arm along with Ray Bradbury's *Something Wicked This Way Comes.*

I skipped along, clutching tightly my new books, journal, and colored pencils but I still didn't know what to buy the twins. I browsed records and disco balls then picked up The Everly Brothers' latest when I spotted it. The perfect gift -- a gold-plated metal keychain of an animal that looked half dragon and half lion -- a Chimera. They left today to find a car and with that car they'd need a keychain and with this keychain they'd never forget the girl that bought it for them.

The twins rolled home that evening in a 1958 Gold Ford Thunderbird with a rag top. I marveled with them at the shiny chrome knobs and soft leather-like interior. "Want to go for a ride later?" Vince asked.

Oh yes! I wanted to go for a ride with the top down and feel the wind in my hair. I glanced at Sara, who smiled and winked. "After dinner maybe we can all go for a ride."

I grabbed one of Vince's hands and one of Jeff's. "Come on," I tugged, "the house smells delicious. Selma made a wonderful dinner and we have presents."

With my urging, and laughter all around, we entered the house and took our seats at the table. We ate homemade lasagna, salad and cheesy garlic bread. Sara said it was 'a carb delight'. I didn't know what she meant and when I asked she chuckled and said 'It's loaded with carbohydrates which growing boys need in large quantities'. Selma also made a chocolate on chocolate cake. My stomach felt like it was going to explode with all the food I stuffed into it.

With large, saucer eyes and joy-filled comments they opened their presents. When they got to mine Vince said, "A Chimera like you," and Jeff pulled out their car keys and tugged them onto the loop.

"This is the best keychain. You're a cool kid Chimera," Jeff said, dangling the keys. "Who's up for a ride?"

"I think you kids should go have fun. I can't handle late nights anymore." Sara encouraged us out the door.

Tucked in the back with Penelope, the top down and the wind blowing our hair crazy, we rode "The Strip". It wasn't quite what I imagined but awesome nonetheless. We took the car on something called "The Cruise". From what I could tell it was going in circles around a central area really slow. People revved their engines and everyone talked from one car to the next while driving, beeped their horns at friends and sometimes one person crawled from one car into another while the cars were in motion.

The twins bragged and pulled the car over into a drive-through fast food place. They popped the hood and a crowd of teens ogled their engine. I was proud to be in the middle of it all. The excitement rushed through my

135

veins even though I didn't have any idea what they were talking about. It was simply magic!

"Thirsty?" Penelope asked.

"Yes, please."

"Come on." She held the door open and I slid along the soft seat and followed her inside. Waitresses on roller skates swished and spun by us. I admired how fluid they were on the skates carrying trays. Their shimmering red skirts swayed as they rushed past us.

"Penelope," called someone. A waitress on skates with her glimmer skirt met us at the counter. She leaned across it, her tight dark curls springing every direction and lipstick as red as Penelope's hair made her dark complexion appear darker. Her deep brown almond eyes twinkled under the lights and she looked charmed.

"I'm having a girls' night sleepover Wednesday Night. You should come." The dimple in her cheek accentuated her smile and pearly white teeth.

"Yeah, I'll be there," answered Penelope.

"Groovy, see you about six o'clock." She sailed off on her skates.

We rolled home by eleven thirty. Sara was upstairs, watching TV -- given away by the flashes of light cutting through the darkness of the living room. I pulled out my new books and couldn't choose which to read first so I did Eeny Meeny Miny Moe which stopped on *A Wrinkle in Time*. Flipping the cover, I read silently, my ears poised and listening. The chimes of the grandfather clock covered the barrels of the locks as they clicked over for the night.

Chapter 12
The Corridor

The days passed, some slower than others. In the evening when the sun went down I'd make my way through the cactus jungle, past the tree and down the hill where I'd play with Timmy -- the boy in the hat. I didn't exactly know where he lived but he assured me it wasn't far. We played games like hide and seek and tag.

One evening while playing hide and seek, running out of good hiding places I snuck into the crypt, walked past the drawers and tried the door on the other end. When it opened I sighed a breath of relief and hid behind the door. It was a good twenty minutes before I heard him on the stairs.

My hands pressed against the door I waited, his footsteps thumped against the ground, moving closer until the knob turned and the door opened.

The ceiling lights glowing against him made him appear paler than normal and his pale eyes carried disappointment. "I thought we decided the crypt was off-limits?"

I chuckled and ran through the long corridor, into the darkness. "Catch me!"

"Scarlett, come back!" he called but I didn't stop.

His steps pounded behind me. We ran through the pitch-black passageway. I'll never know exactly why I chose to do it; an instinct, a forbidden desire. All I know is it wasn't bravery. I was running so fast when I got to the end and it shifted uphill I stumbled and tripped but pulled myself up and faced a solid wall.

Timmy caught up. "We should go back."

I shook my head. "No. What is this? Where are we?" The pieces swirled together in my head. The crypt was at the other end. I was running toward the house. I pushed against the wall. It was wet, cold, and dense metal. I felt it move. "Help me."

He shrugged. "You're impossible." He pushed against it with me and soon it budged. A faded rainbow of colors shone through the widening crack. My curiosity grew and soon the gap was large enough to squeeze through.

The rainbow lights bathed my skin and a spiral staircase wove upward. I glided up the stairs, following the rainbow. On the second floor was a landing, three walls had a window and a door on the fourth wall. The cactus jungle and beyond that the lights of Albuquerque. I turned and spotted the little adobe structure with nothing beyond it then the front yard.

"We're in the tower," I whispered.

"We shouldn't be here," Timmy warned.

I was more interested in learning what caused the rainbow and continued up the staircase as it wound around to the third floor which looked identical to the second. Holding onto the rail I moved upward until I came to a fourth floor. My head just above floor level, my eyes glued on the stained glass windows on all four sides that were responsible for the mystical rainbow. "It's so pretty."

"That's what I like about it," said a girl, startling me. In the middle of the floor was a young girl with long golden hair. The colorful lights floated through her. She stood and the paper dolls she'd been playing with dropped to the ground. "I'm Shari."

I glanced behind me to make sure Timmy hadn't disappeared. He was still there with an angry face as he glared at me. I continued to the fourth floor. "I'm Scarlett and this is Timmy."

"You want to play with me?"

I nodded with delight. I had two friends my age now. Timmy's face softened as we all dropped to the floor.

"How did you know this room was here?" I questioned.

"I've known for a long time. I come here a lot. Can you come here again?" Shari asked in excitement. "I'm alone so much and would love to have more friends."

"Yes! My best friend moved and Timmy is my only friend now. Maybe we can all play together. In the evening we play outside. It would be so much fun to have another person," I said, elated.

Timmy glanced at me, then her, with narrowed eyes. The rainbow washed through him the same as Shari. A smile swept over his face and he said, "It would be more fun."

She smiled. "Yes, yes we have to do that!"

Eleven gongs echoed through the walls of the tower. I knew I was in the house but not in the part of the house I needed to be and I didn't know if heavy bolts would lock us in the turret too. The last thing I wanted was my new friends stuck inside the tower all night. I stood. "We need to go."

Shari gazed at me curiously. "We do?"

"We do," answered Timmy.

When I got to the third floor I tried the door, thinking maybe we could sneak through the house instead of following the cold, damp corridor but the door was locked from the other side. The second floor door was locked too. *Why were the doors locked?* A little frustrated, I sighed and we wound down the staircase until we were back on the bottom floor. We squeezed through the doorway and back into the passageway, pulling the door closed behind us.

Skidding down the hill and running through the corridor my hand brushed against something rough and solid half-way through. I didn't stop to investigate; there was no time. We reached the other end. Light shone through the open doorway and we scampered into the crypt, giggling from the rush.

Once outside I asked, "Can we all meet here tomorrow evening as soon as the sun sets?"

"Oh yes!" Shari responded.

We all waved as we ran in different directions. I made it into the house with time to spare and strode through the living room, using the light from Sara's TV to guide me then around the bend and down the hall to my bedroom. I was ready and lying in bed by the time Penelope and the twins got home.

A week or so later, I was in the kitchen helping Selma which I did every day she joined us. I was in the pantry collecting items for Selma when Sara strolled into the kitchen. At first I thought it was Selma and peeked my head around the corner to ask how many cans of green beans -- usually it was two. She walked to a cabinet that didn't have anything we used and scooted everything out of the way. I scooted further out the doorway and watched her take down a tin like the kind Christmas candy came in. She popped the lid off and stuffed something inside. I couldn't make out what it was since her fist was balled. The item didn't make any noise. She placed the lid back onto it and pushed it back into place inside the cabinet and moved everything else into place.

I scooted back into the pantry so she wouldn't see me and hit the step stool. I fell and it crashed to the floor behind me. The cans of green beans rolled out of my hands and across the floor.

"Let me help you up, dear." Sara grabbed for my hand.

I gulped. "I was helping Selma."

"I see that," she said looking at the green bean cans strewn across the floor.

We picked them up and she left without saying a word about the mysterious tin or what she was doing. I made a mental note to find out what was in the tin later when she retired to bed and the teens were out for the night.

That evening Penelope stayed home and she made popcorn while we watched a rerun of *Twilight Zone*. She liked anything with mystery. After, she read me an Edgar Allen Poe short, *The*

Cask of Amontillado. The character descending into the vault reminded me of running through the corridor. It was creepy but I didn't fear it.

It wasn't until a few days later that I snuck into the kitchen, pulled out the step stool and dug through the cabinet. The tin was filled with one hundred dollar bills. There must have been a few thousand squished into that one little tin. I wondered if she had cash stashed anywhere else. I didn't touch the money but scooted it back into place along with the other dishes which were tarnished silver and looked really old.

A tinkle rang through a teacup as I forced it back into its place, grabbing it I stared inside at a collection of keys. They had loops on the end filled in with an intricate design. *The turret doors?* I remembered the doors were locked from the inside of the house. *How would I get to them without Sara noticing?*

I remembered brushing past something in the tunnel and thought about it. The little adobe structure was locked and in the middle of the floor was a loop and door. I climbed onto the counter and grabbed the keyring then stuffed them into my pocket, grabbed a flashlight and scurried through the cactus jungle, past the tree and to the little empty building. A familiar purr grabbed my attention and I glanced at Salem perched by my heels.

I shoved each key in the lock until I heard the barrel click and turn over, pushing the door open I took a step inside the building. The air inside was cooler than the air outside. I tugged at the loop in the floor and pulled it open and shone my flashlight into the darkness. Its glow illuminated a steep staircase which Salem and I descended into. The corridor was damp and musky and the tunnel appeared to be made of cement stones. A string of lights hung off loops near the ceiling but I didn't see a switch.

This was the same tunnel that went to the house, I was sure. I followed it toward the house and came upon the steep slope and door that opened into the turret. I pressed against the door. It moved easier this time and creaked less. Salem slipped through the crack and with another push I squeezed through and followed the cat that was already bounding up the steps. The rainbow colors shimmered through Salem's silvery coat.

On the second floor I rechecked the door for a lock but it was flush against the panel, as I remembered. The third floor door as well. When we got to the top, Shari was there playing with her paper dolls.

Her eyes lit up. "Scarlett! And you brought a cat." She scooped Salem into her arms. "Hi kitty." She sifted through his piles of fluffy fur to glance at his collar that I put back on him the day I found it. "Salem. What a magical name!"

We played with the dolls as Salem took a seat near a window. The light through the stained glass taking on a dreamlike glow as the moon's light replaced the setting sun. I found all of it odd yet was so wrapped up in having friends my own age and the anonymity

of the house I didn't think about what
my brain told me was true.

Chapter 13
Witchy Witch

I enjoyed the wistful summer evenings playing with Shari and Timmy and missed them when school started again. It was lonely without Lindsey and the other students treated me harshly. At first it was glances filled with suspicion, then quiet talk among them. When I entered the room their chatter stopped but I heard it: 'It's her fault, she started the fire'. But it wasn't my fault. It was Mr. Campbell's fault. He was the evil one and got exactly what he deserved.

The rumors spread like wildfire and the whispers behind my back were said to my face as I walked through the halls. *Wicked girl, murderer, just like your dad.* The word rape came to mind again. I skipped lunch every day and spent my time in the library sinking into the world of fiction. During journal time I continued The Purple Mask adventures. After school, when possible, I snuck downhill to the meadow and played with Shari and Timmy. I told them all about the horrible kids at school.

My birthday came and went with a huge celebration in Sara's home, a place I was loved. I woke to strawberry crepes and a dinner of macaroni and cheese and bacon wrapped hamburgers. My cake was lavender with a purple fairy-like topper stuck in the middle. I'd told Selma and Sara all about The Purple Mask adventures and read them many. They loved the stories, each one of them. For my gifts I got purple wings and a matching mask along with a new journal and a collection of markers. It was a birthday filled with the magic of love and family.

The days came and went and school became unbearable. I stuck to myself as much as possible and didn't look the other kids in the eye. It came to a breaking point one Friday afternoon in late May when I slipped into the bathroom. I didn't go when everyone else was there because of the vile comments and hate towards me, instead I held it, on days I couldn't, I got a pass. I was in the stall when I heard the door open and one set of footsteps walk through the door. They stopped and didn't go into another stall.

I held my breath and let it go as I opened the door. A girl I didn't know but recognized. She was one of the students who gave me the worst time. She was a year older and much larger than me. Her dark hair was pulled back into a tight ponytail. The veins in her head popped out through her light skin. She leaned back against a sink as I maneuvered towards the only other sink next to her.

"You're as evil as your father. One day you'll be in jail too," she said with satisfaction.

I ignored her and didn't look her in the face. When I tried to move past her she grabbed my upper arms and rammed me into the metal wall of the outside stall. "Little Scarlett named for the color of blood." She moved closer to me. Her brown eyes staring into mine. My heart beat against my chest. "You know how I know? Your eyes, even one of your eyes is red from the blood of your mother."

It wasn't true, none of it was true. My real mother and father. Whoever they were, I didn't know them and I wasn't evil. She let go of my arms and punched my stomach. My fear turned to hate as I remembered the evil deeds of Mr. Campbell and without thinking I kicked her between the legs. She dropped to the floor holding her crotch and I rushed past her and to my classroom.

About twenty minutes later I was called to the office where the girl was sitting across from our principal. His green eyes shifted from her to me as I took another seat next to her. He rose and closed the door then took his seat and leaned his arms against the bulky desk, tenting his hands. "Theresa, this is the second time in a month you've been here."

His eyes shifted to me and disappointment washed over his face. "Scarlett, you've never been to my office. Your grades and behavior are always good. The ladies in the library and your teachers have always spoken highly of you. Why are you here?"

I swallowed. Her piercing eyes on my head, I knew I had to lie. I couldn't tell the truth or she'd haunt and bully me for the rest of my school days. "It was an accident. I tripped and fell into her."

The principal's eyes narrowed and I knew he didn't believe me. He wanted me to say she started it. It was all Theresa's fault. I held my ground. The pain from her punch still burning my stomach. His gaze drifted toward her. "Is that right, Theresa?"

She nodded and he leaned back in his chair. The sun filtering through the window behind him, his gray hairs caught in its beams. "That's not what you said earlier." He cupped his hands and waited for her response.

"I was hurt so I didn't get the story straight." She shifted in her seat.

"Then I suggest the two of you get back to class." He waved us off and picked up a newspaper lying on his desk.

We scurried to class and it wasn't until I returned to school the following Monday that I heard. My jaw dropped when I caught what the whispers in the hallway were saying as people parted the way for me to pass: 'Theresa is dead, she was pushed down the stairs. Scarlett's a witch, she did it'.

I blinked back the tears and ignored the burn in my nose as I rushed past the crowd, keeping my head high. That evening after school I rushed to my room, buried my head in the pillow and bawled into it.

Penelope must have heard from her room because soon she joined me. Her hand caressing my head. "Scarlett, what's wrong?"

I hadn't told her anything about the students at school and their hatred of me and the rumors they spread. Choking it out because I didn't want to hold it in anymore I told her about Theresa and the incident in the bathroom and what the kids whispered in the hallways throughout the day.

Her eyes round with horror. "That was an accident, an unfortunate accident. She tripped and fell down the stairs."

I sniffled. "I know."

She pulled me into her chest. "Have these kids been bullying you all year?"

I nodded.

"You hold your head high. You're not a witch but a sweet girl who is the closest thing to a sister I have. I know their older siblings and I'll put a stop to this." Fire and determination flashed through her eyes and her hair appeared as flames.

For the rest of the school year the rumors stopped but their eyes spoke a thousand words as they stared at me like I was a freak. They still thought I was a witch, convinced I was guilty of killing Mr. Campbell and now Theresa.

Chapter 14
A Lonely Highway

That summer started much as the last and I spent most of it with Timmy and Shari, scurrying through the tunnel and playing in the top of the turret. Penelope had been accepted to college with a scholarship and would be leaving in early August. The twins still had another year. By this time I was convinced the social worker had forgotten about me. She'd never returned, never brought anything I had at the Campbells' that might not have burned, or even returned for a visit like she did at the Campbells'.

Penelope spent many evenings working, as did the twins. When she was home we watched summer reruns on TV and stuffed our faces with popcorn and ice cream which is exactly what we were doing the evening Sara got the call. A nagging festered at my gut but with the excitement and pure joy of spending time with Penelope I'd pushed it down until the ringing of the phone broke the magic of the moment.

The color drained from Sara's face and she became white as a sheet as she stumbled over her words. The twins were on their way to see *The Beach Boys* when a truck slammed on its brakes to avoid hitting a car stalled in its lane with its lights out. He hadn't seen the car until it was too late. The trailer jack-knifed as the twins in their Thunderbird slid beneath it, decapitating them.

Their bodies were embalmed and placed into the crypt, along with all the other dead people. Tears filled the eyes of all the students, Penelope, Sara, and myself during the funeral that took place in the meadow.

August came and Penelope left, giving me her address to write as often as I could. We promised each other to keep in touch. Her bus left the station, she waved from her window and I waved back until the bus was a speck.

Sara didn't drive so we took the same taxi home we used to get there.

I was alone. The kids at school didn't harass me but they didn't befriend me either. At home, the house was quiet without the twins' music and my talks with Penelope. I often went into the twins' room and listened and put their records on. I imagined them there, joking and laughing as they called me Chimera.

Penelope left me her collection of books to care for, saying she wouldn't have time in college. I devoured them. I remembered my parents who loved me and my butterflies. I drew and colored one in every color, cut them out and taped them to my wall. Then I drew my parents' faces as I remembered them.

Penelope made it home for my birthday. It was the best present as I ran to her and wrapped my arms tight around her. Only the three of us, the celebration was as extravagant as the last. Selma made her delicious homemade pizza, drizzled in various cheeses and loaded with pepperoni. Penelope bought me a purple diary with a golden latch and lock. It was the most magnificent present -- even better than the collection of new clothes and the AM/FM radio Sara bought me. I used the power within my eyes to snap pictures of that day to last forever.

The seasons came and went. Penelope's visits and my evenings with Timmy and Shari were the light in my life. I often snuck Salem into my room at night before the barrels clicked over and locked him out. My lonely existence continued until shortly after my eleventh birthday when a large boom from one of the floors above me woke me from my sleep.

I jumped out of bed and raced to the stairs. "Sara!" I called several times, but she didn't answer. The flashes from her TV lit the staircase. I'd never been upstairs but made my way that night, standing at the edge of the steps I spotted Sara on the ground.

I rushed towards her, "Sara," and gently touched her back. When I took my hand away a light rose with it until her form appeared in front of me. "Sara?" I asked, pushing up from the floor and taking a step backwards.

She stepped towards me. Her silver hair changing to gold, the wrinkles in her face vanishing until her complexion was taut and she was decades younger. I watched in marvel as I heard Shari's voice behind me, "It's OK, Scarlett."

I turned and watched her form drift through the wall, a gold plate shone through her chest and I realized the wall wasn't a wall but a doorway to the turret. She glided towards Sara who welcomed her in her arms and kissed her head. Sara lifted her eyes, placing them on me. "It's time for us to go."

Their bodies faded into the air. I stood alone in the room staring at Sara's body lying face down on the floor. Ghosts. They were ghosts and I'd known it since Salem first woke me up that morning in my bed but I refused to believe it. The evenings I spent in the twins' room imagining them there with me, so life like I could touch and feel them, their laughter surrounding me. Then I remembered what Selma said about my eyes and having the ability to see and interact with the dead.

I grabbed the set of keys out of the brass tea cup and the cash out of the tin and called 911, attempting to make my voice sound older. I dropped the phone back on the receiver then hauled myself up the stairs. Pushing the key into the secret door, flush with the wall, I turned and the bolt clicked and I vanished into the turret.

The ambulance came and the police. They searched for me but didn't find me.

"It's time to go, Scarlett," Timmy whispered in my ear.

"Timmy." I turned and watched the rainbow of colors shine through him. I took his hand and we walked through the tunnel and into the crypt where I spent the night.

Chapter 15
Fork in the Road

I stayed on the property for a few more days, coming and going from the house through the secret passage. Once Sara's body was safe in the crypt I stuffed a few items into my backpack, checked the phone book for Melissa Jones. Not finding it, I left and went to the public library and scoured the phone books there. After searching through four different area phone books I found a Melissa Jones.

"You're that girl. The one they're looking for," said a dumpy woman with a round face and double chins.

They were looking for me? I thought everyone forgot about me, everyone but Penelope. I watched the funeral from afar, standing inside the little adobe structure. Every part of my being wanted to be there to say goodbye, to feel Penelope hug me, but

I didn't. I figured if I showed my face someone would remember a child lived in Sara's home and they'd haul me off again. I said my goodbye later in the closed crypt. Shaking the thought and mustering my courage I answered, "No, I'm not. My mom is over there." I pointed to a blonde lady in the mystery section. "Go on, ask her," I dared the nosey lady.

To my shock and horror she walked towards the woman. *Oh no!*

"Psst." I swiveled my head and spotted Timmy. "Over here." He waved me towards him. I glanced at the address and recited it in my mind then scurried around the corner. He pointed me towards a side exit and vanished, reappearing by the nosey lady and the woman I claimed was my mother. He pushed several books from the other side and they hit the floor. Both ladies gasped and immediately began to pick them up.

Within seconds he was by my side and we were busting through the side door and running down the street. My

Scarlett Evan's Girls Volume 1

plan hadn't gone further than finding my mother's address. I slid around a corner and ran smack into Kevin.

"Where you going, Chimera?"

I didn't know if it was luck, karma, or something else, but at the moment I needed a ride and Kevin was staring at me with wide eyes. "Can you drive me somewhere?" I glanced around and noted Timmy disappeared again. I admired that ability since I couldn't do it.

"Everyone's searching for you. The only place I should take you is to the police station. People think you were kidnapped. It's in the paper and on the radio." He leaned down and took my hands.

He said *should* which meant *I'm not but it would be the right thing to do.* "I'm here, and look, nobody stole me." *Heck, who'd want me?* "I found my mother's address and need a ride."

His expression soured. "Your mother? I thought she met the great maker in the sky?" We strolled down the street and he pushed a cap over my head. "Just in case, play along."

"Those were the parents who I thought were my parents until the day…" my voice trailed off and I flipped the subject. "This is the mom who gave birth to me."

He held the door of his Impala open for me. "I'll do this but you have to call Penelope at least. She's worried sick."

I agreed. I'd recited the address so many times in my head I spit it at him. I had no idea what I'd say when I got there. I was the baby she didn't want. The rape-child; but it wasn't my fault. It didn't matter I knew what he did to her -- unlawful fornication. That's what Mr. Campbell preached at his church, but rape was worse. It was a violent crime where my father forced my mother against her will to have sex with him. In a way, I got it, why she rejected me. There was a part inside me that day that thought maybe when she saw me she'd have a change of heart. Eleven years can change a person. I clung to that hope as we drove through the city and into the suburb outside Albuquerque where she lived.

"That's it. Should I come in with you?" he asked as we both stared at the small cookie-cutter home.

"No, thank you. Umm... I'll call Penelope later, OK? You can go home." I opened the door and threw my legs over the seat.

He reached across the center console and placed his hand on my arm. "This isn't a good idea. Are you sure you don't want to leave?"

"No." Good idea, bad idea, it was something I needed to do. The walk towards her front door was the longest fifty feet ever.

Strolling alongside me Timmy returned. "I'm here even when you can't see me. This is for us." He grabbed my hand and swung it as we walked towards the foreboding plain brown front door. *What a weird thing for him to say. Us*, the small word echoed inside my head.

I rang the doorbell and almost chickened out but then footsteps halted on the other side of the door and I heard the locks click and the door opened. "Can I help you?"

A beautiful lady with blonde ringlets, as wild as my own, and deep amber eyes inspected me. I felt Timmy near but couldn't see him, drawing on his strength. "I'm Scarlett."

Her amber eyes turned fiery red. "No, this is a joke and a very bad one." She peeked her head outside. "Where are your hoodlum friends that put you up to this? Huh, where are they?"

I was shocked, mortified. "There's no friends, no one, just me. I'm Scarlett, Scarlett Jones. The baby you gave up eleven years ago. Look, we have the same hair." I pulled a strand of curls.

"Get out of here before I call the police!" She began to close the door but I stuck my foot in the way.

My heart dropped like shattered glass and tears poured from my eyes. I'd never really made her out to be anything special in my mind but didn't expect to be rejected to my face. "I'm your daughter. Can I please come in, please? I just want to meet you."

Her face softened. "Well we can't stand here and talk. Once the neighborhood kids figure it out all the pranks will start." She opened the door.

The house inside was cozy. The olive green chair didn't match the blue couch and the end tables were light wood and a black chest was used as a coffee table. The TV dial had tape dangling from it and a small set of cockeyed rabbit ears sat atop it.

"Sit down. How did you find me?"

No milk and cookies? I sucked up my tears. "A long time ago at the home I looked up my file and found your name, so when Sara died and I thought the social worker lady forgot about me I found your address at the public library in one of the phone books."

"What is it you want from me?" Her voice was cold as a frigid Antarctic snowstorm.

"I... I don't really know. I'm not a little girl anymore; maybe you can tell me about... about you," I said softly, fidgeting my hands on my lap.

She swallowed a lump. "There's nothing to tell."

"Or you don't want to tell," I spat.

Her eyes narrowed. "I don't have a daughter. You were a mistake."

The tears swelled in my eyes again. "Why do you hate me? Can you at least tell me that?"

She visibly shuddered and wrenched her hands together. "Hate isn't the right word." That was the moment I realized her actions towards me were disgust and fear as she sank back in her chair like a child. "You were never meant to be."

"I know what happened. Well I understand the harsh word and... and people whisper behind my back. They say awful things. Please don't hate me too." *Freak eyes, murderer,* and the stares from other children swirled through my head.

171

She glanced away from me and brought her hand to her mouth then carefully formed her words. "The rape wasn't the worst part. It was when I learned you were a twin but your twin..." she cleared her throat and her voice shook, "... died in the womb and you absorbed him."

The room became deathly still and silent as if we were in a vacuum. "But that's not possible, is it?"

She shook her head as tears coasted down her cheeks. "You have your father's spirit and he's a wicked man. Your twin was only the beginning; one day you will do hideous things to people."

My jaw dropped. *What was she saying?* It didn't register. I understood her words and they played like a broken record in my head. My body was numb. I couldn't feel anything.

"Your eyes, don't you understand?" She furrowed her brows. "One is yours, the other is his."

I'm truly a Chimera. The nickname I was always so fond of now had a different meaning. I was two people, an evil one and a good one. *Which half would I choose?*

My thoughts were shattered when she jumped out of her chair and stumbled backwards into the wall. Her eyes round and staring to my side. I glanced up and saw Timmy standing beside me. My eyes flashed back to her.

"Get out! Get out!" her voice quivered and shook.

"You see him?"

"Get out of my house!"

"I... I'm sorry." My voice and body trembled as I fled her house and sprinted down the middle of the road.

"Scarlett, Scarlett," called a voice, and firm arms wrapped around me. Blurry eyed, I stared upwards at Kevin. I dropped into him and he scooped me up. Without a word he set me inside his car and took me home with him.

By the time we reached his apartment I'd thought about it all, over and over, and the part that shocked me the most was that my mother also saw ghosts. She had my amber eyes, meaning the green was from my father and my sibling, my unborn twin.

"Are you hungry?" he asked.

"No, I think I just want to lie down."

"You can have my bed. I'll take the couch," he offered, guiding me to a bedroom. The bed cover falling off the side and two puffy pillows strewn haphazardly looked inviting.

I woke hours later. The apartment was silent and the room was dark. I glanced around for a clock and found one on the bedside table. It read one seventeen. "She saw me."

Startled, as I'd thought I was alone, Timmy crawled onto the bed beside me. I pulled the cover over to let him in. I didn't know why since he was a ghost but it seemed the right thing to do. "She did. Do you think the things she said are true?"

He swished his lips and traced the outline of the seams on the bed cover. "She's crazy."

Crazy? I was crazy. Shari was Sara's daughter. *Sharon,* that's what was written on her drawer in the crypt. Shari short for Sharon but what about Timmy? "How come you're still here?"

"Waiting for you," the words rolled from his mouth.

Me, Us. "Why?"

"You needed a friend." He paused and I waited. "You were lonely. Your best friend moved and I thought you could use one."

I nodded and placed my finger beneath his as we traced the seams together. "But why didn't you leave with your family like Shari did?"

"I couldn't. You needed me."

We continued to trace the seams in silence, my finger beneath his, over and over, then he grabbed my hand. "Stop! Listen. There was a time when I was jealous of you. You were alive and I wasn't but when Mr. Campbell hurt you I felt anger. I hated him for hurting you. When that girl hit you I burned inside. I felt white hot rage. You weren't in anyway responsible for killing them, I was."

My best friend, albeit a ghost, was confessing that he murdered people for me? An eerie feeling washed over me. *Jealous?* I hadn't met him when I lived with the Campbells. 'You were alive and I wasn't' his words. "What she said is true. You're... my... twin."

He vanished to let me ponder his words, but why was he my age and not a baby? I was being technical. I understood in a sense Sara returning to a younger age and Shari appearing my age. My thoughts were that they reverted in ghost form to a happier age. Shari was always in the top of the turret with the rainbow colors so I assumed it was her favorite place. Now I rethought that. Timmy grew with me; as I aged, he aged. Maybe he was different because I carried him inside me.

Part 2
Two-Headed Dragon

Chapter 16
Phantom Girl

11 years old 1976

The next morning I awoke and heard Penelope's voice. I jumped out of bed and darted into the tiny living room. She, Kevin, and another person, a guy, sat around the little card table they used as a kitchen table in the folding chairs that came with it.

"Come join us. I made toast and eggs for breakfast," the guy I didn't know exclaimed. His auburn hair catching flames from the morning sun streaming through the window behind him.

I strolled to the table and took the only vacant seat. Penelope wrapped an arm around me and kissed my cheek. Her soft lips warm against my skin. "Don't believe anything she said, you're an important and special person. I love you."

My mother's words and the look of surprise when she spotted Timmy galloped through my head. I didn't want to tell them or involve them in any way. I was a wanted girl and Timmy was killing people for me but I didn't wish death on any of them, no matter how evil they were. *Would he ever hurt Kevin or Penelope?*

"It really eats me up that anyone could be that cruel!" said Penelope as she stood. "Who does that?"

"You always have friends in us," Kevin followed up with, to take the bite out of Penelope's words.

"It's OK, I get it. My mother was raped and I was the product." I swallowed hard.

Penelope's face contorted as her eyebrows raised and her jaw set in a line. She dropped her plate in the sink. "It's still no excuse. It's not your fault."

The guy I didn't know spoke, "How old are you?"

"Eleven," I answered, twisting my fork in the plate of eggs Kevin sat in front of me.

"You ever find out what happened to the man who raped her?"

I was glad he said 'raped her' instead of 'your father'. I couldn't think of someone who did such a heinous act as my father. I shook *no.*

His eyes glazed as he stared at the wall, deep in thought. In a flash he came back from wherever he went and said, "Do you want to know?"

Penelope interjected, her eyes narrowed and blazing into his. "Stop! She's not a case study."

Kevin cut the fire between them and glanced at me. "Rick's studying to be a psychologist. He's interested in all types of human behavior and reactions."

"I haven't ever thought of him," I answered in a quiet voice. It wasn't really a lie. I never did think of him, but now, after meeting my mother, he was on my mind. *Was I somehow like him? Was I worse, like my mother said?*

Rick went to class, Kevin went to work, and Penelope and I spent the day listening to records and watching TV.

My mind wandering with unexplainables, I finally came to the conclusion I didn't care much about the rapist, but wanted to know more about my birth. I remembered what hospital I was born in and figured maybe I could find records in the library -- microfilm or something.

That evening, I decided they needed to take me to Cat and Moira's home. They couldn't hide me out forever; at some point I needed to face my actions and I didn't want them involved or in trouble because of me. Kevin dropped me off, like I asked, a couple blocks from the home and I walked.

When I reached the home it hadn't changed. I opened the front door and children's faces I didn't recognize stared at me, then Moira rushed into the foyer where I stood with my one backpack. I dropped it to the floor and rushed at her, falling into her arms. This place and her arms felt like home.

After a long hug, Moira pulled away and poised her hands on my upper arms, her eyes staring into mine. "We were worried about you. Come with me, Cat will want to see you."

I took her hand and we walked to the kitchen, the delicious spices from dinner lingered in the air. Cat's mouth dropped when she saw me and so did everything in her hands. She rushed towards me and folded me into a hug. We pulled up stools and talked over the food prep island and Cat made me a plate of dinner left-overs. I sat at my usual station, which I was sure now belonged to another child. Life halted and rewound. I hadn't seen either of them since I'd left to live with the Campbells. Neither woman asked where I'd been, only made sure I wasn't injured and had a hearty meal.

Moira rested her hands on the island and her smile vanished. "We have to call the police."

I nodded. I knew that and I was sure the social worker would take me somewhere else -- to a new home, where I'd again have to adjust. "Can I stay the night with you, just one night?"

"I wish, but we don't have any vacant beds," Moira answered.

I glanced from her to Cat. "I can sleep on the couch."

Cat eyed Moira. "Where else is she going to go? They won't have anywhere to place her yet."

Moira nodded as she picked up the phone and dialed the police station. Within thirty minutes two police officers came through the door, one short and thin like a rail with a kind face, the other tall and plump with a gut that hung over his belt. They asked me questions about where I'd been for the past week.

The truth was out and wouldn't be believed anyways, and I didn't want them on a manhunt for a kidnapper who didn't exist, so I told them when I heard the thump in Sara's room I went to check on her and found her face down on the floor. After that I fainted and must have hit my head because when I woke up I couldn't remember anything. I didn't know where I was, freaked out, and ran. I spent the week living on the streets as pieces of my memory came back and I remembered Cat and Moira, then everything else flooded back.

The tall, plump cop eyed me suspiciously and mumbled 'Uh-huh, mmm, uh-huh' a lot. I knew he didn't believe me one iota. The kind, toothpick cop didn't say much but his face never turned sour.

"Someone called 911. Was it you?" asked the plump cop. His tag read Rivera.

I shrugged. "If I did, I don't remember."

"Uh-huh. The caller was a young girl. You sure you don't remember?"

"No, I told you I blacked out and I still don't remember the details of that day except finding Sara." I cupped my hands around my face and cried into them.

Moira cleared her throat. "I think she's had enough. Scarlett is only eleven and this whole ordeal has shaken her." The command in her voice meant business and Rivera appeared to understand that.

"I'll get a social worker out here first thing tomorrow." Rivera stood and the thin cop, his tag read Dumas, followed his lead.

"That'll be fine." She turned from him and faced me with a smile and a wink. "Why don't you get cleaned up and ready for bed?"

The tension in the room thick, she didn't have to say it twice. I dashed to the restroom.

Cat stopped me in the hallway and handed me a folded nightgown. "Here, you can wear this tonight and you remember where the extra toothbrushes are?"

"Yes, thank you."

Small webs creased her smiling eyes. "Tomorrow you can help me in the kitchen."

"I'd love that! Thank you Cat." I collected the clothes from her as I entered the restroom.

I slept on the couch in the study that night. Timmy was nowhere to be found so I rested well and let the past few years drift out of my mind. As promised, the following morning Cat let me help in the kitchen and we prepared waffles and fresh fruit topping. The social worker didn't come by and I spent the week living a dream. Timmy didn't appear either, and I was glad. I wasn't sure anymore what I thought of him, knowing the evils he'd done.

It was a Saturday morning when the social worker made her visit. My hopes of being forgotten and staying with Cat and Moira crushed like a tin can and kicked to a new home. She took me to yet another part of Albuquerque and a new foster family. The home was filled with children of various ages. All of them foster children like me and I blended in and became a phantom.

Chapter 17
Invisible

I was bounced to yet another school where I finished elementary school. The parents, Mr. and Mrs. Kraws, didn't appear to notice much and I slipped in and out of the house, returning to the turret every chance I got. I climbed the stairs and lay in the rainbow at the top, remembering the days when Shari, Timmy, and I played. Cobwebs were already building up in the corners of the house and the lawn was unkempt, but all my good memories were still intact and so were the many books in my room. The house was alive with cheer. Before the clock struck twelve, I'd always leave the house and wait outside for the doors to lock and they did, right on time.

I never knew why everything locked tight at midnight or how it continued to happen, especially since there was no electricity in the house anymore. It was a mystery I'd never solve yet I never stopped visiting the house. Since understanding I saw ghosts I began noticing more but knew what they were so I avoided them, never made contact, and went on my way. I figured they were unsettled spirits waiting for their loved ones to die. That revelation made me think Timmy couldn't pass on until I died and that wouldn't be for many years.

I continued to ponder my mother and my existence, so one chilly winter afternoon I grabbed one of the bikes leaning against the house and pedaled to the hospital where I was born. I wanted to know more about my birth and my twin but wasn't sure how I'd get that information. No doubt, the people at the hospital wouldn't hand me over the records of my birth with a smile.

The hospital smelled of bleach and was colder inside than outside. I walked with purpose down the halls, searching for a map.

"Can I help you?" asked a nurse in plain white scrubs and matching shoes. To her chest she held a clipboard.

I spotted a sign on the wall pointing towards a large office area surrounded by glass with a door. The ladies inside were in business dress with their hair neatly styled. Inside the room, people sat in waiting room-style chairs. A man caught my eye as he sat alone. "Thank you, but my dad's in there." I pointed.

"Well, OK," she responded and walked away.

I slipped inside the room and sat next to the man. He didn't even peek a glance at me but sat with one long leg lifted and poised on the other as his thumbs nervously tapped against the arm rest of the chair. I grabbed a magazine and from the corner of my eye watched the ladies behind the counter. There was another room behind them that they came and went from with folders in hand. I waited patiently for them to leave for at least a few moments so I could slip into the room behind them.

A commotion in the hallway grabbed their attention. A cart filled with food trays toppled, causing a nurse walking past to trip and fall. Timmy stood in front of the cart with a wide smile. The ladies in the office rushed toward the commotion, everyone in the room turned their heads and I used it to slip behind the counter and into the room.

There were shelves of boxes dated by year. I scanned and scanned. The years going backwards; *1973, 1971.*

"1954 over here," came Timmy's voice. I followed it around the corner. *How did he know what I was searching for?* He leaned against the shelf with one leg propped over the other.

I eyed him but didn't say a word. I scrolled through each month and pulled out *November 1954*. I thumbed through and pulled out Melissa Jones. The door creaked open and heels clicked on the tile floor. With the folder in hand I scanned the area. There was a nook at the end of the aisle to my right, covered in shadows, so I plastered against it and held my breath, standing still.

A thin lady with dark, shoulder length hair clicked past the spot I'd stood only moments ago. She stared straight ahead and went down a different aisle. Timmy followed her and they both disappeared from my sight. After a few minutes she returned, her hands carrying a file, and continued toward the door. I let out my breath.

"There's another way out, follow me," said Timmy.

"Where have you been?" I whispered, not that I was happy to see him, more I was curious.

"Around. The door leads to the hallway. I'll make sure it's clear for you."

I stopped. "Not yet." Opening the file I skimmed through and found my mother's birthdate *March 22 1939*. I skimmed the years on more boxes until I found it.

"You want to know if she was a twin too," he stated, leaned against the shelf. *Damn if he wasn't good!* I figured he was just as curious.

"Yes." I grabbed her folder and stuffed them both into my waistband and zipped up my sweatshirt. "I don't want you to kill people for me anymore, no matter how bad they are."

He took a step, his face inches from mine. "I was trying to help." A dark shadow washed over his blazing green eyes, dimming them for a second. "But if you don't want me to I won't.

"How did you know where to find me?"

"I'm always with you, remember." He continued on his way and I followed.

I didn't know what to say to him and I didn't know if I trusted him anymore. He went through the wall. It amazed me how he could do that. With me he was real and I could touch and feel him. He made objects move yet could slip through a solid object at will.

"Coast is clear," he said from the other side of the door.

I grabbed the knob and turned. To my surprise, it wasn't locked, at least from the inside. Not a soul in the hall except Timmy, I tried the door once it closed and it was locked. Timmy walked with me through the hospital to the exit. I didn't speak to him or acknowledge him as I'd look crazy to all the living people. No one saw him but me and plenty of other spirits loitered in the halls. I certainly didn't want to draw their attention or clue them in that I could interact with them.

I pedaled to Sara's house, Timmy perched on the handle bars. I dropped the bike behind the house and entered through the glass room, Salem purred at my heels. I dropped the folders onto my bed and read through them. Timmy is what the report called a *vanishing twin*. He died in utero and the nutrients from his body recycled and absorbed into the living fetus -- *me*. There was no cause written for his death, only that it happens sometimes. What was left of him was flattened and discovered during birth.

"Are you satisfied I'm real?" he asked, staring at me from across the bed.

"I never doubted you were real. I just had to see for myself." I was stunned; part of him had remained through the entire pregnancy. We shared the same womb, well kind of. He was there with me the whole time, in his own little sack even after death and I soaked in part of him. He was part of me. The craziness of it became real that moment.

"What about Mom?" he asked, pointing to her folder.

I lifted the flap and pushed it open, terror seized me as I wasn't sure if I wanted to know, but Timmy pushed me and I read through the papers. He vanished and appeared over my shoulder, reading along with me. Our mother's birth was normal, no twin. I visibly sighed relief.

"So maybe our father," he said, his voice growing faint as he evaporated into the air.

I didn't want to know about my father, our father. He was a violent man and I wanted no part of it as if knowing would make me just as demonic. *But who was the evil twin, me or Timmy?* He killed people, the worst thing I ever did was make Dana ill. The evil lived inside him and that's why he had to die in our mother's womb.

I used to pretend I could use my eyes to harm mean people but always knew it was fake. Now I wondered; was Timmy speaking into my ear, guiding thoughts in my head even then?

I hid the files in the passageway of the crypt where no one would ever find them and pedaled home under the sunset. I didn't figure I'd be missed but I was wrong. Drake, a stout boy a couple years older than me, stared as I came up the road. His arms folded across his chest.

"Where have you been with my bike?!" He scowled as I steered into the driveway.

"I'm sorry. I... I didn't know it was yours." I climbed off and rested it against the garage door.

"Well it is. When you feel like disappearing, don't use my bike." He opened the garage door and coasted it inside.

His words were more of a threat. He noticed when I left and I'd have to be more careful in the future.

Later that night Drake accosted me in the hallway as I was leaving the bathroom. He placed his palm against the wall, his thick arm blocking my path. "Why don't you ever make friends? You always have your head stuck in a book."

I scooted to the other side to step past him but he shifted and blocked my way. I kept my eyes on the ground and hoped Timmy wasn't near and didn't see.

"Something wrong with you?" His body took up the space in the hallway so I tapped his side as if to slide him over but he stepped closer, hovering in front of me.

Two small children squealed as they ran down the hallway. He stepped aside for them and I used that as an opening to squeeze by him. I scurried to my room, feeling his dark eyes on my back. The house contained four bedrooms and I shared mine with two other girls. They never gave notice to me and it was easy to sink into my bed, pull out a book, and read. I was truly invisible in the bedroom. As I read I listened to their chatter about boys and how hot Elvis Presley was in *Harum Scarum*.

Chapter 18
Raury

The next couple years came and went and Drake was sent to another home. I was thrilled because even though Timmy promised me I didn't believe in my heart that he wouldn't kill again. I floated through junior high as the quiet girl no one noticed. I spent my lunch reading and kept to myself. Sneaking to the turret when I could and visiting with Salem. It was the start of high school that changed everything. Timmy came and went but never stuck around.

"Scarlett, right?" asked a boy, his dark brown eyes shining at me and a smile on his face. Tucked under his arm was a textbook I noted as I lifted my face from the water fountain.

I glanced at him then walked away.

"Cat got your tongue?" He caught up and strode beside me. "We're in art together."

I stared ahead as I maneuvered between the other students loitering in the halls during the class change and dodged between them, losing him. But he didn't give up that easy, in art class he sat beside me and talked to me while I ignored him. He wasn't a popular boy or a jock or a nerd, he was somewhere in between and a talented artist. I marveled at his work but only when he wasn't watching. His name was Raury and he had incredible eyes and brown shaggy hair to match. He looked like a rock star.

During a routine fire drill, I was standing with the rest of my class on the outdoor basketball courts. The sun blazing and sweat dripping as our teachers counted heads.

From the corner of my eye I spotted Raury dashing through the crowds of mingling teens. He halted at my side. "By the time we get back inside, class will be over. Come with me, I want to show you something."

I'd never spoken to him. He'd invited me to movies, pizza, parties, yet I kept my mouth clamped. Why would he expect I'd go somewhere now? But the pleading in his voice made me glimpse at him. The sun in my eyes, I squinted. "What do you want from me?"

"She speaks! I want to get to know you. To be your friend, and maybe something more." His lips drawn into a wide smile. I admitted at that moment that I had a huge crush on him. He was about the cutest boy in school and all the attention he gave me made my will power cave in.

"What's so special about whatever you want to show me?" I kept my tone curt and my stance defensive.

"It's the most beautiful place in New Mexico. I promise." He held out his hand for me but I didn't take it.

"If I go with you, will you leave me alone?" Secretly I enjoyed the attention he poured on me and his dreamy eyes but outwardly I didn't express it.

"If you go with me and aren't impressed and never want me to speak with you again then I won't." He peered at me beneath his long bangs hopefully.

I sighed as if frustrated. Inside my nerves were teeming and I was giddy and flattered. "Fine."

I followed him to a Toyota pickup truck that had more dents than the moon had craters in the back of the student parking lot. "Door's unlocked." He skipped around to the driver's side and pulled through the back of the lot and onto a skinny side street.

He drove us high into the mountains along a dirt path and finally parked. "We have to walk from here."

We hiked up a trail, not one made for hiking but one people had worn through the brush and trees, until we came to a peak. "This is it," he said, sitting on a boulder that appeared as if nature had put it there on purpose.

I sat down next to him and stared at the unobstructed view of the Rio Grande. The water captured and reflected the golden and green hues from the plants and brush. The mountains surrounded us, enveloping us in the magic of its embrace.

He shifted and pulled a joint out of his pocket and a lighter then brought it to his mouth. I recognized the odor and it brought back memories of the ghost town Kevin took Penelope and me to. "Here." He passed it to me holding in his breath.

I took it, twirled it my hand for a second, then brought it to my mouth. I'd never smoked anything before and wasn't so sure what to do. I inhaled and smoke filtered into my lungs, choking me. I gagged and coughed.

He chuckled. "You've never smoked before?"

I wasn't sure I wanted him to know that. I'd been around it at Sara's with the twins, Penelope, and Kevin but I never tried it or even asked. "It's been a while," I sputtered, my lungs strangled and searching for air.

He took it. "You don't have to suck it in so hard, go easy and hold it in as long as you can. Watch." He took a long drag and held his breath for several seconds then expelled the smoke in my face. "Take it in."

I inhaled the smoke, coughed a little, then shifted my gaze to the setting sun over the water. Pink and purple hues hung above it, the surface reflecting them back into the sky. We passed the joint back and forth and I got better each time and coughed less.

I blew out and Timmy appeared in front of me suspended in the air. "So this is what you do for fun now?"

I ignored him.

"You get high on a mountain with a boy you don't know," Timmy scolded. His emerald eyes blazing and his lips in a straight line.

Raury grabbed my hand. "Come on."

Leaving Timmy, we ran through the trees hand in hand, hurdling rocks, shrubs, grazing our jeans and laughing for no apparent reason. On the mountain that day I felt free, without the restraints of my past, with a beautiful young man who I liked more by the minute. He fell to the ground in a grassy area and I dropped with him. Our eyes to the darkening sky.

He caught his breath and leaned on an elbow, his other hand brushing the stray blonde curls across my face. "I told you it was beautiful almost as beautiful as you."

I didn't have a response. No boy had ever given me such a compliment; not with the look he held in his gaze. His brown irises beaming and his face a bit flush. With nothing to say, I smiled and immersed myself into the moment. He dropped his face closer to mine and his lips brushed mine in a kiss, then another.

Tingles raced up my spine and I welcomed the sensation as I parted my lips and kissed him. He sank his tongue into my mouth. I met it with mine and explored its ridges and edges, soft as the snow covered mountain yet warm as the sun's heat.

He moved his face away from mine and smiled. "I've wanted to do that for a long time."

I sucked in my bottom lip, dazed from the experience. It was a high better than the pot. "I should get home." I sat up on my elbows.

He nodded and we followed the mountain trail back to his truck. "Are you hungry?" he asked as we neared town.

"Yeah." I was starving and felt like I could eat an entire pizza to myself.

He chuckled. "Pot does that, gives you the munchies."

He pulled into a mom and pop hamburger stop and we pigged out. I had a juicy burger loaded with cheese, bacon, lettuce, and tomato. It was so large I almost couldn't open my mouth wide enough to take a bite. He smothered his French fries in ketchup.

"Yuck," I stated.

"Ketchup goes with everything." He took a fry dripping in the red sauce and brought it to his mouth then took another ketchup-soggy fry and brought it dangerously close to mine.

I scooted my basket out of the way. "Don't you dare," I warned.

"You really don't like ketchup. So, what, you eat them dry?"

"No, I dip them in mustard."

"Mustard. You are weird." He snickered then ate a huge bite of his burger.

"At least I don't eat my hamburger in one bite," I teased. It felt natural being with him that day, skipping school and watching the sunset over the river.

That night, in my dream, we were back on the mountain, running towards the river, laughing and free when Raury turned around and his face melted away, revealing Timmy's. Suddenly I wasn't in the mountains anymore but in a world encased in darkness. Faces illuminated before my eyes like candle flames. I turned in circles; they were everywhere and moving closer.

I dropped to the ground, mud beneath my palms. It oozed between my fingers then turned to red and the darkness went away. I was standing in the middle of a red river. It pushed against me as I tried to climb to the shore and soon took hold of me and I was drifting with it. The sound of rushing water filled my ears and the current picked up, carrying me towards a drop. A tree limb was caught between the rocks and I desperately reached for it, but the realization I didn't know how to swim grasped me and I panicked.

The tree limb grew further away, the current pushed harder. I kicked and paddled my arms, taking a large gulp of air before I was slung beneath the water. My back grazing the rocks below, stinging racked my body and I dropped. My eyes shot open and I was in my bed with a two-headed dragon slithering its tongues at my face, wings stretched and open across its back. One head and wing white while the other was black. They moved upwards, revealing a set of bright emerald eyes staring at me -- familiar eyes I couldn't place at the moment. Breathless, I watched as the eyes of the man with the two-headed dragon tattoo departed, moving away from me and a body and head coalesced around him. Several men surrounded him and jabbed into his gut until he was a bloodied mess on a concrete floor. The other men vanished. I wasn't seeing a ghost, not in the usual sense, more it was like watching a movie -- a gory movie. I closed my eyes and sank beneath my covers, seeing enough and hoping it would go away.

Chapter 19
When Friends Resurface

I walked toward the bus after school when I spotted a familiar face, his body leaning against a new red Camaro waving at me from the other side of the parking lot. I hadn't forgotten about Kevin or Penelope and we wrote back and forth. She was in law school now but Kevin was still in Albuquerque. I hadn't seen him since the day they dropped me at Moira and Cat's but seeing his face I slung my backpack over my shoulder and ran to his car.

"Kevin," I screamed, grabbing onto his chest and hugging him tight.

"Hey, Chimera. What do you say, want to grab a soda with me?"

"This yours?" I asked, admiring the sleek curves of the sporty car.

"It sure is," he winked, "get in. We'll go for a spin."

I admired the fancy gadgets and rumble of the motor. It beat the old Impala he used to drive. He cranked the radio and shifted the gears as we cruised through town.

"I have some information for you," he said as we sat down in a booth with a window. Scent of cooked beef filling the air.

I dropped into the seat and took a sip of my Sprite. "For me?"

"Yeah, I think you're old enough now." He slid a manila envelope my way.

I scrunched my brows and placed my fingertips on the envelope. "What is it?"

"Information about," he paused, "your family."

I searched his eyes but saw only sincerity and concern for my well-being. "I don't have any." Curious, I slid the contents out of the envelope. Xeroxed copies of newspaper clippings about a man who brutally raped several young women, including his own daughter. And a fresh clipping from today about how he'd been brutally murdered in prison, shanked by a group of other prisoners. A double-headed dragon tattoo covered the man's forehead and wings spread over his shaven top. I gulped hard. "He raped my mother."

He nodded. "But you have a sister."

Underneath the clippings was a teenaged girl with swirly golden hair and bright blue eyes. She was striking at first glance but after minutes of staring into her sapphire eyes I saw a deep, resonating echo of myself. "How did you get all this?"

"I'm a paralegal now. Information surrounds me."

I rested my chin on fisted hands. "What's her name?"

"Philmonia. She's in foster care like you. There's a phone number on the back." He took a sip from his soda.

I flipped the picture over. Maybe he thought I was ready but I wasn't. The closest thing I'd ever had to a sibling was Penelope and the twins.

"Thank you." I tucked everything into the envelope and pushed it toward him. "You hold onto it for me."

He nodded as if he understood, but I doubted he did. I'd never been to his house when he was younger but knew he grew up with two parents and a sister and brother, sometimes he'd talk about them.

"When you're ready let me know. I'll drive you to meet her." He placed his hand on mine.

The man who raped my mother died the day of my strange, horrifying dream. I watched his murder as if it was happening in front of me. *What did it mean?* For a while I thought ghosts appeared randomly, and occasionally I'd spot one without explanation, but they didn't attempt to make contact with me so I pretended I didn't see them. The times they made contact with me such as Shari, Sara, and Timmy, it was to fill their void as much as mine. *Was he attempting to contact me by showing me his brutal murder? Did he think I would care? Or was it a biological connection?*

I didn't get the purpose of what I saw, maybe since I was his *daughter* and had the ability to see spirits it wasn't contact but lingering energy connected to me by blood.

On Valentine's Day I waited for Raury on the bench outside the gym. He wasn't usually late and my spirits were beginning to deflate. The boy who tried for months to speak with me and I finally let him in now he was letting me down and I was going to be late for class. For years I'd lived a solitary life and now my everything clung to this one boy. Disheartened, I walked to class, my eyes counting the cracks in the sidewalk.

I went through the day watching other students in the hall carrying stuffed toys and candy. I had nothing; like every other Valentine's Day I remembered. At lunch I sat by myself in my usual spot and opened a book. An arm snaked around my neck and Raury's scent filled my nostrils along with the scent of something else. I turned to see his bright brown eyes smiling at me, one hand behind his back.

"Happy V-Day!" he said, pushing a bouquet of red tulips over my shoulder.

"Raury! You brought me flowers. Thank you!" I grabbed the bouquet and he took the seat next to me. I folded my arms around his neck with the bouquet in hand and kissed his cheek. "I thought you forgot."

"Never. I had to drive my mom to a doctor's appointment this morning and I came to school just to see you." He caressed my cheeks and kissed my lips. "I have something else for you too, but after school."

Raury was like a wild wind that blew from one adventure to the next. That night he took me to the top of one of the skyscrapers downtown. We sneaked through, my hand clutching his as we slipped past the guards and to the elevator that we rode to the top.

I banished the giggles that simmered to erupt as we stole to the very top of the building. "How?" I asked, spinning, allowing the dry air to rush against my skin.

Raury shrugged. "My dad works here." Then pulled a small basket from beside a brick structure jutting out of the roof. There was one on each side. He flipped the top open and pulled out a bottle of blush champagne and two glasses. Pouring the effervescent fluid, he handed me a glass.

I took a sip, the bubbles bounced through my mouth and down my throat. "What else do you have stashed up here?" I asked, gazing at him from beneath curls as the wind blew across my face.

"Music to make the evening perfect." He toyed with a small radio and pressed the power button, finding a local pop station playing *My Girl* by The Temptations, then scooted towards me on his butt. His hands moved upward beneath my blouse and cupped my blossoming chest, singing: "Well I guess you'd say. What can make me feel this way? My girl, Talkin' 'bout my girl."

The sensation of his touch sent frenzied waves of lust rising through me. My hands moved along his neck and downward, exploring beneath his T-shirt. Our lips met and moved together, our tongues swirling inside each other's mouth. One of his hands moved beneath my beltline, caressing my skin and reaching down until his fingertips rested on a sensitive part of my body. He played with the little knob, moving his finger back and forth over it.

He removed his hand as I straddled him, wanting him. Grinding my sensitive area over his growing erection. My panties grew wet and the heat between us flamed as our lips and hands explored the other. His hardness rubbing beneath me as I moved along its length. Our pants the only things between us as we rode the pleasure.

"Stop," he said, pushing me from him, "unless you want more." His brown eyes not hiding his intentions. He wanted full-on sex and so did I, but not yet. I wasn't quite ready and didn't want to get pregnant as my mom had. The circumstances far different, but she was my age when she gave birth to me.

I jumped up and skipped toward the ledge. It was thick. Stepping onto it, I lifted both arms for balance and stared ahead, never looking down. He followed me.

"You're really cool. How come you don't let people see this side of you?" he asked, a few paces behind me.

The wind rushed against my face. "You think I'm cool?" He was the first non-ghost friend I'd had in years that was my age. Since Lindsey. I often wondered what happened to her and Luke but didn't have an address to write them.

"Yeah! Kids at school think you're stuck up. Because you never talk to anyone. But you're not, you're fun and daring."

My ghost brother likes to kill people who wrong me. That sounded *sane* and they'd just have to keep believing I was stuck up. I was used to the whispers and upsetting words. I hadn't paid attention in years to what people thought about me. I cared and wanted friends, but I didn't want anyone else hurt. I took my chances with Raury and crossed my fingers he'd never hurt me. "They can think what they want."

His fingertips brushed against my back. "If they knew how cool you were you'd have mountains of friends."

I'd had enough talk about what others think and friends. I came to the edge and, without looking down, felt for the ledge knowing they met at the corners. Teetering on one leg, using my arms for balance I found it. "Ah, now when she comes walkin' over. Now I've been waitin' to show her.," I sang with the lyrics to the popular song *Crimson and Clover* as it blasted through the radio speakers.

Timmy appeared and floated alongside the building beside me, meeting me step for step as he walked across the air. "That's a choice song," he snarked.

I glanced at him, narrowed my eyes, and blasted him with a not-right-now glare and kept on singing.

Raury sang along with me. By the time the song ended I reached the end, placed my hand against the tall brick structure and jumped down. I rushed to the champagne bottle and took a huge swig. Timmy stood alongside the brick structure, one hand poised against it as if using it to help him stand. I tipped the bottle again and closed my eyes as the bubbles pushed down my throat.

Raury rushed at me. "Save some." He winked as he kissed me. I handed him the bottle. We shared swigs until it was empty. He rolled up his shirt and maneuvered so his back was towards me. "What do you think?"

I ran my fingers over the raised flesh of the fresh tattoo covering his left shoulder blade. The wolf face shifted when he shifted. "Does it hurt?"

"Some," he answered.

"It's beautiful." With Raury, I felt invincible and incredibly free, like the wolf on his shoulder. Now a permanent fixture on his body. Its exquisiteness and the delicate edges of the wolf's fur was a perfect fit for his character. "How long did it take?"

"A few hours." He dropped his shirt and turned towards me. "My uncle did it. You want one?"

"I've never thought about it." It wasn't real lady-like to have a tattoo but maybe a small one in an inconspicuous location wouldn't hurt. A delicate butterfly on one of my ass cheeks maybe.

He lit a joint and sucked down a huge toke. "What would you get?"

I toked on the joint and through spilling breath choked out, "A purple butterfly right on my ass."

He toked again and chuckled then flipped off the radio, stuffed it and the empty bottle into the basket and grabbed my hand. "All right, ass girl. Let's do it."

Within the hour we were sitting in his uncle's tattoo shop, my eyes milling over the various butterfly tats. I wanted something unique, something no one else had on their ass cheek, so I took a flyer from the counter and turned it over and drew my butterfly. The tip of its delicate wings a dark purple, enclosing a fuchsia-purple on top, surrounded in the darker purple, and the lower portion an orchid color with dark purple around all the edges and its head fuchsia with black feelers and an orchid body.

"That's really good," Raury said with a twinkle in his brown eyes. "Like, really good."

I twisted my mouth and thought about its placement. It was far too pretty and dainty for my ass. "Maybe on my boob." I brought it to my chest and he tilted his head, attempting to imagine it.

"I think you should lift up your shirt and place it next to your flesh before I can give you an answer."

I lifted my eyebrows. "You think?" I pushed my shirt up and slowly lowered one side of my bra, quickly placing the paper over my nipple before he had the chance to glimpse it.

He slid his finger underneath the paper, making the butterfly dance, and traced his thumb along my nipple. His gentle touch ignited me with pulses and passion. My chest rising and falling with his touch.

"You ready?" called a gruff voice, startling us. He quickly lowered his hand and I dropped my bra and shirt. A tall man with tattooed sleeves walked from behind a partition.

I nodded and he motioned for us to follow him. I showed him my picture and where I wanted it on the fleshy side of my left breast. Where it would be covered by my bra.

The worst part of getting the tat was the anticipation as he readied his needles and the ink colors. It stung a bit when the needle first entered my skin but after the initial shock my body grew used to it like adapting to the cold sting of seventy degree water. When it was done, I had an elegant and stylish tattoo.

Raury dropped me off at one in the morning. After the tattoo and smoking more weed with his uncle we stopped and ate. Flashes from the TV came through the window as I unlocked the front door. I figured Mr. What's His Name was asleep, like usual.

"Scarlett, sit," said Mrs. What's Her Name. It was bad that at the moment I couldn't remember either of their names. I was really shocked that she knew mine. For years I was no more than a phantom child in the house, coming and going when I pleased. I rarely ate there and usually only used the place for showers and sleep. Guilt crept into my gut as she gazed at me and scooted over so I could join her on the couch.

I sat, but not too close. I left bubble space between us. "Yes?"

She cleared her throat. "I notice you've been spending a lot of time with that boy." *Was she watching me? Did she see us kiss?* My thoughts rolled through my brain as she continued talking. "And you're a beautiful girl. You're going to have feelings and desires."

I wanted to crash my hands over my ears! I didn't need a sex lecture from someone I didn't even know, but her voice wasn't condemning like Mr. Campbell's or harsh or even lecturelike. It held concern, so I stayed quiet as she finished.

"You need to be careful." She squashed several square, plastic, flat bags into my hand. Trojan was written across a circular lump in the middle of the squares. "I didn't have anyone tell me about prevention and when I was your age I got pregnant and had an abortion. Now I can't have children. I don't want anyone to have to go through that."

I suppressed my chuckle. I knew all about condoms and safe sex, the rhythm method, the pill, and the sponge. At this point I wasn't having sex, so all of it was a non-issue. When the time came, I of all people would be careful. I didn't want to be my mom even if the sex was consensual. "Thank you," I stated and ran-walked to my room.

The girls were sitting on one of their beds, eyes painted on me when I entered. Sally flipped her dark, long tresses over her back and with wide, shiny powder blue eyes asked in a whisper, "Did she give you the talk and the Trojans?"

I nodded and opened my palm, displaying the condom collection.

"She's so weird," said Maria, cupping her hands over her mouth. Her dark, thick hair bobbed as she laughed into her palms.

Within a couple minutes we were all laughing together. I'd never talked with either girl, nor wanted anything to do with them, but that day, under those very peculiar circumstances, our friendship was formed.

Chapter 20
And the Floods Came

"Hold in the clutch and practice moving through the gears." Raury placed his hand over mine as he assisted me in shifting through the gears in his truck.

"Reverse is here." Our hands shifted again. "Let it flow natural. You don't want to jam the gears but let them flow."

I followed his words and shifted on my own through the gears a few times until he was satisfied I was ready to move the truck somewhere.

"Reverse and ease off the clutch and onto the gas. Don't pop it." His words guided me through the backing up process as I eased the truck out of the parking space. The clutch wasn't the problem, turning the wheel was. We curved a tight left when I wanted to go right.

"No problem, pull into the driveway and do it again. Turn the wheel the other direction."

I did it and maneuvered the vehicle onto the road in the direction I wanted. The clutch and the gas came natural. I eased off one and onto the other, shifting through the gears, not as smooth as him but with only a few jerky bounces in the beginning. We drove through his neighborhood then onto the main road and through the city. Turning remained a problem. The steering wheel was heavy and stiff. I shifted down before breaking at the light.

"You're doing good, better than I did when my dad taught me. I couldn't get the clutch right and we stalled several times," he said with a smile.

Raury was a guy that seemed good at everything on the first try. I chuckled at the image of him struggling with driving.

"It was that funny but my dad sat in the passenger seat with a poker face and made me figure it out for myself." He slid an 8-track in the player.

"I was imagining you not good at something." I put my energy into guiding the steering wheel and cut that one almost perfect.

He blew out a breath that puffed his bangs. "I'm not good at everything."

"Like?" He made good grades with no effort, created beautiful art, fixed his truck whenever it had a problem, and even though he wasn't an athlete he could dunk a basketball and catch a football effortlessly.

"Like, you wouldn't even talk to me for months. My parents made me take swimming lessons because I always dropped like a brick in the water and I burn anything I cook," he said as if proud of his imperfections.

"I can teach you to cook." I shifted and we lurched a bit as I shifted into third. I headed out of the city and into the foothills. The only place I could think of to go was Sara's. His adventurous spirit, he'd like the turret. I wasn't taking him into the crypt or the tunnel. That was my private sanctuary, but the turret was magical and he'd appreciate it. The large Victorian, out of place in New Mexico, stuck out like a sore thumb on the long street. The few other homes were all common adobe structures.

"Wow! I've lived here all my life and never seen this place." He stretched his legs and arms, his eyes plastered on the large home. The grass overgrown, weedy, and brown.

"Come on." I ushered him towards the back and we slipped through the glass room. At nearly six feet tall the cobwebs brushed his shaggy hair and stuck, pulling with him. I reached up and knocked them off, giggling when he wrapped his arms around me and stole a kiss.

We strolled through the kitchen and into the large living room with a grand foyer and up the stairs. He twisted his neck in order to gawk at everything as he took it in. "Is it haunted?"

I stole up the steps and turned to see him staring at me. Haunted; everything was haunted. That wasn't a specific enough word for me but I could tell he was planted in place at the base of the stairs. "If you mean do spirits live here, I don't think so." That was better than telling him there used to be ghosts but they've all gone to rest. I hadn't told him about my other sight. No matter how much I liked him, some secrets were best left as secrets.

"A place like this has to be haunted." He took the steps two at a time. "This furniture is ancient." He slid his finger along the dusty arm of a chair.

"Ghosts, aliens, they only exist if you believe in them," I stated.

He dropped onto the chair and a dust cloud covered him. "Absolutely." He searched my face. "You don't believe?"

I pinched my face at his comments. "Maybe. We can't be the only life in the universe, right?" I knew there were ghosts. It wasn't a stretch to think aliens existed.

"They might take over our planet one day or just hover over our planet and study us." He flattened his hand and waved it in the air in front of him making beeping UFO sounds.

"What I'm going to show you is better." I stuck the key in the lock and pushed the door open, coating myself in the rainbow colors from the stained glass.

"Shit! Is that the end of the rainbow? Is there a pot o' gold in there?" He jumped off the chair and followed me into the room. "What the hell...?" His eyes drifted down. "What's down there?" he asked, leaning over the spiral staircase.

"Nothing, it's an empty room." I shrugged and climbed towards the third floor.

"It seems like it has to lead to something." He coasted down the stairs.

I wasn't worried he'd find the door. It was flush with the wall. "I'll be at the top when you're done."

He didn't say anything but his feet pounded against the steps until I heard him drop to the bottom floor. I took my usual place in the center of the floor. I'd taped all my butterflies to the walls between the windows and strung some from the ceiling. The colors bounced off them as they flew through the spectral bliss.

Within a few minutes I heard him pound the stairs. He halted on the top step and soaked in my sanctuary. "What is all this?" he asked, turning his head and taking in the glory of the room.

"I come here sometimes."

From the steps he met my gaze then shifted to the door and stepped onto the third floor. His one track mind, he pushed against the door. "It's locked."

No shit, Sherlock. "Yeah, but this is what I wanted to show you." I put my arms and hands out, palms up.

He sat behind me, grabbed my middle and scooted backwards against the wall. "What's on the other side of the door on the third floor?"

I snuggled the back of my head against his chest and collarbone. "I don't know. I never explored it."

"Never?"

"Nope. The magic in the room always beckoned me." I never thought about exploring the third floor. With all the other secrets in the building I never once considered it. When I thought about it now, I couldn't even come up with a good reason why.

He pushed his hands up my shirt and beneath my bra, fondling my breasts. His soft lips caressing my neck with kisses. The familiar tingle of his touch aroused me. I dipped my head and indulged on his tender lips, offering my tongue. His hands continued to caress my chest and belly. The result in his jeans pressing firm against my back.

I wanted him, but was more fearful of sex and pregnancy. With that in mind, I bolted upwards and scampered towards the stairs. "Beat you to the third floor." I giggled and rushed down the stairs, his footfalls right behind mine.

His legs long, he coasted beside me soon and I bumped against him. He caught my arm and pulled me backwards, gaining the lead. I purposely led him away from the staircase and reached the first step when he realized I tricked him.

"I'm soo going to get you. You sneaky, manipulative girl," he said with a smile as he rushed towards me. I wasted no time in scurrying up the steps. My heart pounding from the excitement. A giant dollhouse similar to the house sat in the opposite side of the rectangle room. Shelves of dolls lined the walls and a small wooden rocking chair made for a child took residence in the middle of the room, facing a window. The bench beneath the window was covered with fluffy padding, bleached by the sun.

"This is a little girl's heaven," Raury said as he stopped beside me, his eyes as wide as mine.

Was this all Shari's? Drawn to the dollhouse, I peeked through the windows. All the furnishings were mirrored to those in the house. Chills traced my spine even after all the weirdness I knew existed.

"Look at this," he said with the lid top of the bench open.

"What?" I padded towards him. Inside the chest was a box and more dolls, some made of cornhusks and handkerchiefs. Inside the box were paper dolls. The ones I always saw Shari playing with. We dug further into the chest and endless assortment of toys; a cup and ball, a bag of marbles and wooden building blocks. The further I dug the more creeped out I felt. It was a feeling of dread like none other I'd felt.

I backed away, noting that no dust covered anything in the room, as if it was cleaned daily. The dolls and toys were neat, unlike what a child's room would really look like. The magic of the house was stuck in a time warp in the room. I continued backing away until I reached the steps. "We shouldn't be here." I darted down the steps without looking back until I reached the first floor grand living room. The familiar peace I always felt settled on me and I relaxed. My quickened pulse returned to normal.

A hand touched my shoulder and I jumped.

"Hey, what's wrong?" asked Raury, sincerity and concern flashing in his brown eyes.

"I think we should leave. We weren't meant to be there." His punched lips and scrunched brows displayed his confusion. No doubt he didn't have a sixth sense like I did, but other things about the room had to ring bells in his head. "Look at the dust and cobwebs around you. That room was clean, sparkling clean as if..." my words hung in the air.

"So you do believe in ghosts."

Of course, I see ghosts and visions of death, I thought. "I believe there's something in that room and we weren't meant to be there."

"It was a little creepy," he followed up with, following me through the house and out the glass room door.

"Where's that trail lead?" He stared at the cactus jungle, the path barely visible with overgrowth.

Soft, fluffy fur rubbed against my leg. I glanced down to see Salem and instinctively reached to pick him up.

"What is it?" The puzzlement in Raury's voice alerted me I was about to cuddle a ghost cat in front of him. The lines between the ghost realm and the living realm blurred for that instant.

"Nothing, my leg itched," I gave Salem a quick pet and stood, smoothing my mistake over.

The sun was setting as we climbed back into his truck. Memories of the room hadn't left me. It wasn't just Shari's room; some of the toys were older than those she would have played with, yet they were perfectly preserved.

It didn't make any sense. As many times as I'd been to the house since Sara's death I'd never seen another ghost with the exception of Salem. The energy was different. Ghost energy felt like living energy, what I felt in the room was darker, bolder, and something I didn't have a name for.

An ambulance and police cars rushed past us as Raury pulled over to let them pass. Their sirens filled my ears as he stopped at the sign a couple blocks away from my current living space. We turned onto the street and the slew of emergency vehicles was parked in front of the house. The one I lived in. My pulse quickened, my eyes glued to the haste in their steps as they rushed inside it.

No! I screamed inside. *No!* my brain screamed, my legs pounding beneath me, pushing past the police officers and into the house. A thick arm wrapped around my middle.

"You can't be in here," it said, guiding me outside the house against my will.

He deposited me in the driveway, lights and sirens flashing, emergency workers running past me. Covering my face with my hands, anger burned inside me. I wasn't attached to the What's-Their-Names or anybody in the house but couldn't accept that somebody else in my life was injured or dead... "Timmy!" I hollered, knowing somehow he was at fault. He'd done this.

"Why don't we sit in my truck?" said Raury, his voice stabbing through the fog in my brain. I took his hand and he directed me to his truck.

I crawled through his window and spent the night with Raury, tucked in his arms.

Chapter 21
The Phantom Arises

After all was said and done, Mrs. Kraws died in the bathtub when a hairdryer still plugged into the wall dropped off the shelf over the tub and electrocuted her, frying her guts. The water continued to flow until it poured over the side of the tub and Mr. Kraws slipped in the water hitting his head against the floor, instantly killing him. The hair dryer flowing with the water eventually came unplugged and rested by the door of the bathroom.

None of the children were injured and we were all sent to new homes. My new foster parents were a middle-aged couple. She had a sweet, round face and a bob cut. He had a kind voice and jovial laugh. The modest suburban home was furnished in yellows and golds -- popular decor of the 70s. My room was simple with a twin bed and single long dresser with a mirror.

That night, alone in my room, I summoned Timmy who appeared beside me on the edge of the bed.

"Another home, huh?" he asked as if he wasn't guilty of killing the Kraws - - Mr. and Mrs. What's-Their-Name.

I looked him square in the eye. "Did you do it?"

"What?" he asked innocently but it had his 'accident' handy work all over it.

"Don't play coy. You killed them!"

He turned his head from me and stared at the dresser across the room. "I don't know what you're talking about."

I grabbed his translucent edged face in my hands and turned it towards me. "Why?"

He pushed my hands away and jumped off the bed, taking a defensive stance. "You're wrong!"

"Am I? Is it jealousy? Or do you just enjoy watching people die?"

He shuffled his foot but didn't vanish and I pressed on. "That's it, jealousy. You said it," I urged, remembering the night he told me about killing Mr. Campbell and Theresa. "I lived and you didn't."

He stepped away from me towards the dresser, his reflection didn't show inside the mirror. "You ignore me after I showed myself to you when you needed a friend, helped you, and have always watched out for you."

"So that's why you did it?"

He turned on his heel and faced me. "You're all I have and I'm here as long as you're here."

No, it was more than that. He targeted Mrs. Kraws; but why? I pressed him further and he denied anything other than jealousy but there was something more, something lurking in the dark reaches of his spirit mind. I gave up the battle, urging and begging him to not harm anyone else.

He was a dark spirit, one filled with a burning rage. He died and I lived, maybe because he was the evil twin. I remembered the dragons tattooed on the head of my *father*. Was there a meaning behind them, something significant that would tell me more about Timmy?

With that thought in mind I went to the public library and found a professor who taught classes in mysticism and symbolism. It was his life's work. The campus was large with many buildings. I managed to find a map which led me to his office after several minutes of aimless wandering.

The door was open and a small man with thick glasses, wild auburn hair, and an out of control beard poured over his desk. I knocked and he looked up. "Scarlett, right? Come in and close the door behind you."

His friendly voice reassured me as I took a seat across from him.

"I'm Dr. Kerns. You are interested in something to do with symbolism?"

I nodded, taking in the dreamcatcher on the wall behind his head and the many clay pots, statues, and other items carefully placed on the shelves of his office. I handed him the sketch I drew of the double-headed dragon.

He glanced at it, turning it at various angles. "Where did you say you saw this?"

"In a dream and I get the feeling it means something." I wasn't about to tell him the story.

"Hmm... Dragons mean various things to various cultures. As you can see, I study mostly Native American history but have done research on other cultures as well." He pulled at his crazy beard. "A white dragon tends to mean rebirth and a black one death, but part of the same creature I'd say a fractured spirit. We all have a light side and a dark side. We try to do what's right but sometimes give in to temptations."

"So, you're saying the dragon represents the good and evil inside us. Could it relate to twins? A good one and a bad one?"

"Ahh... I see where you're going. The dragon being one and the two heads part of the whole. It's possible." He leaned back in his chair and placed his hands behind his head. "I've seen that dragon, exactly like you drew, on the head of a convicted rapist who was killed in prison a couple months ago. I dug into his background a bit." He brought his hands to his desk and tented them. "He fathered a child that was given up immediately after birth. You're that child."

I wrenched my hands together in my lap. He knew. I should have figured a college professor would put two and two together. "I had a vanishing twin and I wondered if the dragon meant something. Like I lived because I had the stronger, good soul and he... had to die because his soul was malicious, immoral. Sometimes I feel like he's with me."

"I didn't stop when I found the girl who called me requesting an appointment. The rapist had a vanishing twin too, so if we believe the theory of fractured souls and the stronger twin surviving then we must entertain the idea that it's the stronger soul that survives."

The sunlight caught in the dreamcatcher behind him, sending sparkles across the room. "The stronger soul; so his twin was weak and he prevailed in the struggle inside the womb."

"No one knows really why one twin survives and the other doesn't. Medicine suggests the vanishing twin simply didn't develop and was miscarried. If we look at that and consider the double-headed dragon symbolically it could represent the babies struggling in utero. One will survive and the other won't. Light doesn't always defeat darkness. But we could look at this from another angle. The white dragon represents rebirth and the other death, meaning one soul will die as the other is born. It may have nothing to do with the forces of good and evil, simply that only one can survive." He flattened his hands, his blue eyes searching mine.

"I was the stronger twin and he was malformed from the beginning?" I asked.

"That's what medicine suggests. I'm suggesting he was an evil man, the stronger of the fetuses, and he lived on, his life filled with vile crimes against women. You were the strongest fetus and here you are, curious about the darkness that may lurk inside you. Because one's parents aren't good doesn't mean a child will carry on the parents' legacy. This man wasn't a part of your life. He never raised you. It's a case of nature vs. nurture and I think you are safe from committing the crimes of your father," he said in a cautious voice.

I hadn't thought of my quest for answers in that way. *Was I searching for something that said I wasn't evil like him? Did I blame Timmy because it made sense even though Timmy wasn't alive?* "Thank you Dr. Kerns, you've given me a lot to think about."

He smiled and stood as I did. "Symbolism is an intriguing subject but be cautious what you read into it," he warned.

I pressed the floured roller over the lump of dough on the counter until it was flat, then pressed it onto an olive oil greased pizza pan. Mr. Kerns had given me a lot to think about; maybe Timmy wasn't even real but a figment of my own imagination searching for answers, and all the tragedies in my life were simple accidents.

"Pizza," my new guardian sniffed as I read a book at the table waiting for the oven to ding. "I love the smell of garlic." She took a seat across from me. "Where did you learn to cook?"

"In the first home. I used to help in the kitchen and watched Cat make all sorts of meals." I didn't lift my eyes off my book, *They Never Came Home* by Lois Duncan.

"Well, I'm not much of a cook so the kitchen is all yours. What other things are you good at?"

"I make good grades in school." School was easy and making As was a cinch, something Raury and I had in common.

"So what is it you want to do after school?" she pried, leaning her head against her hand. I knew she was trying to be friendly, parentlike, but I didn't need coddling anymore.

The oven dinged and I dropped my book onto the table. "I don't know. I haven't thought about it." My hands wrapped in oven mittens, I slid the pizza out of the oven and placed it on top of the stove. I grabbed my book and exited the room. It wasn't that I didn't want to get to know her it was more the wrenching pain of how I'd feel when another guardian or person close to me would hurt when she died.

I wasn't one hundred percent sold on Mr. Kerns' explanation. It was possible that the universe was random, but it was also possible Timmy was very real and killing people out of jealousy or some innate need to protect me.

I wasn't forced to change schools, which was good. I'd changed enough in my younger years. Usually I welcomed it, but now I had a boyfriend and I didn't want to give that up.

"The prom is only a month away. Will you be my date?" asked Raury, leaning against the locker next to mine. His eyes smiling, a silly grin on his face.

I closed my locker. "And where am I going to get a dress?"

"At the store. The lady you live with will take you. Ask her?"

Living in foster care wasn't like having two parents that loved you. I mostly wore hand-me-downs, although I was the only child in my current home. Asking her, I'd feel like a schmutz. I still had Sara's money tucked away in the passageway. I'd go to the house, collect some of it and buy a dress. "OK."

"OK, that's it. Most girls are dying to get a date to the prom and you act like it's a sacrifice," he huffed.

"I'm sorry. Yes, I'd be honored to go with you." I curtsied.

"You're such a smart-ass. What are you doing after school today?"

"I'm getting a dress and a flower for your lapel." I tugged at his shirt, placing an imaginary boutonniere on it.

He pulled me against him. "Do I get to see your butterfly?"

I licked my lips. "Maybe. I'll think about it." He'd been pressing me harder for sex but I wasn't quite ready. After I graduated and had reassurances I wouldn't get pregnant. That was what worried me. It wasn't the sex. I wanted that as badly as he did but not the unwanted baby like I was. My mother's words would sting me forever and worse the possibility of carrying on the 'family' tradition of vanishing babies. Being haunted by Timmy was enough. I didn't need an infant haunting me forever. There was no rational way of explaining any of my fears to Raury.

The hotel ballroom was decorated like something from a Disney movie with flowing white sheer cloth hanging over the entrance and fake trees with white flower buds in the corners. White table cloths atop black ones hung from the tables with shiny ball centerpieces.

We strolled through the pristine shiny walkway sprinkled with red rose petals and he grabbed a table. Big red bows were tied to the backs of each chair. I'd never seen anything so elegant.

We danced like it was only the two of us until one of his friends cut in. "After party at my house. The parental units are out of town." His eyes sparkled with mischievousness.

Raury met his rascally grin with one of his own. "We'll be there."

I shoved my elbow into his ribs. "What?" he squeaked after his friend left.

"You didn't even ask me."

"Oh, come on. You need to make nice with other people and stop living like a turtle tucked into its shell."

"Is that what you think?" I questioned, turning on my heel and leaving him alone on the dance floor.

He grabbed my shoulder. "Scarlett, stop. Listen, I'm sorry. I don't get why you won't let anyone in." I halted and listened to his words.

Turning around I met his gloomy gaze. "OK, this one time." If what Dr. Kerns said had a ring of truth to it and Timmy hadn't appeared since then it was my psychological problem and I needed to get over it.

Raury's parents allowed him to drive their car to and from prom since his truck wasn't the right vehicle to put his prom date in. It was a convertible Cadillac El Dorado, as big as a boat and floated on the ground, gliding over bumps in the road. We rode with the top down, the wind rushed through my hair, teasing my senses and furthering my excitement. He parked along a vacant road at the foothills, leaned across the seat and brushed his hands over the bodice of my dress, rubbing a finger over the tops of my breasts.

"You can come out little butterfly," he said as his fingers slipped between the dress and my flesh, over my nipple, squeezing gently.

I shifted in my seat and met his lips as he pulled his hand out of my dress and pressed himself against me. The front seat was so large we lay across the seat as he scooted the layers of my dress until they fell to the side, caressing my legs and the area around my panties. His hardness pushed against me as our lips and tongues eddied together in passion.

His hand left my legs and fiddled with his pants, maneuvering as he slipped them down. He took my hand and brought it to his solid, hard, male organ, cupping my hands around it. It was soft as silk in my palm and I wanted him, more than anything. I let go and he pressed it against me, sliding my panties.

"I've waited so long for this," he whispered in my ear as his hardness pressed against me, willing to find its way in. "I promise to be gentle." He licked my ear. My senses reaching overdrive, uncontrollable overdrive, as I rubbed against him, growing wetter with each second. He slowly entered me, rubbing and rocking as he eased his way in.

It felt so good, I almost let go of my will completely then another voice whispered in my ear, "Do it, Scarlett." I blinked my eyes open and Timmy's face hovered above us.

All the faculties that had left me as I welcomed sexual bliss returned and I pushed and kicked Raury off me. "No, no. We can't do this." I opened the door and ran through the brush.

"You fuckin' tease. What's wrong with you?" Raury asked in frustration.

I continued to run to the top of the small hill while Raury called for me. Ignoring him, I crouched and wept in my hands.

"Stop being a tease. I'm tired of having blue balls and spanking the monkey to relieve the pain!" I felt the agony and desire in his voice. He would rape me now if I showed myself so I stayed hidden until he went back to his car.

"Fine, have it your way. I'm leaving. I'll be at Derek's after party!" he shouted as the motor revved and he pulled away, tires squealing.

I lifted my head and watched the lights of the Cadillac diminish, then veer to the left, silhouetting Timmy. They shone right through him. The crunch of metal as it slid off the road and into a tree echoed inside my ears. "Raury," I called, running down the hill and resting beside his body, tossed from the car on impact. Blood spilled from his head. "I'm sorry, Raury," I cried, the tears rolling down my cheeks. My throat burned and my heart lurched as I choked.

Timmy stood in the shine from the headlights. "You did this! Why?" My parents' car crash flashed through my head. My mother's head bounced against the windshield and my parents' bodies were tossed inside the car as it rolled, killed on impact. The twins; I saw the truck jack-knife in my head. Anger roiled in my gut and rose, spilling out of me. I rushed Timmy and tackled him, punching his face and wrapping my hands around his throat, squeezing with all my force.

He vanished from beneath me. "You can't kill a ghost. I'm already dead," Timmy mocked with a half-cocked grin. Maybe I couldn't kill him now but I'd find a way.

"You killed my parents, the twins, everyone. You're evil. That's why you're dead. You weren't meant to be!" I knew my words stung him. I didn't care. He killed everyone in my life. Now I knew it was him. I watched in horror. My Raury lay dead on the road.

"Why did you live? Your parents. They treated you like a princess and what about me? The forgotten child who died before he had a chance to live. You're a selfish bitch!" His tone filled with rage, darkness, and a deep disdain for his sorry situation.

"Selfish?! I don't kill people. Why don't you fucking kill me?! Why not? Here I am, take me." I placed my hands out and tossed my head back. "Take me!"

His voice softened. "I can't kill you and I won't live, even as a ghost, if you die."

"Then stay out of my life. Forever! I banish you!" I stomped off, leaving him on the road with Raury's body and marched towards the closest gas station, tears streaking my face.

Chapter 22
Mystics and Broomsticks

*A*fter questioning by the police, watching Raury's body loaded into an ambulance. My cheeks drenched in tears. I was a wreck, my mind replaying the events of the night. A warm hand caressed my face and another stroked my hair. I gazed into Raury's deep brown eyes.

He smiled and said without moving his mouth but talking right into my head, *I couldn't go without saying I love you. I'd never have hurt you.*

I love you too, I replied, hoping he heard me. After that he vanished just as Sara and Shari did. My heart felt some relief knowing he wouldn't stay on the earth roaming it as so many other spirits did. He was at peace. I wiped the tears from my cheeks and smiled as the last of him glimmered and was gone.

The self-doubt I felt washed away when Timmy pushed Raury off the road. His sweet brown eyes lingered in my mind. Because of my own fears I halted what would have been my first time. Timmy's face gazing down at me, urging me to do it. The terror of becoming pregnant. I pushed Raury away and ran, hiding like a small child. Raury wouldn't have raped me. If I'd have thought clearly earlier I would have understood that, but the sins of my father lurked inside me.

What didn't make sense to me was Timmy's actions. *Did he want me pregnant and why?* Or was he, in the demented way he did things, toying with my fears and insecurities. I had no answer for either question but knew one day I would find a way to destroy him. Vengeance climbed through my body on suckers and clung, seething and breathing inside me.

School once again became a hostile place. I was blamed for Raury's death, called a witch and other names I'd heard before. Students and even teachers gave me the evil eye and veered to the other side of the hallway to avoid me. I drew further inside myself, spent my time once again buried in books and studying. It wasn't enough I lost my boyfriend but I lost my anonymity.

Dr. Kern was too grounded on Earth, into his textbooks and what they could teach him. He didn't understand that a paranormal realm existed, but I did. I'd seen it. It was Timmy's fault, and time to consult someone who believed in life outside of the physical realm.

A bell on the door went ding ding as I entered Mystics and Broomsticks, a metaphysical shop that did everything from tarot cards and palm reading to crystal balls. Painted in vibrant colors with shelves filled with candles, charms, crystals and gemstones, incense, oils, and books. The purple beads behind the counter were pushed to the side as a woman with flowing golden hair and a flowery headband stepped towards the counter.

"Can I help you?" she offered.

"I think you can." I reached the counter and said quietly, "What do you know about ghosts?"

Her brown eyes sparked. "Ghosts. What an interesting subject." She paused, taking in my facial expression. "Are you being haunted?" The sparkle in her eyes ceased and her face became solemn.

I scratched my head. I really didn't know where to start.

Eying me curiously, she seemed to understand my confusion. "There's no one in the store. Why don't we sit and you can start from the beginning."

I sighed and noted the small, glassy black table to the side. I pulled out a chair as she coasted from behind the counter. Her long, colorful skirt flowing with her and her radiant brown eyes smiling as she sat in the chair across from me.

"I see ghosts and when I was little I played with them. I didn't know at the time what they were." I nervously twisted my lips.

"Relax, I'm not going to judge you." Her soothing words calmed me as I inhaled the sweet scent from the candles on the shelf behind me.

"Well, I realized they were ghosts when my grandmother died and I saw her spirit rise out of her body," I simplified, calling Sara my grandmother instead of attempting to explain my crazy home life. "There was one friend that stuck with me. He was always around. Other ghosts I ignored after that but he already knew I could see him."

"You can see, hear, and interact with them?" she questioned with a raised brow.

"Yeah." I knew it was insane. Selma was right; my eyes gave me sight into the spiritual world.

"Most people can't do all three. They either see or hear them but rarely can do both and interact in this realm. Does this gift run in your family?"

Gift, this was no gift but a curse. "My mother can see them too, but she doesn't talk about it."

"Does she have eyes like yours?" Her eyes darted as they gazed into one of my eyes and then the other.

"No, but I've been told my eyes being different colors allows me to see into the spiritual realm. Is that true?"

She smiled. "It is thought so, but until now I've never met anyone who had different colored eyes and you're the only person I've ever met that can fully interact with ghosts, so please continue." The excited sparkle in her returned and she placed her arms on the table.

I thought about that and spun it in my head for a second. "My *disability*," I didn't know what else to call it, "and the ghost attached to me may come from my parentage. My mother's eyes are amber and my," I paused as I hated to call the man who raped my mother anything but a bastard, "father had green eyes. The ghost attached to me has green eyes and he's not just another ghost but my twin. He died before birth and part of his fetus was found in the placenta."

Her eyes widened. "So you absorbed him and that's how you got your eye color. I've heard of this before."

The absorbing thing wasn't news, but my eye color coming from him, that was new. I'd never thought of it. That's why his eyes and the rapist's eyes were always familiar. We shared the same emerald shade of green. "He does bad things, hurts people, and I want him out of my life."

"This is a first." She stood and perused the shelves of her store. "We recently got in a book that mentions something about vanishing twins. Let me see." She pulled a book off the shelf, flipped to the back and then another. "Here it is!" she exclaimed and placed it on the table between us. "According to this you can only rid yourself of the evil spirit twin in two ways. The first is pregnancy. If you become pregnant, than he can inhabit the baby but he only has a short window in which to do this. It has to be within the same trimester as he passed. The second option is even more bleak -- death."

She squinted her eyes with warning. "That's not a viable option. There's a list of herbs and stones you can use to ward him off and another list to use during pregnancy to protect the baby from possession." The list of herbs included angelica, benzoin, blackberry, boxwood, cinquefoil, sage, and clover. She went back to the shelves and collected various items.

The bell rang as a couple of older women entered the store. She welcomed them to the store then returned to me. "Wear this around your wrist." She handed me a bracelet made of dark stone. "And wear this charm around your neck." It was some type of salmon-colored stone inside gold. She went through everything else, explaining how I needed to burn the incense and sage, waving them around my house and all the other voodoo one would see in a movie.

I wasn't sure if any of the stuff would help me, but she believed and that was enough to at least give it a try. I gazed at all the stuff on the table. "He's never harmed me."

"If he harms you, his spirit will leave this earth with yours. The bracelet is a must to keep him out of your life and if you want to cleanse your home then you need the sage. I'll throw in this bag of gemstones and mixed herbs for free. They will keep your home free from spirits. He won't be able to get to you or anyone in your house," she urged, handing me the items in a small pink plastic bag.

"I'll take the book too, please." Should I ever have children, the last thing I wanted was Timmy's spirit inside my child and the book had other stuff in it that I felt might be useful. "Thank you, for all this and for listening," I said, grabbing the bag.

"You let me know if I can help with anything else." she smiled warmly but her eyes flashed a warning.

My guardians weren't home when I entered the house, sometimes they went out with their friends. I lit the sage and walked throughout the house spreading it everywhere, wafting it with my hand so it drifted into every corner. I put the bag of stones beneath my mattress, then thought again. I didn't need to protect myself but my guardians and the house, everyone who entered it, so I put them in an air vent in the middle of the house. I wasn't sure what to do with the herb samples so I placed them in my dresser. Each one had a tag for what it did. Some were for burning; others were to be kept in boxes or mixed.

That summer I made The Purple Mask stories into comic strips. I wrote in Penelope as The Crimson Flame. Together they saved the world from evil and harm. The Purple Mask saw people and spirits for what they were and The Crimson Flame sent those with hearts that couldn't be claimed to fiery pits of hell using her hair as a whip. I sent a sample to the local paper and waited, after a couple weeks they responded that they liked the comic and would publish what I sent and asked for more. I continued sending them and they published them until The Purple Mask became a regular fixture in the Sunday Comics.

I thought about Kevin and the information he tried to give me. It weighed on my mind. I feared my sister would reject me as my mother had but I worked up the courage and called Kevin. She might have information that was helpful.

He came to my house while my guardian was out. His shoulders broader and a thickening waist, yet still quite slim, he was the same Kevin. He handed me the envelope and asked, "How are you doing?"

"I published The Purple Mask in the Sunday funnies."

He gave me a sideways glance. "I knew they were familiar. Good for you."

"And I graduate this spring," I added.

"Have you looked at colleges?"

"Some." The truth was, even with my impeccable 4.0 GPA, I hadn't applied to any. It was time to change the subject. "How are you?"

"I'm getting married in July." His eye twinkled with the revelation.

I couldn't think of him as married. The goofy, pothead guy who liked fast cars and spooky ghost towns. "Congratulations."

"Do you talk with Penelope much?" He leaned back and placed one leg over the other.

"Occasionally. She graduated from law school and got a job in a law office but I haven't heard much from her since." I didn't make a lot of attempts to keep up with her because of the whole Timmy evil spirit thing. His killing the horrible people in my life was creepy, but his willful murder of those I cared for was unthinkable.

"She's busy and has a nice condo in Boulder, Colorado. After graduation I'm sure she'd love to have you visit."

I was happy for her. She came from nothing like me and worked her way up and was now a home owner. At my age she had already sent her application to various colleges and had a goal in mind which she accomplished. I was floundering and indecisive. It was that moment I realized just how encompassing Timmy was in my life. Everything circled around him, friends or the lack of them, protecting myself from his presence and the cruelty I endured from others. It had been a couple years since Raury's passing and the murmurs in the hall had lessoned since his group graduated but the legacy of death followed me all because of my evil twin. "I might do that."

He unfolded his leg and leaned forward. "I'm still available if you need a ride. You know..." His eyes shifted to the folder.

"Thank you," I replied, then walked him to the door.

On my bed I glanced over all the information once again. When I stared at the rapist's picture, the long dragon heads appeared to move. The black one grew larger and attempted to strangle the white one but it lashed back and freed itself from its grip. *Now you're*

271

seeing things. You are insane. Flipping the picture over, I couldn't bear to look at it anymore. My sister was who I was most interested in knowing, maybe. I wouldn't hold my breath. The address and phone number on the back was from years ago. It didn't hurt to try and I gained courage from the idea her foster life was like mine and she no longer lived there.

I took a deep breath and called the number, nervously twisting the long spiral telephone cord in my hand, loop after loop. The phone rang and a man answered. "Hello," he greeted.

"Hi, uh... is Philmonia there," I murmured.

"No, Philmonia left a couple years ago," he said, lacking any emotion.

"OK, thank you." I dropped the phone onto the receiver and let out a huge sigh of relief. I did it and it was done. She'd just have to be a sister I never knew. As the days passed my mind faltered but I didn't search and stayed fast in that decision.

I've always believed it was my thoughts about her that caused the next major event in my life to happen. It was a hot day in September and, like every other day, I walked to the bus stop when out of nowhere someone called my name. I ignored it the first time but then I heard it again, only closer. It wasn't more than a few feet from me. I craned my neck and glanced, the clearest cerulean eyes gazed at me set inside an oval face, cutting through the crowd of students. Everyone disappeared as if it was only the two of us. Her golden curls bounced against her chest as her body sashayed closer to me.

Chapter 23
Living Like Royalty

My sister glittered from head to toe, from the platinum blond highlights in her hair covering the rhinestone hoops in her ears to the shimmery silver platform pumps on her feet. "Inglenook, Cabernet Sauvignon," Philmonia ordered, batting her blue eyelashes. She motioned the waitress to leave with a flick of her midnight blue acrylic nails. The light from the chandelier catching the huge diamond rock on her left hand. "I'm so happy to finally meet you," she drawled.

I was speechless. What is there to say to someone whose league I'm not even close to. She was flashy as the Silver Porsche 911 she drove, and just as fast and smooth, but she was my sister and came to me of her own free will. I swallowed, shrinking in her radiance. "Me too. I mean, I'm happy to meet you."

Over dinner she continued to talk about her glamorous life and wealthy husband. She described their estate. An estate; she lived in something that grand with servants. It wasn't that I didn't compare. There was nothing to compare. I was a kid who was shuffled from one home to the next, who lost almost everyone I ever loved and hadn't even made a decision about college yet. I was but a speck in her glory.

She batted her cerulean eyes at me and grasped my hands from across the table. Her silver and diamond bangles clinking on the shiny top and monstrosities flashing brilliantly on her fingers pressed against my empty ones. "I'm sorry about what my daddy did. I don't really remember him except," a small tear bubbled in the corner of her eye, threatening to drop, "he would come in my room at night. I was really little."

She cleared her throat and I stared with wide eyes, imagining the two-headed tattooed man sneaking in my room at night. "My mom, she killed herself after they caught him and now he's dead. A group of other prisoners killed him." The tear dropped and she choked back a sob. The tear rolled down her cheek and dropped onto her chest resting in her cleavage surrounded by the blue satin of her form-fitting dress.

"I'm sorry," I squeaked. It was the only thing I could think of to say and it was lame. I wasn't sorry the monster was dead, only sorry he harmed people before he died.

"Thank you," she sniffled. "Let's talk about something more pleasant. You're having a birthday soon, right?"

"Yeah, next month."

"And you'll be eighteen." Her teary eyes dried and brightened quicker than I could snap my fingers.

I nodded.

"You need to come to our house and we'll throw you a grand party."

Was she joking? She wanted me, little reject girl Scarlett, to walk on the marble tile of her house. "That would be nice."

She rolled her eyes. "You don't get excited easy do you?"

"What?" I wasn't sure what she meant by that statement. My life didn't fizz and twinkle like hers.

"I offer you a party and you answer with 'that would be nice'. Jump out of your seat, give me a hug, tell me I'm the best." Even her teeth sparkled in the light between her smiling lips.

I considered Timmy, the dark twin, but in her glow my shadow grew larger and for the first time I considered maybe I was the dark one. He died, I lived, and now I was in the warmth of a beam of sun scented in a flowery perfume. "I would love that!" I beamed, nowhere near as dazzling as Philmonia but it was a start.

For the next month she picked me up from school or met me after school at least twice a week. She asked me all kinds of questions about what I liked, didn't like, from food to colors to decor. She always glimmered no matter what she wore. Even her jeans looked like royalty.

She took me shopping. Her philosophy was 'your body is an ornament and should only be adorned with the finest'. I imagined no matter what she did she always looked perfect as a picture. Philmonia tossed money and waved her magic wand, people jumped and did exactly as she asked. If it wasn't for the obvious physical characteristics between us I wouldn't have believed for a second that we were sisters. I finally had someone, family, a sibling who wasn't a crazy, obsessed ghost.

Timmy hadn't shown himself in years since I visited Mystics and Broomsticks. The herbs and gem stones did the trick and every so often I recleansed the house with sage. My life was finally on an upward spiral, like climbing the turret stairs and reaching the rainbow.

My birthday fell on a Sunday that year and my birthday extravaganza was planned for the weekend prior. Philmonia was picking me up from school Friday and, only because she insisted, I was spending the night with her. She had huge plans for my hair, face, nails, and clothing so I'd be the belle of my ball. I gave her the right of way, enamored with her presence.

Friday came and she waited for me in her shiny Porsche with the top off. *American Pie* by Don Mclean played on the radio. I slipped into her car and she sped off. "This weekend will be the time of your life. I promise. I'm absolutely going to spoil you!"

I never told her I knew anything about her before she wrangled and took over my life like the blazing whirlwind she was. I told her nothing of my past, only highlighting the few bright moments in it. With all her talk and sparkles I didn't know much about her either. At the time I didn't care.

A thick, wrought iron gate swung open. "Welcome to Poppy Hills," she bubbled.

My jaw dropped as I took in the vast, manicured space before us bursting with golden poppies. The long driveway made a horse shoe. She pulled the car in front of the massive double doors of the house. A tall, thin, blond man came running and she tossed him the keys. He caught them in midair.

"Thanks." She winked at him and clutched my hand in hers. "It's beautiful, isn't it? Wait until you see inside!" Her cerulean eyes widened.

She thrust the doors open. The entryway melted into an enormous wide space bathed in sunshine from the skylight in the vaulted ceiling. A corkscrew staircase opened up to the second floor. Straight ahead, on the other side of double sliding glass doors, water from an inground pool shimmered. Aztec rugs and a large salmon sectional were inviting. "You live here?"

"Of course. Wait until you see my birthday gift." She lifted her shoulders in excitement.

"Hello, darling," said a man from the stairs. I assumed it was her husband, Evan O'Conner. He wasn't an attractive man; wisps of dark hair covered the nearly bald spot on his head. The thick bulk of his body gave him a square shape and he was short in stature. His vibrant blue eyes shifted to me. "You must be Scarlett. Philly talks about you all the time." He strolled down the stairs.

"Hello, Mr. O'Conner."

"We're family, please call me Evan." He smiled and took my hand, then kissed it with his old, wrinkly, dry lips. He was at least forty years my sister's senior. I wanted to cringe at the touch of his prune-ish lips but remembered my manners.

I slowly pulled my hand back as he lowered it, ready to have it at my side again.

"Dinner smells delightful." She turned towards me. "Mrs. Kurl is theee best cook," she said, making overexaggerated facial expressions and squeezing her hands together.

"That she is. Why don't you check on that and I'll give Scarlett a tour?"

From the corner of my eye I spotted her lift the corner of her mouth in a half smile before she kissed his cheek then he whispered something in her ear.

I cleared my throat. "What about my bag?"

"Drop it by the stairs. I'll have Mr. Kurl bring that to your room for you," said Mr. O'Conner. "Shall we?"

"Yes, this house is like a palace. I'd love to see the rest."

He chuckled. "It's not quite a palace but it's very nice and suits us well." He tucked his bulky arms behind his back and clasped his hands.

He rushed me through the downstairs of the house then pulled open the sliding glass doors. We strode past the pool and he stopped, the vast expanse of his land stretched out before us. "Your sister was a lot like you when we first met. She didn't have an easy life. She'd never tell you that now. It's been my mission to erase the atrocities of her past and allow her to flourish."

"I'd say she has."

He chuckled. "Yes she has, but she still has nightmares and overcompensates. You'll know what I mean when you see your gift." He winked.

I could only imagine. She was glitter and gold, everything sparkled, and who knows what awaited me. I smiled, unsure what to say. I was happy for her that she found a man who treated her like a queen, yet something about him was off, something about the entire situation, but I was so filled with awe I didn't accept the hints my intuition was sending.

"Her wish is my command," he said in a light tone that carried a hidden warning.

That night, after dinner and a couple bottles of wine, she bounded from her seat. "The suspense is killing me. I can't wait anymore." She pulled the scarf from the waist of her dress. "Turn around, I'm going to blindfold you."

I wasn't crazy about the idea but didn't really see any harm in it. She wrapped it around my eyes and guided me out of the kitchen and up the steps. Mr. O'Conner's cumbersome footsteps trailed behind us. A door creaked open and she said, "Ta-da!" as the sash fell away from my eyes.

Before me was a room, decorated in white and lavender, delicate sheer curtains flowed from the windows and above the bed. A shiny silk comforter draped over the sides of the mattress and several puffy pillows in orchid, fuchsia and violet perched against a lavender fabric backboard. White furniture accented the room. I covered my mouth in shock.

"Happy birthday!" She draped herself around me.

I welcomed her thick-scented perfumey hug and when we parted I stepped into the room. "This is for me?"

They both nodded earnestly then Mr. O'Conner spoke, "We want you to consider staying with us. I know it may be a shock now so spend the weekend with us and consider it."

I stepped into the room, dumfounded and flattered that somebody, anybody, especially a sister I only recently met, would go through all this trouble for me.

"Oh, you haven't seen the best yet." She pulled the closet doors open. Racks of shoes filled the open space beneath the rods of clothing.

I was reserved, my sister was flamboyant, and this was too much for me to process as I stood gawking at her moving across the room to another door she pulled open. "And you have your own bathroom."

"I… uh..." I stuttered, unable to get a word out.

"You don't have to say anything yet. No pressure. The room is yours whether you decide to stay or not." Mr.

O'Conner's voice was soft and again carried a warning.

The next day was filled with the royal treatment that blew my mind; the hair, the makeup, all of it was too much for me. I just kept thanking them for lack of anything else better to say. The house was filled with people for the party, people I didn't know. I dressed in a silver bodice-hugging dress that opened to a wide-flowing skirt with a sexy slit up the back. My unruly blonde curls tamed in an up do and flashy make up on my face, a silver choker that fell in layers against my chest, I felt like a princess.

Out the large sliding glass doors a teenaged boy caught the corner of my eye. I glanced and spotted him beyond the pool. The moonlight bathing his pale hair. My heart skipped as he turned, thinking it was Timmy. I wore my bracelet and brought my bag of gem stones, but I hadn't burned any sage here. I didn't want my sister and her husband to know I was haunted by the ghost of my evil twin brother.

His head turned in my direction, our eyes met. Under the moonlight his eyes appeared as azure stars, burning bright and hot. My heart thumped against my chest, realizing this wasn't my brother. No, this was a beautiful young man, tall, muscular, and a sensation similar to what I felt for Raury pushed within me and sped through my veins at lightning speed. My gut said to rush outside.

"Scarlett, have more wine," said Philmonia.

I glanced away from the boy for a split second and gazed at my sister in her bright red taffeta gown. She pushed a crystal goblet filled with deep red wine into my hand. When I returned my gaze to the boy he was gone. *Was he a ghost?* He didn't have the usual translucent glow about his edges.

My sister had taken control of my life. I was but a prisoner of the kind of luxury I thought only existed in Danielle Steel novels. The music and spirits flowed freely as I floated in pearly white heels as flaxen as my hair.

I didn't know what to say. My gut said to go home, but my brain said to stay and indulge.

The following morning I woke up, after not remembering going to bed, in a stuffy room. The air thick, I forced my heavy lids open. The room was black so I assumed it must still be night. I tried to scoot my arms to lift up but they wouldn't move; something was wrapped around my wrists, holding them in place. "Help! Philmonia! Help!"

Chapter 24
All Consuming Darkness

My screams went unanswered. I shifted in my position but a strap around my chest prevented much movement. My feet felt as though they were dangling and spread-eagled. I listened to the intense silence, my eyes unable to adjust to the pitch black surrounding me.

The air was thick and musty, like the crypt, only it was hot. Tiny drops like pitter patters echoed from beside me and a stinging sensation burned against my arm as I twisted it right then left. I perked my ears and concentrated on the drops. They came at regular intervals and again the stinging sensation in my arm. I was hooked to an IV, but why? *Did something happen? Was I in a hospital bed?*

No. The thick, musty, hot air told me another story. I was trapped, a prisoner, and if I didn't find a way out something more horrifying than anything I'd experienced was going to happen. Every bone in my body screamed to be released from the straps binding them and run, never look back. Drip, drip. My mind grew fuzzy and the blackness consumed me.

The next time I woke I heard voices, long and distorted. I couldn't make out the words. My heavy eye lids refused to part so I concentrated on what my ears could tell me, attempting to paint a picture in my mind.

"Thaaat's iiit, po-op her chay ray, po-op it." I focused all my energy. Sweat or water rolled down my forehead, my throat, my body was soaking and the voice came again, it was female. "Po-op thaaat chay ray." My mind sorted the elongated words, attempting to make sense of them when suddenly they came into focus. "Pop that cherry, slide it in."

A stinging sensation like a million needles bored into my vagina and I screamed in pain, but the sound never left my lips.

"Is it bleeding? Did you do it?" asked the disembodied voice.

"We did," was the response, a male voice.

My brain didn't recognize either voice because it refused or I was pumped full of too many drugs. "Oh doctor. You turn me on. Take me here," moaned the female voice.

Then a slapping sound and groaning filled my ears, burying them in the sounds of sex. Wet, slicked, naked bodies smacked against one another. Moans ricocheted off the walls, "Oh, oh, ohhhhh doctor."

"Nurse Philly." Followed by a growl that sounded like a wounded wolf.

I willed my mind to think of something else, anything else, and slipped into the turret surrounded by my butterflies. Their bright, colorful wings reflected from the rainbow lights. Shari, Timmy, and I played hide and seek in the meadow.

Timmy. Where was Timmy? Surely I wasn't protected from his evil spirit here in this vile place. I willed my mind to reach out to him. *Timmy, Timmy where are you? Timmy, if there was ever a time I needed brotherly protection it's now.*

Nothing. He couldn't hear me or the drugs my body was filled with prevented communication. I overexerted myself and fell into the darkness again.

I awoke when something cold touched my thigh. It startled me awake, my heavy eyelids stuck closed. "Stick it in there, squeeze it... swim for home babies, attach to that egg, you can do it. Ohh Dr. O'Conner."

What was she talking about? Dr. O'Conner? Everything began to fall into perspective, *Nurse Philly.* The wet slapping bodies pressed against each other, a ting hit the floor and echoed. It was something metal and the floor was hard like tile. No, not tile. Tile would give a hardier ting. This was a muffled ting; wood. It was wood. More rattles sounded against something metal; a cart, a tray. I attempted to listen between their moans for clues, anything.

I willed my eyes to open, concentrating all my energy. Slits formed and the darkness was now immersed in a soft light. More tinging caught my ears and I shifted my slitted eyes in the direction of the noise. Two fuzzy forms cleared as my sight adjusted. A large, naked ass with dark curly hairs was surrounded by poles, no legs with feet.

Ting, ting. "Ohh. that's it, ohhh yes, yes!"

"RRRRRR... RRRRR... Phillly!" The cart hit hard against the wall as the bare, hairy ass thrust hard.

I closed my eyes and shifted my head, looking away as the horror of my sister and her husband having sex on a surgical cart blinded my vision. When I creaked my slits open again another surgical cart was to my right, on it lay an elongated tube with a narrow end, something like a turkey baster, only thicker, and the fatter end an open bag.

No, it wasn't a bag, it was rubbery and had tubular flaps.

I squinted my slits to make out the narrow end, something shone from it. Little beads of cream dripped, a tiny puddle of the liquid formed on the metal tray beneath it. The rest suspended on the end. My mind couldn't fathom then what they'd done to me.

Bulky footsteps moved toward me, stopping between me and the surgical cart. "Her eyes are open, hand me another bag," said Mr. O'Conner. His penis wrinkled like a raisin hanging over his testicles that sagged between his hairy legs.

I closed my eyes, lacking the energy to move my head again. My mouth heavy and unable to form words or sounds. The pinching in my arm tingled and soon the blackness consumed me. I welcomed it.

I woke next to the pitch darkness. My mind processing what it'd seen. I was the subject of some type of twisted sexual fantasy between my sister and her husband. Bile rose in my esophagus, burned as it climbed my throat and hurtled out of my mouth, leaving a sour taste. My body shook and my head lurched with dry heaves, thrashing in convulsions. The straps against me lifting and creating a clinging sound that ricocheted off the walls of my torture chamber.

My sister, my flashing, sparkly sister whose glow I absorbed in her radiance was just as maniacal as the father whose sperm she was born from. The two-headed dragon took on another meaning. She was the dark head and I was the white. An innocent victim, like my mother. A tear slid from my eye followed by more. My body trembled again and everything went black.

For days my foggy mind went in and out of consciousness. The rubbery, elongated object slipped in and out of me until a warm liquid coated my insides followed by a deep growl from Mr. O'Conner. I welcomed the black and slipped into the turret whenever it became too much.

Bright light shone against my eyelids and I forced them open with more strength than I'd had for days. Sheer purple fabric surrounded me and I instantly knew I was in the room Philmonia designed for me. It was my new prison as I twisted to free myself but I was still strapped. The mattress beneath me hard. This wasn't the bed she'd bought for me.

I lifted the only part of my body I could -- my head. Leather straps bound my wrists and ankles and wrapped across my chest and thighs. I mustered my energy and bucked, but it wasn't enough. I was helplessly glued to the bed beneath me.

Drip, drip. A sound that had become familiar echoed in my ears and to my left was an IV with a long tube stretching to the crook of my arm. The liquid inside it clear. The door creaked and small footsteps pattered against the floor. I closed my eyes, unwilling to look. I needed a plan, a way out.

"Scarlett." Philmonia's face was above mine. I felt her warm breath, smelled the mint of her toothpaste and flowery scent of her perfume. She jabbed me gently, "I know you're awake."

I didn't move, not a finger twitch, only allowing my lungs to take shallow breaths.

"I'll be back." She fiddled with the IV. I felt the stinging sensation I abhorred in my arm.

My mind raced as I became more lucid and reached my fingers out to feel anything near me but all they felt was air. I twisted my head and pulled upward. To my dismay, there wasn't anything near me except the IV stand and the tube. I moved my head to the side toward the tubing but it was out of my reach, stretching my neck as far left as I could I still couldn't reach it.

"Scarlett, honey," said Philmonia, parting the sheer curtains. "For your safety and the baby's we have to keep you strapped. The first trimester is most detrimental for the health of the child and we don't want anything happening to our perfect little human growing inside you."

What the hell was she talking about? Then the rubbery tube and shiny drops, the burning, pinching sensation and the warm liquid coating my vagina came into focus. They raped me and purposely implanted a child in me. Bile ascended quickly, rushing through my esophagus and through my throat projecting outward. I turned my head in time for the yellow liquid to spew onto Philmonia's chest. It dripped between her cleavage.

"Oh, how dare you!" she screamed and slapped my cheek. It stung my soul more than my flesh. "You wretched little bitch!" She huffed and stomped out of the room.

A few minutes later thick steps broke the silence and the sheers parted. Mr. O'Conner's wrinkly, square form stared at me. His blue eyes sent icy daggers into my flesh that stung all the way into my soul.

Fury raged inside me. "Get the fuck away from me you nasty, wrinkled bastard."

He stood with squared shoulders, his face expressionless. "Is that the way to treat me? We were successful and you are the first person the experiment has worked successfully on. You are a success."

Success, is that what they called it? I wasn't the first. A horrifying thought rushed into my brain and stung so hard it was worse than brain freeze. They had tried this before. *How many others?* Involuntary shudders riddled my body as I convulsed.

"Philly, Philly come quick," he called through the tunnel that threatened to take me.

Tendrils of darkness swirled through the light, coming for me. I welcomed them, my soul easing and the shuddering stopped then the lightness came back. "No!" I screamed. I wanted the darkness, to feel its chill on my skin.

They stared at me and Philmonia's curt voice sent all the darkness packing. "You can't do that. You scared us."

"How many? How many before me?" I spat.

"It doesn't help your situation to know. All that matters is that you were a success," Mr. O'Conner said in a firm voice.

After a few days I realized my hate wasn't going to help my situation. I was carrying their 'miracle child' inside me. If I wanted to play their game and free myself I needed to take their side. "It can't be healthy for the child if I'm tied to this bed. It prevents my blood from circulating properly."

Philmonia eyed me suspiciously. "You'll run."

"No, I won't. There's nowhere to go and I'm done fighting. This blessed creature," I choked back my bile, "needs me to move around. My blood needs to pump and circulate through my body," I repeated.

She narrowed her cerulean eyes and turned on her heel, leaving me alone in the room. After a few minutes heavier footsteps followed by quiet ones moved towards my prison room and the door opened. They strolled beside my bed and unbuckled my wrists then placed my hands together and wrapped a single strap binding my wrists.

Philmonia unbound the strap around my chest and the one around my thighs while Mr. O'Conner lifted me upward and reached around me, his hot breath against my neck sending eerie cold chills across my spine. With a bulky arm he shifted my legs and Philmonia caught them and pulled them off the bed.

Mr. O'Conner tied a thick strap around my neck and Philmonia undid the strap around my ankles.

"Stand up," he ordered.

I pushed, my legs weak and falling beneath the weight of my body. The strap around my neck jerked and my head thrust backwards. Philmonia shot a horrified glance past me into Mr. O'Conner's eyes then pulled me upward and wrapped an arm around me.

"Baby steps. You've been lying for quite some time and have lost muscle mass in your legs." Gently she stepped forward and my frail legs attempted to make the step. I lifted my leg only far enough to drag my foot along the ground. Mr. O'Conner wrapped a thick arm around my other side and together we took one step and another.

My feet dragging with each step. I willed my legs to work and gathered my strength, but after a couple circles around the room I was out of breath.

A week passed and then another. My walks came more frequently and my diet changed from soup, mushed vegetables and fruit to solid food. I played their game and built up my strength and their trust. Waiting for the day they took off the leash and didn't strap me in bed.

After a month I talked them into allowing me outside. The leash kept me from going far and they were always close but I welcomed the fresh air and the chill it brought. I basked in the glow of the sun and they were becoming more careless with me. Leaving me chained to the door like a pet while they sucked whipped cream and strawberries off each other. Philmonia engulfing Mr. O'Conner's penis in her mouth, white cream dripping down her chin as they recklessly had sexual relations in front of me.

Their sexual fantasies didn't end with food. They'd strap and whip each other, wear collars, and tie each other up. Her favorite get up was a black leather bodice with no underwear and fishnets that rose just below her ass. She took on the dominatrix act better than he did an alpha. She was in control. I remembered his words as she lashed the whip beside him, splitting the air: 'Her wish is my command'.

Chapter 25
Summoning a Ghost

*A*t the height of their morbid sexual act I became invisible, a casualty of war. Fisting my hands together, my wrists bound, I punched my stomach hard, harder, until I knocked the wind out of myself, dropping to my knees. I wanted the little beast inside me out, gone. It was a monster. Breathless, I toppled to the floor, my stomach bouncing off the tile.

"Something's wrong!" shouted my sister in a wretched scream.

Thick arms lifted me off the ground as I choked for air, denying my body's will to breathe. If only it would give up, quit and let me die, the vermin inside me would die too. Warm breath was sent into my lungs. I opened my eyes to see Mr. O'Conner's lips pressed against mine, filling me with air.

I choked out a scream as terror gripped me and scooted out of his embrace. I tucked my legs between my arms.

"It's OK, it was a scare. We're taking you to your room." He gathered my balled-up body into his arms and marched me upstairs, Philmonia behind him. My eyes met hers and dread teemed inside them.

He laid me down on the bed and lifted my shirt then pressed a stethoscope against my belly.

"Can you hear the baby?" she asked.

"Not at this stage." He moved around the bed and pulled my legs apart.

My eyes widened in horror as I fought against him. "I'll have to do a pelvic exam."

A what? I thrashed and kicked my legs free, hitting him in the chest. "You'll do no such thing. I need a real doctor!"

His eyes blazed at me and Philmonia grasped my hand. "She's

right," she said, squeezing my hand between her jewel infested fingers.

He narrowed his eyes and let out a defeated sigh.

Within the next hour Mr. O'Conner barged into my room. "The doctor will be here soon," he fumed then stomped out.

Philmonia entered. "You will be me. I'm taking the straps off and you're getting dressed in my clothes. I'll fix your hair and makeup. You will do nothing to endanger the baby or give the doctor any idea that you aren't me. Evan will be in the room with you the entire time." She stomped her foot and folded her arms over her chest. "Am I clear?!"

"Crystal," I seethed, narrowing my eyes into slits and wishing a painful death on her.

"And we have to do something about your odd eyes." She marched out of the room and came back with a makeup case. She brushed and braided my hair which was platinum, hers was a dirty, darker shade of gold but her chunky platinum highlights made it appear much lighter in a well-lighted room.

"Put these in," she ordered, handing me a small case. I opened it and stared at a set of contacts.

"I've never worn contacts. I don't know how to put them in."

"Watch." She took a contact out, placed it on her fingertip and pulled her eye open with the other hand. "Then you pop it in. Do it or I'll do it for you."

She undid my wrist straps and I fiddled with the tiny lenses until they were in my eye. They hurt and were probably in all wrong. My eyes watered.

She wiped my face. "I can't put the makeup on with all that liquid leaking from your eyes. Dry it up!"

It wasn't voluntary. As she completed the makeup, dressed and undressed me I made a decisive plan. If the book I bought from Mystics and Broomsticks was correct then Timmy could inhabit the soul of this wicked little monster growing inside me. I read the book cover to cover and knew exactly how to rid ghosts and evil spirits from my life but not how to summon them.

Mr. O'Conner stood in the doorway the entire time she primped and prodded me. All her glitter came with a price and I was going to sell the baby to the devil so to speak. They moved me to their room and she stuck several bangles over my arms, hiding the marks left from the straps.

I was compliant with the doctor. Mr. O'Conner stayed beside me, holding my hand in his cold grasp, creased with excessive lines from his saggy skin. I brought my mind back to the book and read through each page using my memory as a visual guide. It warned against using primrose and blackthorn, saying they were harbingers of bad souls.

Items belonging to the spirit or having meaning to the spirit could be used to alert it and was thought to increase spirit activity. I'd get them to buy the herbs, suggesting they would ease the baby. I'd have them buy lavender, angelica, rue, and sage.

"That was a hard fall," said the doctor as he gazed at my bruised stomach. His eyes searched mine as if he was looking for an answer. *Could he tell they were fist marks?*

I gave a half-smile. "I don't know what happened. A strong pain shot through my belly and I lost my balance. My stomach tightened and it became hard to breathe."

He narrowed his eyes in disbelief. "I can't tell you what happened but the baby appears fine, Mrs. O'Conner."

I cringed inside but acted the part, sighing and sweeping my forehead in an exaggerated movement. "Oh, I'm so grateful. You're sure?"

"The baby is fine," his eyes shifted to Mr. O'Conner, "but she needs to visit me regularly, monthly at least, until the third trimester. The baby will grow rapidly then and I'll need to see her weekly."

Mr. O'Conner's face showed relief when the doctor said the baby was fine and he agreed to monthly visits. I was getting out of the house once a month, and more when I reached the last couple months. I couldn't help but smile.

The O'Conner's agreed to getting me the list of herbs after I explained the calming and healing properties of them. I also convinced them to leave the straps off and lock my door when I was alone at night. Baby steps, just as Philmonia said. They still didn't fully trust me, I saw it in their faces, but they worried about the parasite inside my womb, giving me the control.

I finally saw things clearly. They were at my mercy. I mushed the goji berries, anise seed, and wormwood together and drank it to abort the baby. That was my first plan. I puked all night and spotted, a glop of blood and flesh dropped into the toilet and I thought surely that was the beast, but when we made it to my first doctor's appointment the little monster's heart beat strong. Its sound haunted my ears.

My next step was to summon Timmy, appeal to his soft side. The part of him that craved life. If the book was correct his spirit could enter this baby and I'd get my revenge on him and Philmonia at the same time. At the next full moon, at the close of the first trimester, I paired the primrose in a bundle of thirteen and spread the blackthorn over the room.

I sat Indian style on the floor and pleaded, "Timmy, I know I've wronged you. All you ever wanted was a chance to live, to breathe, to be seen and noticed by others. I want to give you that gift." I waited with no response.

"Timmy, you hear me. We are connected in a way that can't be undone. Show yourself."

A breeze swept from behind, blowing my hair over my face. A finger caressed the nape of my neck. "I'm here," Timmy whispered.

"Is this all for dramatic effect?"

He materialized in front of me and pointed his fingers at the primrose and blackthorn. "Is that for dramatic effect?" He was much taller now and filled out. His platinum curls unruly and his emerald eyes more vibrant than I remembered.

"I pushed you away from me. I was scared after Raury's death but I see now that all you wanted was to protect me. Be my brother. I'm sorry," I pleaded for forgiveness, beginning my manipulation of Timmy Jones.

His eyes widened and filled with rage. "Do you know what it's like to have a barrier between yourself and the living realm? You and I are connected. There's no way to sever it and for the last few years I've lived bottled in a magical tube!"

I would have suggested he keep his voice down but nobody could hear him but me. "I'm sorry, but I think I can give you a chance to live."

"Because you thought your sister was somehow going to be better than me but turned out as wicked as our father? I see what's happening from the glass walls of my bottle. You've tried to abort that baby twice," he seethed in a melancholy sing song tone.

I swallowed. "You're right, I have tried, but this baby doesn't want to leave. It's strong and in the next couple weeks I'll be in the second trimester. I think it's waiting for you."

His nose twitched. "What exactly are you saying?"

"I'm saying I'm inviting you to enter the soul of this baby so you can finally be born into the world. Sure, the O'Conner's are strange and into S & M but they love this baby. It's the apple of their eye and the only thing that melts their heart. You'll be born into all this wealth and luxury." I enticed him as he raised a brow.

"You want me to possess that baby?"

"Yes." I nodded enthusiastically. "Exactly!"

His eyes shifted as he soaked in the splendor of my prison. "It is a nice house and they are rich -- stinking rich."

"And they love this baby. You'd have a perfect life," I said in a soft, assuring tone.

His tone changed. "I already considered this option you know, but I can't yet, not until your twenty-fifth week. That's when my heart ceased to beat and I died."

The book said the same trimester but maybe it was incorrect and the window of possession was narrower. "You have fourteen weeks to think about it then. Stay here with me, keep me company. Live with us," I urged.

He vanished. The next couple weeks I played nice, wrapping them around my finger with baby needs. I got out of the house and enjoyed my doctor visits even though I had to wear those horrible blue contacts, concealing my identity.

It was in the fifth month that Timmy returned while I was sleeping. He brushed over my swelling belly and that's what woke me. "Timmy?" I asked, rubbing the sleep from my eyes as I sat up in bed.

"It's time." His emerald eyes glowed in the darkness, the light from the moon shone against his translucent form. He was completely see-through except for his eyes. Like a small tornado he spun, the wind kicking against my face. I didn't look away and laid back, welcoming his soul into the baby.

The wind stopped and a black mist surrounded me and slipped in through my belly button. It seared like hot coals as it shot through the umbilical cord and into the growing fetus. I cringed and clutched the bed sheets to keep myself from screaming out in pain.

After a couple minutes it was all over. My brother now inhabited the little demon child. A wry smile spread across my face.

Chapter 26
The Crimson Flame

"*Y*ou've been perky lately," said my sister as she felt the baby kicking in my belly. Only I knew what had happened. I'd rid myself of Timmy and given her a future filled with torture. This child would be the end of her. I knew it then and couldn't wipe the smile off my face when I thought about it.

"I guess pregnancy is working for me." *What they didn't know!* There was a lot I didn't know either such as: *is Timmy's spirit going to mesh with the baby's? Does the baby even have a spirit yet?* I believed it did since Timmy was the ghost of such a baby. *Would their spirits fight? The strong one winning the battle and in control of the physical body?*

There were too many questions and I didn't care what the answers were. What I did know was Timmy could no longer haunt me and Philmonia would have to raise the little monster who I knew would one day turn his back on her.

"Well, don't get used to it. We are keeping the baby," she smarted as if her words stung.

Yes, you are! He's all yours. I shifted my eyes down. "I know," I countered in a soft, mournful voice as the baby did a summersault in my belly. Its little claws stinging against my womb.

That afternoon she left my room while Mrs. Kurl was vacuuming. They were really particular about when and where she cleaned and I doubted she even knew I was there. From the corner of my eye I spotted Mrs. Kurl take a quick glance in my room as my sister closed and locked the door.

A couple weeks later my sister and Mr. O'Conner went out to dinner and left me alone, untied, in my room. I watched out my window, soaking in the massive slice of land they called home. Headlights shone against the field, illuminating the brush as it moved toward the house.

I watched in curiosity as the headlights bounced over the field, stopping beside the patio. It was a golf cart and Mrs. Kurl stepped out and walked towards the door. Another form that I couldn't make out stayed in the cart.

I listened as the door unlocked, her feet pattering against the tile. She went back to the cart and the second person stepped out. I expected to see Mr. Kurl and was shocked when I saw someone else, tall and blond with broad shoulders. He lifted his head, spotting me in the window. Our eyes locked.

The young man I'd seen outside during my party. The night before my nightmare began. I recognized his eyes. It was him. I'd thought he was a dream, part of my drug-induced visions. He followed Mrs. Kurl inside. Their footsteps thumped up the stairs, my heart quickened. I ran to the door. "Hello?"

"I'm Amelia," said a sweet voice like honey drizzled on a biscuit.

"I'm Scarlett, Philmonia's sister. Can you get me out of here?" I pleaded, desperate to step out of my prison at least for a moment.

"No, dear. I don't have a key to this room. I brought my son, Jenson, with me. He told me months ago and I had suspicions they had someone trapped here. They've been very cryptic--"

He cut her off, "Is there anything we can do for you?"

I stumbled over my words. People, normal people, were here talking with me. It was a life line and I needed to think quick before the O'Conners came back. "I uh... I have a friend. Um. Do you have a pencil?"

"Not on me," he said, his voice strong and confident. "I see their headlights. They've returned, but I'll be back."

"Penelope Fischer in Boulder Colorado," I spat out.

"We have to go," Mrs. Kurl urged.

"I'll find her," he said, then his footsteps pounded the stairs and they were gone.

I rushed to the window and watched them climb into the golf cart. He waved at me as they headed across the field.

I had no wish to leave yet and be stuck with the baby. I wanted friendship and a companion. Alone all my life, I'd never been more alone, but Jenson brightened my days as he would glimpse at me from the field, our eyes and bodies making conversation. His firm jaw and the straight line of his nose showed confidence and strength.

When the O'Conners left he stole to my room and we chatted. He was the light that pressed me forward. Excitement effervesced and my heart raced with his every smile, eye lock, and movement. My emotions swept off their feet and overcome with desire. As the time neared for the monster's birth they left me alone less and kept me in their presence for too many excruciating hours every day.

When my birth pains came three weeks early, they dressed me and stuck the painful blue contacts in my eyes. Mr. O'Conner escorted me to the hospital. Several hours of pain that I bore, my solace was being free of the little beast and knowing what they'd face as he grew.

With a final push, a wail cut through the air and the doctor pulled a bloody, screaming blob out of me. They cleaned *it* up and *it* stopped crying then the nurse tried to lay *it* on my chest. I pushed *it* away. "I'm tired. I need rest."

It was in that moment I realized why and how my mother could hate me so. I carried that sentiment for the tiny wailing blob. I was raped and forced to carry the tiny beast who refused to let go even after I tried to abort it. I considered the ball of fleshy blood that hit the toilet during my spotting. *Did the beast have a twin? Did I make it vanish?*

If so, I hadn't been haunted by it. Maybe it was a certain age when a fetus gained a soul and it hadn't yet reached that point. The doctor said nothing of a vanishing twin in the placenta but if I aborted something it happened in the first trimester. I'd never know the answer.

The nurse's eyebrows rose and she wrinkled her nose as she handed the tiny beast to Mr. O'Conner who held *it* as though *it* was a priceless artifact. I closed my eyes and slept, too tired to think about escaping.

Mr. O'Conner refused to leave my room and even left the bathroom door open when he drained his pruney penis. They tried to get me to breastfeed the monster and put *it* close to my boob. My skin crawled with the touch of *its* flesh and my butterfly wilted *its* fragile wings. I'd turn over and say I was tired.

"You will let this baby suckle. Do you hear me?" Mr. O'Conner buzzed in my ear, stinging like a wasp.

"You will not bring that little monster near me, not if you want *it* to live," I seethed, narrowing my eyes. "Now let me rest. My job for you is done."

Shoulders squared and face deeply webbed he huffed and set the little bastard in the tiny plastic bassinet, then the nurse wheeled *it* to the nursery.

I lay in the bed, facing away from my captor. Familiar blue eyes winked at me from the hallway. Jenson. He placed his hands beneath his cheek and tilted his head making a sleeping gesture then pointed to Mr. O'Conner.

I glanced at the sleeping old man and crept out of bed. He took my hand and heat exploded through my arm and down to my toes. We scurried down the hallway to a darkened corner. "Listen, I got hold of your friend. The lawyer -- Penelope."

I studied the horizontal and vertical lines of his face, and ran my fingers over his smooth-shaven cheek, his mouth, and chin. This was the first time we'd touched, met face to face, and he was beautiful. The connection between us charged and thrilling. If karma existed, and I believed it did, then he was the reason I was taken prisoner at Poppy Hills.

His gaze met mine. I brought my mouth to his chin and kissed it and he folded me in his arms, his lips pressed against the top of my head. "You're the most beautiful woman I've ever met."

I pulled away and met his gaze again. His soft lips found mine and excitement shot through me. He pulled away. "I'm sorry."

Grabbing his shirt, I pulled him back, "Don't be," and pressed my lips against his. He welcomed my tongue and for that moment I let myself slip away and considered leaving the hospital and running away with him.

"She's... bargaining a... deal with... Mr. O'Conner's... lawyer," he said between breathless kisses.

"What?" I lowered my eyebrows and pulled my lips away.

Our noses touching, his breath mingling with mine, he said, "You'll walk out of that house and be free of them forever."

Freedom. For the past nine months I'd been a prisoner. I wrapped my arms around his neck. "Thank you."

Wrapped in his arms, I permitted the magic of the moment to sweep me away. It was like nothing else I'd felt ever in my life. I breathed in the fresh scent of the aftershave and raked my fingers through the back of his short blond hair, almost as platinum as mine.

"Since I first saw you, my heart gravitated to you like the tug of the moon on Earth. I can't imagine what life without you would be like." He nuzzled against my face, his words mimicking my own thoughts.

"Have you seen my wife?" The words stung deep in my heart and I needed to head back and continue the charade. My life hinged on Jenson's words. In my heart of hearts I knew he wouldn't let me down. I'd never trusted another soul as much as him.

I stepped out of the shadows. "I'm here. Taking a stroll."

Mr. O'Conner stood at the nurse's station. When he heard my voice he turned, wearing a warning on his face, networked with deep lines. I strolled up to him. "I didn't mean to worry you." I looped my arm through his, cringing from the prickles of his cold flesh. "Can we go see the baby?"

He played along and I choked back my gag reflex as his prune-ish skin brushed against mine. We stopped at the nursery. *It* was tiny and appeared innocent, but *it* wasn't. A great evil lived and breathed inside *it* and I didn't know anything of the baby's spirit before Timmy possessed it.

The beast turned *its* tiny head and stared straight into my eyes. A shadow passed over the blue irises, turning them black. A shudder ran up my spine and the hairs on my arm prickled. In that moment, I knew Timmy was in control.

Part 3
The Chimera's Bite

Chapter 27
Marine Corps

June 26, 1973 18 years old

The morning of June 26, they released me from the hospital and I endured the ride back to Poppy Hills with Mr. O'Conner. Mr. Kurl flashed a glance at me through the rearview; a knowing glance that carried an entire conversation. It wouldn't be long now until I was free.

We entered the house and Philmonia came running, swooning over the evil little creature who was the devil himself. "He's perfect!" She carefully placed him in her arms, her eyes sweeping over him. "We made him." She brushed his cheek and he began to wail.

She brought him to her chest. "Shhh... mommy has you." His wailing didn't stop but grew louder as though he sensed how corrupt she was.

"He's probably hungry," Mr. O'Conner said, giving me the evil eye. "Your sister refuses to breast feed him."

I folded my arms over my chest. It wasn't my job. I gave the beast life and now I was through. Philmonia eyed me maliciously as though I was the revolting one. The one who raped my own sister with a machine, ejaculating my husband's sperm into her body. No, that was her, and my job was complete.

"You fake little whore!" she smarted while bouncing *it* within her arms.

I scowled at her, The Purple Mask's eyes searching her soul. It was dark as a starless night.

Mr. O'Conner's steps vibrated against the floor as he clomped out of the room, returning with a device.

"You will pump your milk into this." He shoved it at me. "If you refuse, we're done with you and will dispose of you."

That was definitely a threat but I didn't care and I'd use the device so long as *it* didn't have to touch my breast. "Fine," I seethed, "but you will give me privacy." I grabbed it then glowered at them.

They met my glare with shocked expressions. They hadn't broken me; my backbone and will were too strong. All the death and sadness in my life raged forward, filling me up, giving me the strength I needed. "I'm not returning to my room and you're not pumping me with any more drugs because they'll end up in the breastmilk."

My sister handed Mr. O'Conner the crying creature, *it's* screams slowed to a whimper, and stepped towards me, her face inches from mine. "Who do you think you are?"

"I'm *its* mother and unless you're storing milk in your tits I suggest you do what I ask." My words distinct and to the point.

Her eyebrows raised and nose twisted as she backed away from me. Mr. O'Conner whispered something in her ear and they left me alone. I followed them with my eyes as they walked up the stairs. Once they disappeared, I plugged the breast pump in and attached the monstrosity to my breast and pressed a button. It pulled on my boob, sucking and making kerchunking noises.

Drops of a thick cream dropped into a glass bottle. When I drained the first boob I attached it to the second. The butterfly on my breast gently moving with the suckling action. My mind drifted to Raury and the day I got it. The roof top and his sweet ways, until my ghost brother took his life.

The phone rang drawing, me out of my memories. Mr. O'Conner clumped down the stairs, glimpsing me on his way to the kitchen. "Hello... What?... That's not possible," a few expletives and, "Fine!"

He stormed into the room. "Whatever you think of us, Evan is innocent." He grabbed the device and bottle filled with the thick cream. "Gather your stuff, you are leaving!"

Isn't that sweet. They named the baby after his daddy. Evan O'Conner Jr. or was it the second? I didn't really care. "Where's my backpack?"

"Your what?" His brows shot upward.

"The backpack I came with. Where is it?"

Through clenched teeth he said, "We threw it away."

"Then I have nothing." I stood and marched to the front door, twisted the knob but it was locked with no visible bolts to unlock.

"You thought you'd just waltz out the door?" His sardonic chuckle chilled me to the bone.

I wasn't going to show any weakness. No, I was in control, not him, or at least I had to make him believe that. "Better get that milk to Evannn while it's warm."

Icy daggers shot from his eyes then he turned on his heel, carrying the milk to the beast. *Its* wails slowed and eventually stopped. I waited on the plush sectional, watching. The hallway of the second floor fully exposed. Mr. O'Conner left the creature's room and disappeared into another then reappeared many moments later with a small duffle bag. He lugged it down the stairs, my sister on his heels.

I took a defensive stance, squaring my shoulders and planting my feet at shoulder width. It couldn't be this easy and I didn't know what was in the bag.

Philmonia slithered to me and lifted her hand to touch my face. I slapped it away. "Some sister you turned out to be. You're your father's child through and through." My words sent daggers into her, drawing on her weakness, bringing back the days when *Daddy* snuck into her room at night.

Those words hit her hard and her face lit up. "You're the rape child. The reason my mother killed herself!"

Now the truth was out. The motivation for her deplorable actions. "No, your father, my mother's rapist, is the reason she killed herself. She was weak!"

She slapped my cheek. The stinging ignited the rage trapped inside me and I caught her arm and twisted. Bones cracked and she screamed. Mr. O'Conner flew to his wife's side but I pulled her in front of me, her twisted arm behind her back. "Doesn't feel so good, does it?! What's in the fucking bag?"

He unzipped it, dropped it to the floor and slid it to me. "It seems someone is watching out for you. Take it and leave my house." It was filled with money.

I forced my knee into her and pushed. She stumbled forward and fell onto her hands and knees. The lock on the door clinked so I grabbed it, twisted the knob then turned on my heel and called, "Timmy, you will do well here. Take this gift and your second chance and flourish. Become the man you were meant to be."

They wore twin dumbfounded expressions, clueless to the meaning in my words. With the heavy duffle bag in hand I sprint-walked towards the gate which opened when I reached it and closed after me. Once through it I inhaled the fresh air and scent of freedom.

My head held high, I marched down the road. A voice from the trees beckoned me, "Scarlett."

Leaning against the fence, covered by the shade of a tree, was Jenson. His jeans loose around his legs, arms resting against his chest.

"Jenson." On instinct I ran towards him, dropped the bag and pounced him. Clinging to his neck, he wrapped his arms around me. I smothered his face in kisses and dove my tongue into his mouth.

"We need... to... leave," he said in between ragged, passionate breaths. He set me down.

"Where?" I searched his eyes.

"Boulder. I'm taking you to Penelope." *Why couldn't I stay with him? We could go anywhere together.* As if he read my mind he followed with, "I enlisted, next week I'll be North Carolina at Camp Lejeune training to be a Marine."

My heart dropped and I swallowed hard. "You're going to war?"

"My country needs me and if traveling to Vietnam is what I have to do then I'm doing it." His words, solemn and proud, hung like a dark cloud in my heart.

This noble, wonderful man plummeted into my life and now he was leaving it. "Will I see you again?"

He cupped my face in his hands. "You will definitely see me again."

He picked up my bag and we strolled down the road. With him beside me, nothing could touch me. The patter of footsteps on the road behind us forced me to turn and glance, my pulse quickening as I squeezed Jenson's hand. Behind us were several young women, translucent glows surrounding their bodies.

Why hadn't I ever seen them before? *Was I too trapped in my hate and defiance?* I stopped and faced them, "You need to move on. I know what they did to you and me but I've taken care of it. I've avenged us all. Inside that house is an evil worse than the O'Conners. A killer who will show no mercy."

One stepped up to me, her hazel eyes smiling as bright as her lips. "Thank you." The group of women, all blonde with green, hazel, or blue eyes wrapped me in a tight hug. Bit by bit their spirits vanished, leaving twinkling stardust until even it was gone. The words, "use his weapons against him," clung to the air and rebounded in my head.

That was the first communication I'd made with ghosts besides Timmy in many years and I realized they didn't all stick around waiting for family as I'd once thought but to complete unfinished business. They watched as I suffered the same pain as them, waiting, hoping, maybe even they knew I'd be the one to free their spirits. That's why I hadn't seen them until now.

I turned back to Jenson who eyed me with confusion. "There's a few things I should tell you about me."

We neared a small truck. "You can tell me on the drive. We have about eight hours, give or take."

And so I did. He was the other half to my soul. I told Jenson all about the ghosts, my family, my past. He, on the other hand, lived a relatively normal life. Mr. and Mrs. Kurl were as nice as they seemed and they protected him from Mr. O'Conner's ways until he was old enough to figure it out for himself, but I imagined there were plenty of indiscretions they knew that he never would.

His eyes filled with sorrow. "I don't understand but I won't let anyone harm you ever again. I promise that."

I knew it was an impossible promise but the words lingered inside me and I knew he meant it. "I believe you." I slid across the bench seat and pressed myself against him. His strength and honesty melting into me.

We'd traveled through the mountains, trees and barren nothingness slipping past us as the sky took on pink and purple hues. For the first time in my life I was escaping New Mexico.

"You've spent years avoiding spirits but after what I witnessed today, your words, maybe they come to you because they want to move on but are stuck."

I'd never thought of that, not really. I was strange enough, a girl who death followed both in the physical and spiritual realm. Acknowledging their presence only heightened my awareness that I was a freak. His words, he meant them, and without judgement. "You're saying my freak ability is a gift?"

"Yeah. Sometimes I think we all sense ghosts on some level, like smelling your grandmother's perfume after she's gone, but most people aren't open and perceptive enough to interact with them. You have vision into another dimension or realm of sorts and I think you're meant to use it." The ramifications of his words held limitless possibilities.

Chapter 28
Miss Lenure

*W*e stopped for dinner at a truck stop. The pink and purple hues obscured by falling darkness. The green paint of the building faded from the sun and neon lights blinking half the lettering. The yellow booth seats white around the edges and cracking from the harsh rays that beat on them day after day. "Are you planning on driving all night?" I asked.

He swallowed his bite of steak. "No. There's a motel just down the road. I think we'll call it a day and finish our trip tomorrow."

That night I wrapped myself in the comfort of the bed and his arms. He caressed my hair and dropped gentle kisses on my neck, shivers of pleasure coursed through me. I wasn't yet ready for sex but was ready to allow this man into my life. In his arms, curled tight against him, I slept that night better than I had in a very long time.

The next day a nagging sensation tugged at my gut. The further from Albuquerque we drove the more it poked at me. I ignored it and we made it to Penelope's by lunch. She'd stuck a key in a planter beside the door. Her place was simple and inviting, decorated in warm, earthy tones and modern sleek furniture. Hungry, I raided her refrigerator and cooked us lunch.

Rubbing his full belly he leaned back in his chair. "I've never had the occasion to say this before but your cooking is as good as Mom's."

I dumped the dishes in the sink and took a seat on his lap, pulling both my legs over his. "Is it?"

"I think I'm going to pop."

I giggled at his response. "Oink, oink," I teased.

He grabbed me up, one arm under my legs and the other supporting my back and dumped me on the couch. His fingers tickled my sides and I

341

thrashed against him, grabbed his shirt and pulled him on top of me.

"Scarlett?"

We both shot upward. Penelope stood in the doorway, a wide smile on her face, framed by her flaming red hair.

"Penelope, this is--"

"Jenson," she finished my words and padded towards us, dropping her purse on the kitchen table.

He righted himself and put out his hand to shake hers. "Yes Ma'am. Pleasure to meet you," he said. I expected a salute but that didn't happen.

I drew her into a long hug and she squeezed me tight.

"I think you have a lot to tell me," she said.

I swallowed. "I do, but first how did you get me out of there?"

She wrapped an arm around my shoulder and clucked her tongue. "Let's just say Mr. O'Conner didn't get rich because of his honesty and work ethic."

The Crimson Flame she was, fiery and bold. "Your turn."

I told her the story, starting with Kevin giving me the information and ending with the expression on the O'Conners' faces when I exited Poppy Hills.

"Kevin did the detective work and dug up the trash on Mr. O'Conner. He was promoted from paralegal to investigator." Kevin; now a married man. I missed his wedding.

"How was his wedding?" I asked, taking the conversation a full one eighty degrees.

"It was nice, his wife is very sweet. You'd like her." She unbuttoned her white and black suit jacket, exposing the ruffled collar of her blouse. Her tight, knee-length skirt exposed her long, stockinged legs.

We dropped Jenson at the train station that night. He left me his truck as a promise of his return. I lost myself in his embrace, framing the moment in my mind. Allowing the warmth of his touch and the pound of his heart to imprint on my soul.

Living with Penelope brought back old times when we were kids, even though she worked ten to twelve hours a day which gave me a lot of free time. I found another mystic store in Boulder and bought protective stones to send to Jenson. Juggling them in my hand, the weird sensation that had been with me since leaving Albuquerque disappeared.

I reached for more stones. No doubt it was related to my extra sensitivity and ghosts. I remembered Jenson's words and his suggestion to assist spirits. If I warded off all spirits I wouldn't be able to help those I chose so I brought my hand back. A rack caught my eye and I decided on a pendant made with peridot, black onyx, and bloodstone to protect me from only the evil spirits.

While there, I thought to get another copy of the book. I examined the spines of every book and to my dismay it wasn't there. I approached the cashier dusting the shelves. "I'm

looking for a particular book and don't
see it."

Her heart shaped lips smiled.
"What book are you looking for?"

I told her and she responded, "I
don't recognize the name. Do you
remember the author or the
publisher?" She strolled to the counter
and from a shelf beneath it pulled out a
large book.

"Mildred Lenure."

She tapped her fingers. "I've heard
that name." She licked her finger and
flipped through the pages, finally
resting on one. "Yes! She lives local
and speaks at conventions and such. I
can order the book."

"She's local?" It was more than
coincidence that brought me to this
store at this moment.

She nodded. "There's an address
here but it's a P.O. Box." She scribbled
it down and handed it to me.

"Does she have any other titles?"

"Just that one," she said.

"I'd like to order it, please."

345

She bit her lip as she wrote up the slip then shifted her eyes from the paper to me. "I really love your eyes."

My eyes, the distinguishing marks upon my face that set me apart, made me different than the rest of the world. "Thank you."

"I'll get the order in this afternoon and it'll be about two weeks. Do you have a number I can contact you when it arrives?"

I gave her Penelope's number and took the address. It was in Denver. When I got home I searched the house for a map, finding one I located the street. It was on the outskirts of Denver, about a forty minute drive, but most likely a post office or postal depot run out of a gas station or something.

I wrote the letter, explaining how I'd found her book, and told her a bit about my vanishing twin. The next day I took it and the protective stones I bought for Jenson to the post office and mailed them with a letter that said *'Keep these with you, always. They'll protect you and bring you home'.*

For the next few weeks, each day when the mail carrier arrived I bolted out the door waiting impatiently for correspondence.

I received Jenson's letter first, thanking me for the stones. He promised to keep them with him at all times. The rest of his words devastated my heart. They were sending him to Vietnam. I knew in my heart of hearts it would happen but seeing it in print finalized the deal. I wasted no time in writing him back, sending him my love and strength. It was a couple more weeks before I got a letter from Miss Lenure.

Clutching it in my hands I slid a butter knife under the flap and pulled out the letter.

Miss Jones,

Thank you for writing and sharing your experience. There is so little known about vanishing twins and how the living twin is affected by the one who passed. I have spent years researching and still have no further information than I did when I published that book. I would be pleased if you'd be my guest for dinner, six p.m. this Saturday, at Palaggo's.

Sincerely,

Mildred Lenure

That Saturday I drove to Denver, excitement burst inside me. Her book, which came just in time, lay on the seat beside me. If I was going to meet her she was going to sign it. When I arrived, the hostess guided me to a corner table away from the bustle of the other patrons, lit by a large candle in the middle.

An older lady sat at the table, her hair salt and pepper. Small lines crinkling around her eyes deepened with her smile. "Miss Jones, it's such a pleasure to meet you," she said as I took a seat across from her.

"The pleasure is mine," I answered, placing the book on the table. "I'd be delighted if you'd sign my book."

"Of course, in time. Let's talk. I believe it was fate that brought us together and I'd like to know more about your experience." A welcoming atmosphere enveloped me in her presence.

I relayed my story, except the most gruesome details.

"You welcomed him into the child so his spirit is trapped in a physical body?"

I hadn't quite thought of it that way. "Yes. I shouldn't have done that?"

"On the contrary. I'm not sure; most people don't welcome evil spirits. In this form he has power in the physical world which is stronger than that of the spirit world in many ways. He can also be killed and sentenced for crimes whereas the spirit world doesn't hold those boundaries." The candle wax melted, running down the side. A small puddle forming in the wide brass base of the holder. "I also have to wonder if his spirit is in control or the child's own spirit."

Were two spirits living inside the child, fighting for supremacy? The two-headed dragon surfaced in the folds of my brain. "But what will happen to his spirit now should he die?"

"That question can't really be answered now can it?"

"No, I guess not," I said thoughtfully.

"There are few experiences people have with their vanishing twin. Most people aren't as sensitive as you. They may be haunted once or twice in their lifetime but you formed a relationship with yours. Do you see other spirits?" She swirled a glass of blush wine.

"Yes, many. I've avoided interacting with them, most of them. I wore a bracelet made with black stones and burned various herbs after reading your book to keep the spirits away from me."

"Where is the bracelet now?"

"I don't wear it anymore. A friend suggested I use my *talent* to help them but I'm not sure yet if I want to do that." Hesitation lingered in my voice. I pulled the pendant that lay against my chest out of my shirt. "I wear this now."

After sipping her wine, she placed the glass onto the table. "Why is that?"

I leaned in as if it was a secret. "Not all of them are good and I want the protection from the evil ones." The candlelight reflected off her eyes. Blue and green; different colored eyes like mine.

She smiled, noting my shocked expression. "Yes, I had a twin too. That's what sparked my attraction and interest in the area of vanishing twins. You see, when they die we are still here, their flesh becomes our flesh, their spirit meshes with ours. You have gone further than I. Your insight and extrasensory perception is a blessing."

I stumbled over my words. "You had a twin. Were you ever haunted?"

"There have been many unexplained events in my life, a misplaced brush, a missing pen, small things, but each one, petty as they were, saved me from harm. When I was much younger, a child, a ferocious storm hit us, lightning, thunder, and wind whistling through the trees. I had placed my favorite baby doll in a chair by the window. When the storm hit its peak I returned to get her. A bolt of lightning hit the chair, illuminating it, and she was gone. I turned to leave the room and something crashed through the window. A large branch had fallen through it and my doll appeared on the floor beside me." Her twin saved her from harm but not in the way mine did. No; Timmy caused harm to others.

"Have you ever seen him or her?"

She smiled. "Once. I was visiting my grandparents for the weekend and, as an only child, I was bored and lonely. We played in the field behind the house. Her name was Ingrid. Of course it wasn't until many years later when my parents told me I had a twin that died in the womb. My mother suffered many problems during pregnancy and delivery, that's why I never had another sibling."

That brought me back to the unwanted pregnancy, still fresh as only a couple months had passed since the birth of the beast. "I told you how I tried to abort him but it didn't work. I spotted, a large glop of blood came out of me. It was small and fleshy but I've never been haunted by it. Do you think maybe I..." My words hung in the air.

She finished my sentence, "Aborted a twin? It's possible or it might have been a blood clot."

No doubt her words were meant to soothe me but they didn't. "Do you have any children?"

She raised a brow. "Heavens, no. I've spent so many years searching for others like me that I didn't have time for love and marriage."

Our food arrived. When the waitress left I asked, "Nobody?"

She sighed. "You are a curious young lady. There was one. A young man I was deeply in love with, head over heels for him. We were going to get married but I lost him -- WWII. I knew the moment it happened. My knees grew weak, my heart stopped for a split second, and I saw his face. After that I didn't have the desire to replace him."

She was sensitive like me, not as much so but she had a foot in the spirit

353

realm and I thought of Selma and Sara's house. Timmy was adamant about not going into the crypt. Was there something there that wanted to deny him access? "Is it possible to seal a room in a house and the house itself?"

She dunked her spoon into her gravy-soaked mashed potatoes. "Oh yes. One can either keep spirits in or out with the right spells, but it can be dangerous. One must be sure they know what they're doing. If done right the seal will hold until the person who placed it repeals it or passes to the other side."

I didn't ask any more questions as we ate. My brain teemed with thoughts. They moved too fast for me to catch any but I knew eventually they'd settle and I'd have answers and more questions.

After the waitress took our dishes she dabbed at her mouth and placed the book on the table next to her where she signed it. She dropped the pen and met my gaze. "I have a business proposition for you. Would you be interested in assisting me with a second book, all about vanishing twins?"

Flabbergasted with honor by her offer, I answered, "You want my help?"

"Yes." Her eyes widened. "Your insight could help many others like us. I'll pay you and you can stay with me. I have a house far too large for just me, or I'll put you up in a hotel." She tented her hands and laid them on the table. Her gaze never left mine.

"Yes," I answered without another thought.

"Wonderful, I'll have a contract written up and delivered to you. Once you have signed it we'll get to work." The peace and comfort that warmed me in her presence was the love and kindness in her heart. It was a risk, since my last ordeal with my sister and captivity, but I was stronger now, smarter, and the calm I sensed with her told me no harm would become of this, only good.

It was destiny or karma. All the horrors in my life brought me to this place and taught me trust in my family was a sliding scale from heartbreak to malevolence, sliding mostly to the malevolent side. They were the bringers of violent acts in the name of their own selfishness. But now I could right some of those wrongs. I never expected my extra sense to pan out to more than heartbreak.

Chapter 29
My Calling

A few weeks later, contract signed with Mildred Lenure, Penelope took me out for a pizza and a movie. We both laughed at the irony when we saw the life-sized poster for *The Exorcist*. We chose *American Grafitti*.

"That reminded me of the time I went cruising with you and the twins," I offered as we walked out of the movie theatre, giggling at how I was just a little kid.

Penelope sighed. "That's right, when they bought their car. We were smoking pot and you just hung like you were one of us. You were, just a lot younger. Oh, I miss the twins." She stared off into nothingness for a few seconds. "Those were good times." She paused. "We explored the house when Sara wasn't home this one time."

She unlocked the car door and got in, leaned across the passenger seat and unlocked my door. "We wanted to explore what we were told not to. Typical teens," she chuckled. "Anyways, we went to the second floor and found the door but we didn't have a stinkin' key to unlock it so we went to the third floor. Boy was it creepy; like ghost creepy," she cringed. "I didn't mean like that. It spooked us all so much we never snooped again."

My thoughts lingered on her words and Miss Lenure's, giving me the answer. "The third floor isn't right and neither are those locks that automatically click every midnight. They still do, or at least they did the last time I was there."

"That wasn't right, those locks. I figured Sara did it to maintain some control and keep us out of trouble, but we never found a timer or any device that controlled them."

Miss Lenure's words repeated in my mind. "That's because it was done with magic. Spells can keep things in or out. I think the third floor was protected by magic to keep ghosts and people out, all except Shari or Sharon, Sara's daughter." I heaved my chest to continue my story but Penelope stopped me.

"Sara's daughter?"

I guessed it was time to tell her and I was pretty sure I understood the enchanted workings of Sara's house. "Yeah, I used to play with her ghost before I knew the difference. They have translucent edges and living people don't. That entire floor was a red alert for 'go away'. No ghosts, but an intense desire to flee the room. I went there with my friend Raury. We both felt it. To him it was just spooky. For me it was more. A warning, but not a spirit. It was different than that. I think it was magic, a spell that someone put on the room to preserve and protect it."

Penelope's eyes lit up. "And the bolts that locked us in every night; that was part of the spell?"

I grimaced. "I think so. The bolts weren't to keep us in but to keep other spirits out, so magic was used to seal them and the windows. Remember how they wouldn't open? They were sealed with a spell that didn't extend to the turret, only the main house." I paused for a second, rethinking it. Shari was always in the turret. "Maybe it was a combination of spells, like levels. The only ghosts I ever saw were Shari, because she was trapped there and attached to her mother, Timmy who was attached to me, and Salem the cat. There are plenty of spirits roaming the earth but they avoid that house." Everything clicked as it rolled out my mouth.

"Do you think Sara was a witch?" she asked.

I shook my head. It wasn't her, but someone close to her. "No, Selma's the witch." I wasn't positive about that, but sure enough to suggest it. "She worked there for years. They were friends and she helped her, trapped her daughter so Sara could stay close to her until the time of her death and they'd pass into the afterlife together." It sounded crazy but made perfect sense. Selma knew herbs and was the first to put the notion in my head that I was sensitive to the otherworldly and the house and room remained sealed after Sara's death. They'd remain so until Selma passed, according to Mildred Lenure, anyways.

Penelope pulled her car into the driveway. I pushed my door open, the air chilled my arms and caused them to erupt in goose pimples. The street lights and stars faded. Two blue orbs at a near perfect width from each other moved closer. My mind was no longer in the living realm. The orbs drew closer until I recognized them as eyes. The familiar eyes of my captor, Mr. O'Conner.

I reached to my chest, searching for my pendant, but it was gone. Then I regretfully remembered I took it off before my shower. It was lying on the counter by the bathroom sink. "What do you want?"

His blazing blue eyes stared at me, unmoving and unblinking. A shadowy bulk formed around them and his body took on shape. His arm a willowy tendril shifted over his eyes and I was transported to his bedroom. He and my sister were in a cockeyed erotic position. His hands handcuffed to the bedposts and her hands covered in leather gloves she wrapped around his neck. Her torso undulating above him. It was like watching bad porn with no sound, but I didn't need volume control to know what she was saying. I'd heard it for over nine months in the torture chamber they locked me in.

Mr. O'Conner's body shook beneath her, smack in the middle of her climax. It was priceless and I felt my body shake in laughter as I closed my eyes and grasped my stomach.

"Scarlett, Scarlett," a voice from far away called and came into focus.

Tears running from the corners of my eyes, Penelope came into focus, eyeing me strangely. One brow lifted higher than the other and her voice faltering she asked, "Are you OK?"

I noted I was still halfway in the car. "Um... Yeah."

"You completely zoned out like your mind went somewhere else. It really scared me."

I grimaced as I finished pulling myself out of the car and took her hands. "I was somewhere else. Mr. O'Conner is dead. He showed me." It was in that moment I recognized the pattern; evil spirits attached to me, in death they showed me their final moments on Earth. *Did they pass on?*

We walked to the door arm in arm. She paused. "Do you think your sister will look for you?"

Philmonia; she killed her husband with sex. It was too ironic and quirky for words. "I don't care and I don't think she's smart enough to find me. Tomorrow I'll be in Denver."

She pushed on the door and it whooshed open.

I arrived at Miss Lenure's by noon. I'd thought twice about this arrangement since my captivity with my sister but the sensation of calm and peace around Miss Lenure made me feel comforted. Her intentions direct, with no hidden agenda. At least, not something intended to harm me. She lived in the boonies with breathtaking views. Her modern chateau garnered two levels, appearing as steps for a giant. The angles and sleek edges were complimented by the four peaks of the roof.

The afternoon sun was beginning to fade, and the room grew a shade darker as she toured me through the main areas of the house. The house was so large and extravagant it was difficult to imagine why someone would live here alone. My room was on the second floor. It was a suite with my own balcony, bathroom, and sitting room. There were no locked doors or rules. I reminded myself I was an adult now and the only rules I had were self-imposed, but in someone else's home I expected something but there was nothing. She also lived a few miles from the closest house and further from the closest gas station.

It was my first night as I settled into bed, soaking in the night. The moon's light and stars above, so bright. My door creaked open, assuming it was Mildred I tilted my head, realizing then it wasn't her. The form was similar to hers but with edges bathed in lunar brilliance. A smile passed over her lips. "You can see me."

I nodded, obvious to me she was Mildred's twin. Her gentle face and mellow glide as she neared my bed brought tranquility on my soul, nothing like that of my own twin.

"It's been so many years since I had someone to talk with, not since we were small children." She floated on the air at the foot of my bed.

It was my chance maybe to ask questions but I didn't want to be too hasty. "Hello, Ingrid. Mildred told me about the time when you played at your grandparents'."

Her smile curved higher up her cheeks. "When we were little, yes."

"Do you like to read?" I asked, grabbing the book that I'd placed on my nightstand.

She sat on the edge of the bed, her body pushing into the mattress as if she was solid. "Can you read to me?"

I opened the book and began reading. Every night we did this and talked. I built her trust that way but wasn't sure it was even necessary as she'd come to me searching for a friend, a companion. After a few weeks she'd appear during the day as Mildred and I worked on the book. She listened intently, talking to me as Mildred jotted down my notes, my insights.

Over the next few months we fleshed out a framework and a few chapters for her next book. The idea of being part of that made the suffering and oddness of what was "normal" in my life purposeful. It was a frosty day in February, the snow outside piled high and still falling. Flames licked the iron gate around the fire place as we neared the end of our work for the day.

Over the days and months, Ingrid gave me insight into life from the vanishing twin perspective and I began to understand Dr. Kern's words, his perspective. Nature made us twins and took one away but that alone didn't make us evil. Our paths were cut from our experiences. Mildred and Ingrid were loved, grew up in a wonderful home. Even though Ingrid was lonely she didn't hold hate in her heart because of nurture.

Ingrid was never truly alone; she and Mildred were attached in a way that would never change. Relaxing on my balcony we conversed. "Would you ever consider possessing someone, so you had the chance to live and communicate with Mildred?"

Her eyes widened in horror. "No! Never." She bowed her head. "I listen in on all your sessions. I understand what you did and your brother was an evil spirit but now he resides inside a child and he will never have full control. Their spirits are in conflict, but to your mind the child's spirit was never good."

"How do you know this?"

A cold wind blew against us, rustling the colorful leaves on the trees and I tucked the blanket under my legs, "How do you know this?" I repeated.

"I have visited the child. There is a darkness in him that rises to the surface when he's angry. His soul was never pure, but yours is. You don't give yourself enough credit." Her words clung to the chill in the air.

"Do you think he will one day remember me?"

Her words embraced my soul. "A part of him might. There may be remnants of memory left, tied to Timmy."

Mildred wrote several words in flowing cursive before she glanced up at me through the spectacles she wore during our sessions. Her eyes distant, something was on her mind, having nothing to do with the book. Behind her a white cloud formed and took shape. I shifted my eyes away, watching from the corner of my eye, knowing it was Ingrid. Her jade eyes peering at me from behind Mildred. She combed her hands through Mildred's hair, kissed the top of her head then stared directly at me. Mildred shook her head as if she felt the gentle caress but continued her work. She glanced up, her eyes poised on mine. "You see her, don't you?"

"I... yes. I do."

"She is here right now."

I nodded confirmation. "She's always with you." I remembered Timmy saying just that. He was always with me. "Do you feel her?"

Her lips curled into a smile. "I do. I only wish I could see her like you do."

After several uncomfortable seconds she didn't shift her gaze so I met it, stared back at her. Ingrid's lips curled into a smile as she parked herself on the armrest of the chair. Her arm draped over Mildred's shoulder, I smiled. The love she had for her was real even though she was dead and Mildred was alive. It wasn't a jealous love but a true love.

People always believed ghosts were attached to places, and maybe some were, but from my experience the majority were attached to nothing -- wanderers -- the rest were attached to people. Humans they loved before death. Ingrid's spirit rose, she kissed the top of Mildred's head and vanished. There was something more I was meant to do here, a deeper purpose.

That evening I strolled to the kitchen, met by a frenzied Ingrid. Her form swirling around me. "Quick, it's Mildred. Come!"

I followed her into Mildred's room where she lay on the floor. I dropped. "Mildred." Grasping her wrist, I felt for a pulse. Feeling a weakening thump, I rose and glanced around her room, my heart pumping hard inside me, blood rushing through my veins like a river. A phone was set on the nightstand. I wasted no time in dialing 911.

The operator walked me through steps to keep her heart pumping and stayed on the phone with me until the ambulance arrived and she was carted to the hospital. I followed in Jenson's truck. *What would have become of her if I wasn't there?* And Ingrid, who sat next to me in the car, cared so much she wrung her hands in anxiety. She didn't want her sister to pass on and join her.

"It's not her time. It's not her time," she repeated then grabbed my arm. "You think I'm wrong but she has unresolved issues. She can't go yet. She can't."

Her words seemed so far away, inside a tunnel, and I didn't get them then. It was later when we went back to the house, Mildred stable, that Ingrid showed me and it all came together.

In Mildred's room, on the top shelf of her closet, was a small leather box with a tarnished latch. I took it down at Ingrid's beckoning and opened the lock. It was filled with pictures of a young Mildred with a handsome young man. The one that got away, died far too young.

I opened a letter and read.

Dearest Mildred,

You are the sun that warms my world, my strength in hard times. I think of you every moment and I know it's you I want to return home to. I'm sorry for the pain I caused but I won't make it out of this war and this land alive without knowing you forgive me. Guilt worms its way into my heart. Please say one more time you love me.

Sam

I read letter after letter. "What is all this? I don't understand."

Ingrid curled on the floor next to me. "Mildred and Sam fell in love at first sight. Their hearts were drawn together but it couldn't be. Before he met her he got another young woman pregnant and he was pushed into marrying her but it didn't happen as he was sent to war before it could pass. Mildred was so broken-hearted she never returned his letters yet read every one of them. She wanted nothing more than for him to come home, but in her heart she knew the best thing was for him to return to the other woman and baby."

The story cracked my heart in two, its fragmented pieces shattering on the floor. I thought of Jenson and how much I loved him. Regardless, I'd want him to return to me. I sucked back my own fears and insecurities. "What happened?"

"He never returned but was killed shortly before the end of his tour." Her eyes dropped to the picture of them that lay on the floor in front of her.

Mildred's smile vibrant, love emanating from her eyes; and Sam, something about the shape of his face, the arch of his cheeks tickled a memory buried in my mind. For minutes I stared, unable to grasp it, dangling from the edge of my consciousness.

That night my dreams ruffled my memory as I was back in New Mexico in the mountains running through the wildflowers and between the trees with Raury. His dimpled smile reflected in his soft brown eyes that suddenly changed to blue. His face was replaced with Sam's, Mildred's beau, and the woods and flowers vanished replaced with dense trees and thick, wet air. I crawled on my belly, a large rifle in one hand.

"Hey, dummy!" seethed a voice I hadn't heard in many years. I glanced to see long, straight, dirty blond hair, oval face, and deep blue, almond-shaped eyes planted next to me.

My eyelids fluttered open with recognition. Dana's father's name was Sam Courier. I jumped out of bed and threw open Mildred's closet, grabbing the leather box and one of the letters: *Sam Courier.* He was Dana's father. I closed my eyes and thought back to the day I snuck into the office. With my mind, I reached into the file cabinet and pulled it out, opened it. Her mother had given her up at birth because her family made her. *Did she love him?*

I needed to find out more. Drifting my mind back to her birth certificate;

what was her mother's name? I let out a deep breath and rested my mind, focusing on the words. They slowly came into focus -- Sherry Pritz.

Ingrid appeared beside me. "What are you doing?"

"I thought I remembered something." Sam, I recollected the familiarity of his name at the time, but why? *How did I know him?* At that young age my life centered around my loving family and G-e-n. That was it. Her last name was Courier! She told me about him during our card games. Every so often she'd bring up his name. Gen was his mother. The world in all its vastness and complexity swirled into a central point. "I knew his mother!"

"How?" Ingrid played with the edge of her dress, pulling and squishing the fabric together.

Her nervous fidgeting gave it away. "You knew this already."

Her mouth curled into a half smile. "I did. I watched you at Palaggo's when you met Mildred and I knew you had to come stay with us. That you could settle my sister's troubled soul and reunite them."

"But he's dead and she doesn't have my sight. How?"

She heaved as if sucking in a deep breath. "I've always been with her and witness to her breaking heart. It tore mine apart. She's never dated since him. He was her one and only. Mildred is stable for now but doesn't have much longer. She needs to know everything and you have to find it for her."

Gen was dead, Sam was dead, Dana really had nothing to do with this. She was the unwanted baby, like me. But her mother. I'd find Sherry Pritz.

The next day I stopped by the hospital. Mildred was awake and alert but weak. Her heart was having difficulties. I cupped her hand in mine. "I'm making a short trip out of town for a couple days and when I return you better be strong enough to go home. We have to finish the book."

Her head and torso raised in the mechanical bed, she attempted to squeeze her fingers around mine but her strength was depleted. "I will be. You go on." Her words carried a ring of awareness as if she knew what I was up to.

Chapter 30
A Medium's Job is Never Done

I called Kevin, knowing he could find her. I arrived at his house, a simple square home in the suburbs, painted light green with a white door. A lady answered and invited me inside. The decor was simple and the aroma of fried chicken filled the house. She introduced herself and brought me a glass of lemonade when Kevin strolled into the room.

He immediately drew me into a hug and we sat. "I have good news and not so good. I'll start with the not so good. Sherry Pritz passed away several years ago due to a horrible accident. She was traveling on a train when it derailed. She was one of many casualties." He swallowed. "She does have a daughter and gave her up soon after birth. The child, Dana, also died a couple years ago when she was beaten and brutally murdered. She was living in Oregon and it was all over the papers there."

His words halted my breath. "They're both dead?" I hated Dana but got my vengeance. I never wished such a horrid death on her. "You said there was good news too?"

He nodded. "Yeah, the good news is Sherry's parents are still alive. They live in a rest home in New Mexico." Kevin placed a file on the couch between us, his eyes filled with warning. "Be careful."

I bit my lip, contemplating what I had to do next. I didn't even know why I had to do this. Sam was dead, case closed, but an urge nagged at me. "I will. Pinky promise." I held out my little finger and he wrapped his around it.

I continued driving through the night until my heavy lids forced me to stop at a small motel off the highway. The bed was lumpy but the room smelled clean and I slept peacefully until the morning sun streamed through the crack in the curtains. I walked to the diner next door and ate a small breakfast before finishing my drive.

In the truck, I pulled out the map and checked my route. Leaving it open I drove straight to the rest home. It was a large building with many stories. The trees bare now due to the unusually cold winter. Snuggled in my jacket I strode up the wide cement steps and into the building. An ambulance pulled in and went around the building.

I suppose that wasn't unusual for an old folks' home. The place smelled of honeysuckle and was painted in a cheerful baby blue. I stepped up to the front desk and was greeted by a lady with beautiful caramel skin and deep brown eyes. Her long, thick hair rolled into a bun. "Can I help you?" she asked in a heavy Spanish accent.

I smiled. "I'm here to see Mr. and Mrs. Pritz."

"Lucky for you visiting hours aren't over for the day and they're in the courtyard," she said with care as if she knew where each resident was at every moment.

She came around and brought me through a hallway lined with calming pictures of scenery, into a glass room filled with plants and a waterfall in the center. The sun on her skin made her almost transparent. Several couples and groups sat at the tables, some playing games, others talking quietly. We finally stopped at a table and she introduced me.

Their eyes widened and I took it they didn't get much company but, with a dead daughter, a granddaughter given up at birth and now dead, there was no one. Here I was chasing someone else's ghosts and it brought me to this couple. Her pale blue curly hair accented her blue eyes, lines webbed her face giving away her age and Mr. Pritz had only a few thin wisps of white framing his long face.

I sucked in a breath with no clue how to start this conversation. They looked at me expectantly while I stumbled over my words. "Hi."

Mr. Pritz raised a brow. "Did you know our Sherry?"

I let out a deep breath. "No. I uh... I knew Dana your... ummm..."

"Grandaughter," finished Mrs. Pritz, the wrinkles in her face were also webbed over her throat.

I nodded. "Yeah, we shared a room at the orphan home."

Through the glass I viewed two bodies laid on stretchers and wheeled toward the waiting ambulance.

His eyes glazed over and met hers. After that everything flowed as if they had to cleanse their souls before the harbinger of death stole them from the Earth. It turned out Sherry had what they called 'episodes' or wild mood swings, high in the heavens to rock bottom low. It was during one of those highs when she became pregnant. She swore the boy loved her, but they knew better. She'd seduced him with alcohol until he was docile.

He promised to do the right thing, but they knew Sherry was in no mental shape to take care of a baby and they'd all live a painful life. It was shortly after the baby was born that she became very depressed, no highs just lows, and she couldn't take care of herself much less an infant, so they placed her in a psychiatric hospital and gave the baby up. It wasn't only the shame and disgrace having a bastard grandchild but the father, Sam, died shortly before the adoption was final. He never knew.

Shadows dropped onto my soul. Dana liked to think she was born out of love, we all did, but instead her past was as deformed as my own. We sat so long the sun set on the horizon, a crimson shade shone through the glass falling over us and through them. Their spirits rose and dispersed in the beautiful sunset.

I left with a tug on my heart and tears in my eyes. I wasn't sent here for Mildred but to save the souls of this couple. The world so vast was small. I followed the well-worn path of my life and ended up at Sara's. I hadn't been there in many years. It was now grown over with weeds, hidden from the road.

I entered, knowing instantly something was different. It wasn't the thick covering of dust or the musky odor. The calm peace I always felt there was gone, replaced by something menacing.

I turned on my heel to leave when I heard Selma's voice calling me. Every time I'd been to the house she was never there. "Scarlett," she called again. The pendant against my chest vibrated and I knew I was amongst malevolent spirits. "Scarlett, up here," she called. I traipsed the stairs to the second floor, then sucked in a deep breath to the third floor. The uneasy feeling was gone and it was now collecting dust.

She was standing in front of the window gazing at the vast valley below us. The lights of the city twinkled, muting the glow of the stars. "Selma?"

"I always knew you had a second sight." Her face much younger without any lines and wrinkles. Her thick, dark hair fell over her back and shoulders. Her eyes didn't stray from the window.

"What are you doing here?" I knew
she was dead and the spell gone, letting
the evil spirits inside.

"It's very complicated."

"What? What's complicated? I
don't understand."

"Many years ago after Shari died,
Sara and I sealed this house and this
room," her voice wistful, her eyes still
gazing out the window.

I knew that already. "What
happened to Shari?"

"Sara married a man more beautiful
than a god and wealthy. He built her
this home. It was her design and when
she became pregnant they were happy.
When Shari was born she was their
everything, but he wanted a boy and
when she couldn't get pregnant again
he started drinking, becoming angry,
very angry. I was Shari's nanny and had
become very close to Sara during that
time." She shuddered with a sigh.

"What happened?"

"I was standing right here. Sara was
out at a luncheon when he came home,
stumbled in the house. Shari was in her

room downstairs when he thrust her door open. I heard the commotion and raced down the stairs but I was too late. She was lying slumped on the floor, her head limp to her side. I froze. When he saw me he rushed past me, pushing me against the wall, knocking the breath out of me. Once I caught my breath I crawled to Shari. Within a few minutes Sara came home. Her father was found a week later at the bottom of the mountain. His body bloodied and ravaged by animals. He wasn't buried in the family crypt but a potter's grave. Sara inherited everything."

I touched her translucent shoulder, something nagged at me. "Is that why you sealed the house?"

"Partially, but it was more. Like you, I have a sixth sense, but not sight. I hear them and everyday I'd hear Shari. I knew her confused spirit was still here, lingering in the house and we didn't want her father to return so we spelled her play room." She finally shifted her eyes away from the window and met my gaze. "She loved this room. Then we spelled the house and the grounds. We used powerful magic that could only be undone in death, our deaths. Now that I'm gone, his spirit has returned." She pointed to my pendant. "Take it off and go down stairs."

"You have to leave," I urged.

"I can't. Over the years he's grown very strong and refuses to let me leave. When I died, my soul came here. It wasn't my choice." The only reason I could think she'd return to the house was unfinished business.

I had to help her so I closed my eyes and slipped the pendant off, resting it on the window sill in front of her. I opened my eyes and was alone in the room. Swallowing, pushing my heart back into my chest, I grasped the handrail and took the steps in the darkness, each creaked in the eerie silence of the house. "Hello," I called in a quivering voice. My instincts said to leave, vacate now, but I couldn't. I had to do something and save her soul, and maybe his.

The still air answered me. I stepped onto the second floor, glancing around me for movement in the blackness of the room. Glass shattering on the first floor broke the silence and I jumped. *Don't be scared, don't be scared,* I repeated in my head as I coasted down the stairs. I wanted to run and never return but I couldn't leave Selma there with him.

Keeping my chest high and back straight, I strode through the room. The worst thing would be for him to feel my fear. When I reached the steps I felt her chair on one side and the handrail on the other. Clutching the rail, I stepped on the first stair then the next until reaching the bottom floor. A heavy wind blew my hair, almost knocking me over.

I continued and moved through the living room and the long hallway as if I was going to my room. *Think of the peace you always felt here, push him away, out of the house.* I reached the twins' room, my hand against the door frame. It slammed, grazing my fingertips. I jerked them away. A light shone beneath the door of Penelope's room. When I pushed it open a tall man with broad shoulders and short, dark hair held Shari by her face in his hands. She wheezed and struggled against him but her strength was no match for his.

I acted on instinct and rushed toward him, landing on his back, but I slid through and dropped hard on the floor. He was showing me a vision as if his own guilt and shame had built up over the many years. "Let me help you."

The door slammed shut and the light dimmed. Shari clutched her throat sprawled on the floor by the dresser; broken pieces of lamp lay next to her. I scooted towards her. Shouts from next door, from my room, halted me mid motion. I scurried to my feet. Shari was already dead, there was nothing I could do.

Throwing the door open, I watched as Selma and the man fought. "This needs to stop!" he shouted, pushing her against the wall.

"Tell her!" Her piercing voice ricocheted off the walls as she struggled to push his hand away. When it remained firm against her chest she kicked him, her two inch heel poking into his leg. When she brought it out, blood trickled onto his shoe, dribbling to the floor, and he let her go. She scrambled from the room.

He chased after her, Shari lay in her room gasping, reaching toward the top of the dresser. Perfume, a hairbrush, and various odds and ends covered the wooden top. She continued to grasp for something. I moved closer and scanned the dresser's surface again; a metal object with a pump lay on the edge. Her fingers drifted upward, scaling the drawers, then dropped. She had an asthma attack.

I ran through the dark house. I knew the house so well light wasn't needed. Through the glass room, following the cactus jungle. The man fell over the edge of the cliff. Selma looked on, her hands over her face. *Did she push him?* It all came together at that moment. They were lovers; Selma and Sara's husband. That day they fought and Shari heard it, bringing on a stress-related asthma attack.

I sprinted toward Selma, but she vanished before I arrived. The cliff, cacti, and tree disappeared and the walls of the house dropped around me. I was shrouded in blackness so thick I couldn't see my hand in front of my face. It was my passion for life that got me in trouble. Why couldn't I have left, followed my instincts?

I fumbled my surroundings, attempting to decipher which room I was in. I pushed against the wall and felt along it until I came to an opening. Lowering my hand, I felt for the ground but touched a step instead. Feeling around the floor I was sure I was on the first floor by the steps that led to Sara's room. Taking a step forward, my shoe hit the solid floor. I dared to take more steps until I came to the front door. I grasped the knob and twisted but it was locked.

They'd trapped me inside. My
pendant; it was on the third floor
window sill. Rushing toward the stairs
and grabbing the rail I jogged up them.
The front door burst open, an intense
wind blew against my back, knocking
me down. It sucked at my legs. I
crawled on my belly, forcing myself to
move against it until I reached the next
flight of stairs. Pulling myself upward
against the wall, I grasped for the
railing. The wind clutched at my feet
and legs.

With all my energy and pure will to
survive I dragged myself up the steps
and across the floor. Reaching the
window, I plastered my back against
the wall and slid upward. A cold, chill
shot against my back and something
soft graced my face. I batted it away
but it was only the curtain blowing
from the air coming from the open
window behind me. Creeping my
fingers along the window sill, the frigid
air against my back, I felt the chain
from the pendant and clutched it tight.

Everything stopped; silence smothered the air. Gripping the pendant I walked back downstairs and toward the front door. Thrusting it open the moon's light glowed around me, silhouetting the car, but my job wasn't done. "Selma!"

"He didn't kill her. It was an accident -- asthma. She had an attack and couldn't get to her nebulizer in time."

The tall man appeared before me. His eyes narrowed and brows drawn inward. "It was an accident?"

"Yes." He stumbled backwards in shock. "Have you been reliving this all these years?"

He stopped and gazed into my eyes then smiled. "It was an accident. I didn't do it." Disoriented, he spun in circles. "I didn't do it."

Selma then appeared next to him. She wrapped her hands around his. "I'm sorry."

After a few minutes I got them settled and we talked. He came home drunk, that's what they were arguing about. She'd smacked him across the face, that's when he pushed her against the wall. The lamp in Shari's room fell, breaking over the floor as she let out her last gasp of breath. He grasped her face in his hands and Selma misunderstood, assuming the worst. When he saw her face he ran out of the house. Drunk and unsure what he'd done, he jumped off the cliff, killing himself.

They weren't malevolent spirits, but lost. The age of the crypt was my first clue that Selma's story was off. My second clue was that Sara's husband was buried in the crypt as well. She wasn't remembering things correctly, possibly confused by her own guilt, and brought back to her place of shame. Inebriated at death, he relived the scene day after day. Shari was forced to die over and over, stuck on auto play, that's why she sealed the house, to give her peace and to keep him out.

Chapter 31
Soul Saver

*I*ngrid didn't send me on the wild goose chase to only save the Pritzes' souls. She knew about Sara's house. Vanishing twins were different than other spirits. They lived in the world of life and death, growing with their twin but seeing life through dead eyes. She still had an ulterior motive which I would soon figure out.

Several weeks later, Mildred was home and doing well. I assisted her whenever needed and she began building her strength. Like all winter days, it was chilly on the mountain. The snow from the previous week not completely melted. I sat on my balcony in the early morning, wrapped in a thermal blanket, admiring the views. The white capped peaks of the mountain taken hostage as a brilliant orange light spread its rays. The disk crawled over the tops of the mountains, reflecting off the snow in muted shades of pink.

A breeze swept my hair from behind, pulling it upward, startling me. "You make her happy," a soft voice whispered in my ear. I turned my head to see Ingrid standing beside me. "As hard as she tries she doesn't see me. When I touch her the sensation leaves an imprint. When I talk she stops as though attempting to hear but her vision isn't as astute as yours. Can you help us connect?"

Connect? That was it? Mildred, like me, was a twin and a chimera, why did she lack the skills or was it something else? *Fear of the unknown?* Maybe in a small way she feared what might happen if she actually allowed her sister into her world. "I don't know what you mean."

The sun caught her translucent edges circling her in a blush halo. "I want her to see me like you do. I want to talk with her. All these years I've been here watching out for her and she knows. She understands the signs when I'm near but her mind is a barrier."

Jenson's advice pressed on my mind. I should help them. My New Mexico experience was still fresh but I wasn't dealing with a sad or distraught spirit. Ingrid was something else -- a twin. The book would be done soon and I'd be on my way. Finding her book all those years ago wasn't luck. I was meant to be here at this place, at this moment in time, and use my skills to help these wayward sisters in different realms find each other and possibly something more. "I'll try, but I'm not sure how I do this. I've always just seen spirits and been able to interact with them. But I will try for her and for you."

"Thank you," she said as her form vanished.

I didn't have the first clue what to do and the landscape, breathtaking as it was, gave me no answers. There was a time when I conjured Timmy but he was already there just waiting for me. Ghosts showed themselves purposely when they wanted or maybe they didn't have as much control as Timmy made out they did. That would be like him.

That evening, when our work was through, I asked her if she ever attempted a seance to converse with her sister and she replied that she had considered it and almost went through with it but stopped. 'It didn't feel right' she said.

Her lips curled downward and the lines around them deepened. I tried to comfort her as tears threatened to fall from the corners of her eyes. "Most of my life I've been alone, had to fight my own battles and been surrounded by awful people but even before that I felt dread, gut instincts, and intuition. It was when I was truly alone that I began seeing spirits in a house sealed with magic. They were my friends and gave my lonely life sustenance as I gave back to them. I think we are born the way we are but most people are happy and sound in their lives and don't have evil twin ghost brothers hanging around.

Ingrid is kind and sweet, you are lucky."

She smoothed her chin. "I've tried."

"Have you tried everything?"

"Of course I have." She narrowed her eyes and shot me a defensive glance as if I was suggesting she was somehow at fault.

"The full moon will be soon and spirits have more energy, more power. We don't need a special ceremony. I can call her as easily as I can talk with you, but she wants to connect directly to you, not me."

Her eyes took on a faraway stare then she spoke as if in a trance and began scribbling on her notepad; *frankincense, quartz, blue lace agate, moldavite,* and a few other items. "The full moon, of course, and a March moon is considered the last of the winter moons so it's a time for rebirth and I have you, someone who can see her, to call her to me." Her eyes lit up as ideas swarmed through her mind.

That full moon we sat in a circle, candles glowing around us, mingling with the light streaming through the windows. She was prepared with every item in her repertoire known to help spirit awareness and open the mind or 'third-eye'.

We held hands so she could draw on my vision and I called for Ingrid. Without the hullabaloo Timmy used, Ingrid appeared. What happened here didn't take me by surprise, my intuition and sight was stronger than ever. "She's with us."

Mildred who'd closed her eyes to further her senses and assist her concentration opened them now. She glanced to me and around us. "Where?"

"Relax, let out any tension. Let her in," I soothed, rubbing the backs of her hands.

Ingrid stood in back of her sister and whispered in her ear. Mildred jerked her head to the side, searching for her. "I feel her. I hear her."

"What's she saying?"

"She repeated your words and added I love you."

"Let out a deep breath, close your eyes, imagine you're with her."

She nodded, tilted her head back, closing her eyes. Ingrid whispered further into her ear and Mildred's face lit in a smile. After a minute or so Mildred opened her eyes, Ingrid stared down at her and a tear dropped from the corner of Mildred's eye as she reached for her sister. "I see you."

Ingrid stepped in front of Mildred and held her hand out. "It's time, sister. Take my hand. We'll do it together."

Mildred took her hand and stood, her physical body drooping as it collapsed to the floor. Together the light enveloped them.

My calling was saving spirits and sending them to the peaceful beyond, but I still had a lot to learn. I sent Mildred's finished book to the publisher and walked out of her house with fond memories.

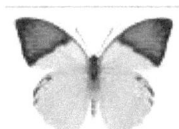

Jenson returned home and was given a few days to visit his family. Our eyes met and a light sparked between us as I ran to him, wrapping my arms tight around him, inhaling his scent. Our lips found each other and meshed into a fervent kiss. He'd made it home, alive.

That night I gave myself to his gentle touch and the smooth kisses he dropped on my body. His fingers caressed my nipples. "I love you," he whispered in my ear.

"I love you. I want this," I urged through deep breaths.

His nose pressed against my cheek, his fingers relentlessly scouring my curves, he asked, "Are you sure?"

I traced a path to the button on his jeans. "More than anything." My worries in the past evaporated at that moment. I tugged the button loose and slid my hand downward beneath his briefs.

"I'll be gentle," he reassured as he pushed my skirt up and slid his fingers between my legs.

He pulled me on top of him, his erection belonging to me as our bodies moved slow and tender until he was deep inside me. My toes curled in pleasure as we rode the waves, gently rocking us into an overwhelming bliss.

Chapter 32
Quantico

O ver the next several years the gnawing and yawing in my gut pushed and nagged relentlessly for me to find it, follow it. *But what was it?* Jenson traveled the world. He went wherever they sent him with pride and honor. Into the darkest areas. His sniper skills unrivalled, he became a killing machine, but always the enemy. During his times of absence I spent my days assisting ghosts, settling their souls and leading them into the afterlife.

Earth's Wanderers is what I called them. They are the chilling breeze that sweeps through someone on the hottest summer days. The bone chill in the winter leaving a person icy all day. Most of them dying such tragic deaths even their spirits refused to accept it. I help them; together we find solace, but first they have to face their deaths. For some they become very angry and want revenge once the memories fill their spirits but that will only send them to the underworld and the fiery pits. Talking and soothing them into acceptance and an afterlife in the bathing sparkles and light is at times difficult.

It was ten years after the birth of the monster that my badgering gut could be ignored no longer. The feeling inside sent me on a wild goose chase -- a direction. It was like a compass and I followed it to Horn City, North Carolina. Without a clue what I'd find, it found me. It led me to the doorstep of a suburban home. Crime scene tape and police swarmed the house. Through the cars' headlights I watched them haul a boy, yelling profanities, out of a house and tuck him away into the back of a police car. His blond, unruly curls stopped my heart.

From the back seat his teary sapphire eyes stared into the headlights of my car. My back tensed and straightened like an icicle -- Evan. I parked my car and turned down the lights, scrunching in my seat I watched. Evan was taken away and a young girl, two or three, was carried out of the house, hysterical, and put into another car. Memories of the day my own parents died flooded me. I was that little girl so many, many years ago. *What would become of her now?*

Through the tears that clouded my vision I watched them carry out three black bags. One held someone; a small child. Bile rose in my throat. I did this. Timmy did this. Now in human form, he could be killed. What would become of his spirit, I didn't know, but he could be killed and I vowed that moment to make sure it happened.

A young boy with blond curls walked through the commotion, his head turning in various directions as his eyes inhaled the scene, stopping on the little black bag. He cocked his head then shot a glance at me as if he knew I could see him. I met his gaze and he moved towards me then an arm reached out to him, halting his movement. Philmonia's head jerked my direction, her gaze boring into me. My breath caught and I stepped out of the vehicle. She was not taking him wherever she was going.

I strode towards them with purpose and the boy lowered his brows, gazing from her to me as if he knew he had to make a choice. Ignoring my sister, I squatted when I reached him. "Hi, I'm Scarlett."

His sapphire eyes widened. "I'm not supposed to talk to strangers," he said in a tiny voice as he leaned into his mother -- Philmonia.

"Leave him alone! He's mine. Look, you did this. It's your fault and you won't have this one!" Philmonia spat as she wrapped an arm around the boy and took a step to leave.

I grasped his arm to stop her. "I'm your aunt and I'm here to help."

"Miss, this is a crime scene. I need you to step away," said the firm voice of a police officer. The lights spinning from the police cars illuminating his badge, Officer Cunaway.

My hand firmly grasping the boy's as I stood and stepped backwards. "I'm sorry."

He gave me a cockeyed glance and shook his head. No doubt he thought I was insane. *After all, who was I talking to?*

Philmonia had other ideas and tugged the boy in a different direction. He squirmed in her hand. "I want to go with the lady, Mommy. Let's go with her."

She glanced down at him, her jaw tight she stated in a firm voice, "We are not. I am your mother and you belong with me."

I squeezed his hand again and as if he felt my positive energy he wiggled his hand from her grasp. "I don't want to, Mommy. You're dark and she's light. I want to go with her."

Officer Cunaway glowered at me. I continued walking backwards, when I heard the boy's words and saw his hand free from her. I scooped him up then ran to my car. Inside it I had stones that warded off evil spirits. Philmonia wouldn't be able to enter.

She didn't chase after me but appeared in front of me. I ran through her. The frigid air of her spirit and the murky pit of her soul froze me to the bone. He clung to my neck as I thrust the car door open and pushed him inside. She grabbed for his leg.

"Mommy, it's pretty in here. It's like a nightlight. I want to stay with her." He kicked to free his leg from her grasp but she pulled him. "No, Mommy," he whined.

I pushed against her. "Leave him be, let him go into the peace."

She seethed, "He will go with me."

"You have always been a selfish bitch. You want him for you and I'm not letting you drag him to hell or make him aimlessly wander the planet with you. Let him go!" I seethed then turned towards the boy. "Grab the bag on the passenger seat and hold it tight."

He reached his arm across the seat but her tug on him pulled him far enough away he couldn't reach. His little hand caught the compartment above the gear shifter. "Hold on," I called as I ran around the vehicle, thrust the door open and tossed the bag at her.

It hit her in the chest and went through her as she disintegrated before our eyes. I let out a deep sigh. "Climb over here." I patted the passenger seat.

He scrambled into the seat and I rushed to the other side, grabbed the bag and tossed it to the floor by his tiny feet.

"How dare you take both my boys?" hissed Philmonia's voice as it cut through the air.

The little boy tucked his legs between his arms as if the ice in her voice chilled him. Maybe it did. She was, after all, his mother and who would know her better than her own child? I turned my car around and headed out of the housing development and into the far outskirts of nothingness. Surrounded by thick trees, I pulled the car over and turned towards him.

"You feel the warmth and see the peaceful ever after, close your eyes and

welcome it," I soothed the boy,
cupping his tiny hands inside mine.

His lips curved in a smile. "It's
pretty and so bright. I can go there
now?"

I nodded. "Yes."

"What about my Mommy and
Daddy?" His brows shot up in concern.

"When they let go of their hate,
maybe then they can join you." I
remembered Sara's husband but didn't
think that applied to my sister who was
beyond malevolent. My goal was to
help the innocent and let the wicked
rot in sorrow on Earth.

His smile grew as his little fingers
disappeared in my hands and his body
vanished, leaving behind the sparkles
that told me he'd passed on. His spirit
was forever in a good place. It was my
fault he was taken too soon and that
weighed heavily on my soul and always
would. Knowing he was in a place filled
with love lightened my burden and
maybe he was in a place that was far
better than anything he'd experience on
Earth.

I drove back to the crime scene and circled the subdivision. I needed to find the boy's father and try to save his soul. With my logic and knowledge of spirits I figured if he hadn't immediately gone into the *peace* then he was an Earth Wanderer but I couldn't assume anything except the fact that I hadn't seen him. I didn't even know if his spirit was good or evil. He may have passed into the darkness, swallowed by his own vile deeds.

I drove slowly through the area, more coasted through with my foot off the gas, but didn't see the spirit of a man near the house or in the area. Another possibility was Philmonia found him as I was saving her son. My soul downtrodden, I checked into a hotel.

Lying on the bed, staring at the popcorn ceiling, the day spun in my head like kernels of corn popping on the stove, jumping from the heat. My mind grasped at them, catching one, I now knew what the irritating wrenching in my gut was -- Timmy.

Now that he was in a human body, the cells inside us were connected. Flesh to flesh, as Miss Lenure always said, only it went deeper. The iron attached to his blood as it pumped through Evan's body worked as a compass. My blood drawn to his. We were connected on a spiritual and physical level.

The little monster, Evan, was sent to a psychiatric facility in the mountains of North Carolina where he spent several years. Tucked away from the rest of the world I continued my work, nevermore ignoring the nagging -- the compass -- that connected me to my twin.

His baby sister, Emily, with her cute, bouncy, golden curls and a smile to light up the world was adopted almost immediately by a well-to-do family.

In those years I returned to Poppy Hills with Jenson to spend time with his family. Mr. O'Conner, even in his death, paid them a salary to maintain the house and grounds. They refused to live inside it but continued in their little cottage at the edge of the property. It was home to them.

The house, large and foreboding, was a dark, haunting shadow on my soul. A place I hadn't thought of since the day I left. I now entered it, Jenson's hand encircling mine. I swallowed hard as my eyes drifted up the stairs to my room. No longer did the light shine on the purple fabric, bathing it in a lavender hue.

"Are you sure you want to do this?" He squeezed my hand and little lines formed over his brow in worry.

"Yes," I answered, lifting my foot onto the first step and then the next. As we grew closer I saw a little white cradle and blue coverings. They'd turned my princess prison into a nursery. Tiny clothes still filled the drawers and hung in the closet, stuffed toys lined the shelves. Mrs. Kurl informed me Philmonia had vacated after meeting another man, the talk and rumors in town made her paranoid.

The floorboards creaked outside the room. I turned first to Jenson whose face was twisted in anger, his eyes glowering at the little white cradle. Behind him stood Philmonia. The sun shone right through her edges and her lips perverted into a demonic smile. One hand on the door frame, the other at her side, she stood in the doorway as if I couldn't walk right through her.

She wasn't an Earth Wanderer who aimlessly rambled the planet. She had purpose. My lips curled upwards into a smirk. She was powerless now. I walked right through her body and down the stairs. It was that night when I brought up my encounter that Mrs. Kurl admitted something I never expected.

She hated the house, could feel their spirits inside it, worse now that Philmonia was dead too. She felt as if they were watching her every move. The night of Evan O'Conner's death she couldn't take it anymore, watching them flit around the house with their abnormal sexual activities and flaunting the baby. The child they created from their own deviousness. She knew what they did and made a conscious choice to poison him with over-the-counter weight loss drugs. She crushed them up and dropped them into his drink. It worked and Mr. O'Conner's heart stopped.

My jaw hung slack. Mrs. Kurl was the last person I ever expected to do something like that. She was sweet and kind. It was her gentle soul that hated him and her own guilt that allowed her to feel his spirit and watchful eyes in the house. He'd passed on. I was sure of that as he'd shown me the vision of his death and I hadn't seen him since.

Killing Philmonia and Evan at the same time might have drawn too much suspicion. An old man dying of a heart attack didn't raise any red flags. Mr. Kurl planned on rigging the brakes in one of the cars, but Philmonia vacated before he had the opportunity. They wanted to leave a good year or so

between deaths so they wouldn't draw
suspicion, but never got the chance.
Evan did it for them, and killed his
younger half-brother in the process.

The details of Philmonia's death
were morbid beyond measure. What
he'd done to all of them was sick, more
than Timmy-sick. It was calculated and
done with a weapon, a thick blade. The
weapon was never found and the
slaughter remained unsolved, but I
knew it was him. Furthermore, I felt his
spirit wasn't in full control but split
time with Evan's natural spirit.
Together they were abominable.

The next several years passed
quickly and Jenson moved up in rank
and was stationed stateside at
Quantico, Virginia. Those years I
stayed with him, we never married but
did make a beautiful, perfect child
together. It wasn't long after
Philmonia's death when we learned I
was pregnant. It wasn't planned
because of his crazy life in the military
and my even more insane ghost
chasing, spirit-freeing existence, but

was welcome. A baby made through our love for each other.

Devlin was born Dec. 5, 1985 in Manassas, Virginia. Our pride and joy. He was perfect in every way and his smile melted his father like nothing I'd ever seen. Jenson bought a house in the mountains when he learned he'd be staying put for his final enlistment period. The work he did was top secret and he had a fairly high security clearance. I never asked, as he was forbidden from discussing the details of his work.

Our home was a simple ranch-style house with three bedrooms, a kitchen and dining room with sliding glass doors that opened to the deck, exposing the views of the valley in the winter and thick woods in the spring and summer. In the fall the leaves changed into all colors and coated the ground. Devlin loved to jump into them after we raked them into piles. He'd laugh and move onto the next one, making a huge mess until he'd finally scoop them up and toss them down the mountainside with his father.

From an early age Devlin was groomed to be a Marine, to follow in his proud father's footsteps. Jenson was a tough father who demanded respect and got it in spades but also had a soft heart that he only showed to us. He was taught to love and appreciate the country he lived in, to accept our freedoms as a gift -- a precious gift. Those years were my favorite, watching our boy grow and living together in sheer bliss. My favorite, for all the small reasons that spelled L-O-V-E, was observing my men get their hair cut. Devlin had to do as his father. He was a mini Jenson in every way.

Like all good things, eventually it came to an end.

Chapter 33
Hurricane Chloe

*D*evlin was six and a half years old when my internal compass went wild. A hurricane spiraling in the ocean not far off the outer banks of North Carolina blew onshore causing complete devastation to the little island town of Billows Hollow. My gut churned with each twist of the storm, Jenson encouraged me to follow my internal compass. He always supported the impossibilities in my life and understood on a level I've never comprehended that it was my destiny. I was attached to Evan because only I could stop him. Leaving my little Devlin for any amount of time broke my heart, but Jenson was right. He was always right.

I made it to the island, after the devastation from the storm. It was the craziest scene I'd witnessed to that day but have seen more since. Evan was a ruthless storm that blew onto the shoreline, shattered lives, and escaped. I was too late to stop him, but I heard the news of his presence. People didn't know; they assumed it was the storm, but I knew better. He killed an innocent family, leaving behind a little girl.

Traipsing through the wreckage, I assisted in cleaning the beach. A hat on my head and dark sunglasses covering my eyes, I searched for the family. I didn't leave in time to stop Evan but I could save the souls of those he murdered and send them to the peaceful beyond. They hadn't moved from the wreckage of their home. Huddled inside the arms of the father, I found them, all four.

The only thing keeping them there was Eilida Tate, their daughter. They had to know she was safe before they would move on. I found the little girl in a shelter and brought them to her. Once her aunt and uncle picked her up, they welcomed the *peace*. From that moment, I became the protector of the girls. Evan would never harm them again.

The Billows Hollow residents' talk mingled between the loss of the Tates and a miracle baby, Dillon Thomas Findley, born during the hurricane -- a life for four deaths. I listened intently to the conversations, soaking in all the information I could, almost immediately feeling an attachment to the child. I continued to keep tabs on the little boy as he grew, knowing one day he would be instrumental in Evan's demise. Born from death and devastation, it was his destiny.

I stayed in touch with Penelope and Kevin. Over the years she and a couple other lawyers built their own firm in Boulder. Kevin, the chief investigator. I fed him information and he returned with the whereabouts of the girls. The families who took them in, adopted them. I made sure they all went to homes where they'd be loved. It was all I knew to do for the havoc I'd unleashed on the world.

Jenson retired from the Corps and accepted a position with the Secret Service. With the highest level of security clearance in the country, including his family, we finally married. It was a simple wedding with only his parents and our closest friends.

On Evan's twenty-first birthday he gained the Poppy Hills Estate. His father had left it in the will. It was as if the house needed a sinister occupant to live and breathe. We received regular updates from Jenson's parents as they continued to work on the estate. Mr. O'Conner had provided nicely for them in his will but now they had to work for his vile, abhorrent son. A child born of my womb after he and my sister acted out a sexual fantasy using me as their incubation tube.

Every three years, Hurricane Evan blew in and out with storms. I was always too late to stop him but managed to save the souls of the families and see that the little girls were placed in homes, loving homes. At least I hoped, but I had no control over how they were treated and I couldn't erase the nightmares Evan thrust on their tiny souls. Many times I wished he'd have killed them too instead of forcing them to live with the terror of his ways. His sick, malicious ways. Tears stained my pillow many nights. My solace was that he could be killed.

1998. Devlin was seventeen and a half when my internal compass sent me on a wild goose chase from one stop to the next, not giving me time to catch up. I didn't know his reason for deviating, but felt relieved I had time. Maybe I could stop this one.

I coasted my car into the woods, alongside the long road to the house, and through the pouring rain and winds pushing the trees, their branches scraping against my skin. I scampered toward the house, dodging the boughs and limbs as they bent in precarious positions as if trying to stop me, ducking behind a bush and watched as Evan stood at the doorstep. A thin, dark-haired man answered, I couldn't make out the words but he closed the door on Evan and my heart did a little dance, hoping maybe they wouldn't allow him in. That was always the problem; his victims invited him inside their homes unaware of his sinister ways.

After a few minutes the man returned to the door and led Evan to a two story garage beside the house. The man looked frail, almost sickly. I stayed squatted in the woods. The man returned alone, entered the house and that was it. My legs cramped from the awkward position, I stood and moved along the tree-line searching and contemplating what I should do. Tucked in my waist was the 9 mm Jenson had bought me and taught me to use.

It was far too risky to run across their driveway towards the garage. The wind and rain eased and I slipped through the woods and around the back of the house and edged in the direction of the garage. I pasted my ear to the side and listened. Rustling and footsteps echoed through my ear. He was downstairs, no doubt plotting a way in.

"So, what, you think you're going to stop him?" Philmonia hung in the air, a loose low-cut gown clung to her large round breasts. I glowered at her. "You did something to him. You made him this way. It's all your fault." Her words filled with hate and sarcasm, but she was partially right it was Timmy's dark soul mixed with Evan's true soul that created the monster.

"Shut the hell up and go away." I took a few steps along the garage and heard the floorboards creak beneath his weight.

"You sound like him, always pushing me away."

I considered her words for a moment. "When you were alive?"

"No, now. He shouts at me, forces me to leave when all I want is to love him." It was something about the way her voice clung to the word *love* that sent tingles flying up my spine but I was more concerned with the idea

Evan had my curse or gift depending on how one thought of it. He saw her.

"When he was little his eyes had rings around the irises melting into the blue. It reminded me that he was yours." She seethed then vanished.

A crash followed by shattered glass ricocheted through my ears. I followed the sound and peeked around the corner of the garage where a large tree limb lay against the wall. My eyes followed the siding upward until they halted on the broken window.

Quickening footsteps squished against the soft earth and I ducked around the building and back into the forest covering. My back against a tree, I slid my face around the side and watched as the man escorted Evan into the main house. That was it. He created a diversion and now he was in, let his sick games begin.

The blood in my veins rushing as a heavy stream during a storm I moved through the woods and towards the house, listening, hearing my own rushed and raspy breath. The gun neatly tucked and cold against my skin. I slid along the house and cupped my hand around the back door knob then twisted gently, carefully, but it was locked.

Voices inside begged my attention, closing my eyes I listened. A rustling through trees forced my attention elsewhere. In the woods were several young boys motioning for me to join them. *What did they have to tell me?* Their edges, catching the glow of the moon.

When I approached they stepped backwards until we came upon a raised patch of earth. The boy who'd beckoned me, his dark eyes solemn, pointed to it. "That's me." He raised his arm and swung it around in a circle. "We're throughout these woods."

Another boy with a green ball cap stepped forward. "She did it and they're going to do it again unless *he* stops them."

Evan preyed on the innocent but, for whatever reason, he'd deviated from his original plan. He was now in a house of horrors. The game changed and he was the hunted. The prey lured into the occupants of the sticky web. *Who would walk out alive?*

I considered the man I saw, his fragile body no match for the stout, muscular man Evan had grown into. "Who else is in that house?"

Another boy answered, "A woman. She's the one."

It was karma that led him to this house, maybe something good would come of this. "How many children are in there?"

The same boy responded, "Three. One of them will end up just like us." He shot a quick glance at the first boy I'd seen, the one who beckoned me. In return he made a quick nod of his head.

The first boy, I noted he was a bit taller and thicker than the others, maybe older, spoke up, wind kicked against the trees, splashing water over him. "His heart is black and he hates. He will destroy them."

His, Evan, yes he was but a black hole upon the planet. It wasn't the parents I was worried for but the children. They were innocent, victims of circumstance. My thoughts halted and switched course, no ghost had ever told me they saw human souls. There was something special about this one or was it Timmy's spirit, partially meshed with Evan's?

I glanced from one to the next, fear and rage filled their eyes. They weren't evil spirits but wanted vengeance for their souls. I needed to pass them into the *peaceful beyond,* but first I wanted to understand how he knew. "Can you see his soul?"

The boy nodded.

"How?"

The wind whipped with a squall and a branch raked against my back.

"I just do. His is black and fractured like glass. It's also fluid and the fissures move in waves." His dark eyes wide and his hands fidgeting at his sides. Even I couldn't glance into someone's soul. I sensed immoral and revolting ones but couldn't actually see them.

In the folds of my mind I'd heard it before, a fractured spirit, then it came rushing forward. The professor I asked about the two-headed dragon: 'I'd say a fractured spirit. We all have a light side and a dark side. We try to do what's right but sometimes give in to temptations', but was his soul more than fractured, shattered and fluid as more than two souls fought for dominance?

Nonetheless, I had to pass these boys on, lest their hate grow and turn them into dark spirits. "Revenge is a trap. In a violent death it's easy to hate and want to get revenge on those who harmed you, but all you will get for it is to wander this Earth forever or..." I paused because the alternative was far worse, "a darkness filled with anger and fire. Let go, welcome the *peace*."

The soul-sighted boy folded his arms across his chest, stubborn and unwilling to let go of his hate. The other boys glanced to each other then to him, seemingly unsure or seeking his approval. *Was he the reason they were all still here?*

"It's OK. I promise. I've watched many spirits pass into the afterlife," I begged.

A little boy with springy brown curls smiled large and asked, "We can go?"

Soul-sighted lowered his brows and squared his shoulders, glaring at the boy.

"Yes," I encouraged and the little boy's spirit evaporated. One by one they all followed, except Soul-sighted. "Why are you still here?"

"I can't go," he stated, still maintaining his defensive stance.

He was holding onto hate. "Let go, welcome its warmth."

He raised his voice, "I can't go. It won't let me. It's not my time."

I'd never heard that before and didn't get it then. How could a soul not go? Unless it was malevolent, and I didn't sense that about him. "Can you explain?"

He shrugged. "It's not my time, not yet."

"What do you need to do? I can help you."

Lost in the effort of saving the boys I nearly forgot about Evan, or my mind willingly pushed his evil deeds aside to let him destroy the couple who killed innocent children. There was no remorse to be felt for them. A door shut and I twisted my head in that direction, tiny feet scampered through the mushy ground, squishing as they went.

When I turned back around the boy was gone. I'd saved them all but one. I picked up my feet and ducked beneath the heavy limbs, dodging the fallen branches. A little boy no older than eight or nine headed down the long drive towards Evan's car. He'd saved him. I stopped in my tracks. He rescued the boy. *Why?*

Did the child not fit into his scheme? Did he have a heart in there somewhere, buried beneath the muck and hate, or did he have other plans? Heavy footsteps splashed against the dirt road -- Evan. I shrunk down, hiding behind a stack of fallen branches and watched. He hummed *Oh My Darlin' Clementine* as he strolled down the road, confident and pleased with himself. The little boy thanked him, then Evan opened the driver's side door and in an even tone that sounded like his father said, 'Don't speak. Get in.' The boy followed his instructions while Evan popped the hood, fiddled with something then dropped it and joined the boy inside it.

This was the first close-up glance I'd had and seeing him sent shivers quivering through my body. His bald head, shaved clean, and his bulk identical to that of Mr. O'Conner. He was beyond a doubt his son. Once his car turned I darted across the road to mine. It was deep enough in the woods the trees surrounded it. Cranking the engine, I followed from a safe distance.

He pulled the car into an empty gas station. The little boy bounded out of the car and to a pay phone then climbed back into the car. I followed them all the way into a subdivision. He pulled the car alongside the road and the little boy got out and stopped in the street, waiting as Evan pulled away. Once his car was out of sight the boy scampered across the street towards a house. I gawked. Evan hadn't killed him but took him home. A woman pulled the boy into her arms.

I didn't follow Evan. My job wasn't finished. I wasn't saving the parents, but the boys said there were three children; one was the boy who was now safe at home with his family, the second most likely a girl, but the third would be a boy. I had to see that his spirit was sent into the *peace*.

Smoke filled the air as I followed the road towards the house, maneuvering my car back through the fallen branches that littered the road. The closer I got, the worse it became. I parked my car a distance down the road and wandered through the smoldering air, unable to see further than a couple feet in front of me. I searched for a boy. Coughing and gagging, I continued deeper until I spotted the house in flames. Tendrils of fire shot from it and spiraled in all directions.

Sputtering, smoke choking my airway, I halted my search, dragging myself back to my car. It was the next day I learned he'd left a child, a girl, behind just as the others. Chelsea Mora was her name and she was found heavily drugged outside the home but a safe enough distance away she hadn't inhaled too much smoke and was alive. I drove to the hospital and strolled through the halls. It was a small enough town the hospital wasn't too large and it didn't take me long to find the girl.

She lay in the bed, peaceful and sleeping, but a disturbing sensation clenched my gut. Certainly not this little girl with her cherub cheeks.

Chapter 34
Karmic Roles

*D*evlin turned eighteen and joined the Corp just like his father, leaving us with an empty house and time to contemplate. Jenson left the Secret Service and rejoined the Corp on a special assignment. I knew nothing of the details. His parents were our eyes into Evan's home but he kept them at a distance which we considered good. It was scary them living on the same patch of ground Evan inherited. We needed another set of eyes in the house, one who could get close to him, earn his trust.

During those years I learned more about the first Evan's lawyer, Mr. Fritz; a clammy, slimy man with few morals. I broke into his house and beneath a brick in the fireplace found the weapon Evan used to murder his own family -- my sister. Dropping it carefully into a bag I collected it, already planning Evan's demise.

It was 2007 when my internal compass pointed again to the southeast and a familiar name surfaced. I followed it like always, this time arriving as someone else, a gangly blond teen, approached the house. I watched in horror as he strolled right in. I drew closer, hoping to get his attention. It was bad enough he already killed the family. Then I remembered the boy he saved. *Would he spare the teen?*

Without thinking, I moved closer to the house. The teen entered the bedroom, my heart stopped. His eyes widened in terror then he grabbed something off a dresser and smashed it against Evan's head. He dropped. *Did he kill Evan?*

My mouth agape. Evan wasn't moving and the teen exited the house, running like wild through the woods, the object still in his hands until he stopped and dropped it. I approached him. "Are you alright?"

His blue eyes vibrant and wild,
filled with tears. Not for his actions,
but for the loss. He knew the family
well enough to enter their house
without knocking. He was distraught
and lost, somehow I convinced him to
come with me. I was staying in an FBI
safe house, Jenson gave me the keys. I
didn't know then that I was part of a
much larger plan that fit nicely with my
own.

After a bit the teen calmed and
when he told me his name, Dillon, it
sparked recognition. I didn't press him.
Whoever this boy was, I needed him.
He took a risk, an emotional one,
acting on instinct and knocked Evan
out. I knew he wasn't dead. My internal
compass was as sharp as ever and he'd
wake up in a hissy, maybe make a
mistake or get caught. That evening,
after the boy went home, I called
Kevin.

I returned to the scene and sought
the spirits of those he slaughtered.
They embraced the *peace*. I followed the
same protocol with the girl. There was

also a car fire, a diversion set up by Evan. Unexpected; he'd never killed outside his code. The OCD was the Evan side because Timmy didn't care. I remembered the ghost's words in the woods outside the Moras' house of slaughter. Evan's spirit was black and fractured like glass. The two halves to him, one as vile as the other and fluid, suggesting to me maybe there was a third. I searched for the man who Evan scorched in the car fire but he was nowhere to be found.

Kevin returned my call within a couple days. The boy who I met was Dillion Findley. The same boy who was born during Hurricane Chloe. It could only be karma that put us together and this was his role in Evan's demise. Over time I gained the boy's trust and when I returned home Jenson and I discussed it. It was the first time he ever conversed about work with me.

The FBI was on the case, Evan's case, alerted by an ex-Billows Hollow cop and a retired Jag Officer after Evan's diversion clued them onto another suspect. They started the ball rolling, only they weren't brought into the conspiracy to capture the Hurricane Killer. I was the key to its success. Jenson informed his commanding officer of my spiritual ability and I was brought in. First sent on a mission to prove myself. I had to find the children murdered and raped by a child predator. Once I found them I saved their tiny souls and relayed all the intel. It was gory and almost as revolting as Evan's dirty deeds.

From that point forward I hunted Evan and my anonymity was solid; Scarlett Jones no longer existed. My name erased from record, a thick black line on a page.

Over the next few years, Dillon and I continued our relationship. Evan killed every three years like clockwork and the time was running close. I let my compass guide me as he scouted the area, hunting for his next prey. He had a particular liking to a neighborhood, one he revisited. The family fit his modus operandi. I used a vacant house to pull off a very clever ploy, tricking Evan. This wasn't part of their plan, but mine. I wanted Dillon's eyes and ears in the house.

My rogue act worked like a charm and Evan welcomed Dillon into his home. I was nothing more than an informant. It was Jenson's friendship, connections, and openness about my abilities that gave me a way in. My connection to Evan was never disclosed to the FBI only my spirit vision. But I didn't doubt they knew more about me than I knew about myself. I was scolded for my actions, but nothing more than a slap on my wrist. Over the next few years, Dillon corresponded whenever possible, but Evan stayed dormant. He'd gained a liking for the boy.

My devoted special ops son, Devlin, was chosen for the mission due to his exceptional abilities. I wasn't sure I liked the idea of my beautiful boy trotting such dangerous territory but it was who he was, proud and courageous like his father.

It was Evan's attraction to Dillon who now went by Tommy that eventually stopped the beast, but not without more casualties and ghost rescuing. His final victims, his own sister Emily and her family; leaving them in a bloodied mess. Erica, her daughter, the sole survivor, whimpering in the corner of the kitchen. My own guilt eats at me for what I did. The gory scene embedded in my mind.

Evan planned a romantic getaway for Tommy but it wouldn't end the way he imagined. In order to track and trick a killer one had to be a few steps ahead. Tommy held the dried, flaky bloodied knife Evan used to kill my sister to the throat of the beast. Like I knew he would, he dropped the knife and rushed out of the cabin. My darling Devlin followed on his heels and snuck through the unlocked back door, slicing his brother's neck as was his assignment.

The monster was dead, gone. His flesh no longer attached to mine, our

DNA no longer connected. I was free and so was the world.

Chapter 35
One Haunted Night

I knew death wasn't an end but sometimes a beginning. Evan was dead, but what about his and Timmy's souls? I prepared my home for their arrival, removing the stones and herbs I kept around to protect my family from the horrors and spirits. I placed them in a spot to be used later. Until this point, I hadn't truly waged war with an evil spirit, most were simply confused, but this was something more. A spirit who was wicked from conception. I begged Jenson to leave but he refused, saying we'd battle them together.

As a soldier he wasn't a stranger to war, but not this kind of war. His weapons would do no good in the spiritual realm. They could take every bullet fired at them and each swipe of a blade would sail through their translucent bodies. Not even the heaviest artillery grenade could slow them down. This was a different kind of battle. A battle of spirit and will.

The winds kicked up that night and rain pounded against the roof. We sat as usual together on the couch, watching TV until the power went out. Jenson lit a candle and we snuggled together as the light bounced off the wall. A rush of wind and a shadow blew out the flame and I knew they'd arrived. I clutched Jenson's hand. "Timmy, is that you? No need for the drama."

In the blackness, falling objects hit the wood flooring, echoing off the walls. "No, Timmy is gone!" said a satanic voice that froze me to the bone. I took a deep breath. "Evan?"

The candle lit and Evan's stout form, broad shoulders, and eyes filled with black as dark as the deep ocean appeared. "You," he seethed. "You and her did all of this."

The candle flickered and went out. The couch we sat on scooted across the floor, moving fast towards the wall.

Jenson tugged at my hand and we jumped off seconds before it crashed into the wall. "Where's Timmy?" I demanded.

The lights above our head rattled as I led Jenson out of the room and down the hall. "Where is he?!"

"You abandoned me and left me with her!" His voice rattled the house to the foundation, shaking, pictures dropped to the ground surrounding us. Jenson wrapped his muscular arms around me as if he could protect me from the demon spawn.

Where was Timmy? Had their spirits merged? I wasn't going to get anywhere with him unless I played along. "I'm sorry. Let me show you."

The room lit up and a little boy, a young Evan with curly blond hair sat in a tub, Philmonia leaned over the side. Jenson, who'd witnessed death and destruction first hand, scrunched his face into a look of disgust as she touched the boy in places no one should, whispering sweet nothings, comparing him to his father. A father

447

he didn't know. The scene disintegrated, followed by a man, his hair dark, whipping a belt across the young boy.

Tears ran down my cheek as I covered my mouth in horror. A young boy with innocent amber eyes and platinum curly hair stood before us. "I'm sorry," I choked out between sobs. "I'm so sorry. I didn't know." I reached my hand out for him to grasp. At that moment, my mother's own words rushed back to me, 'The rape wasn't the worst part. It was when I learned you were a twin but your twin died in the womb and you absorbed him'.

Evan's vanishing twin, the reason he saw spirits and at an early age, had multi-colored eyes. Eyes that continued to change throughout his life. His fractured soul, this child the fluidity between Evan and Timmy. He took my hand and a rush of horror and revulsion gripped my soul. I froze to that spot unable to open my mouth and speak.

I brought my mind back to a dark place it never wanted to return to -- the dank, black, hot room where I was raped repeatedly. I cast the thoughts at him. The only weapon I had was to show him as he'd shown me. I struggled against the straps that bound me. The collar secured around my neck, keeping me from escaping. The boy let go of my hand, his body suddenly formed into that of a grown man; attractive, tall, and muscular.

He opened his mouth and in a trembling voice said, "I never left the womb and in the first few years was in control until *she* did things to me and *our* drunk, fake father whipped me, hated me because of who my father really was. My own hate grew and their spirits rose to the surface. They took control, forced me to take a back seat as they seethed and plotted together." He ran his tongue over his lip.

My mouth was dry as I attempted to swallow. "You saw what they did."

His lips curled into a smile. "Yes and now I understand. She treated you as she did me. A toy for her sexual fantasies."

"I was your demon but now you know the truth and you can leave." The lights in the house flickered back on and the winds and rain died down.

"I was the only one who knew you, remembered you, and I closed those memories inside me so they wouldn't know, wouldn't find you." His revelation brought a sense of clarity. Evan wouldn't come looking for me. He didn't know anything about me or even if I existed.

"What is your name?"

His green eyes flickered and a satanic smile tugged at his lips. "Evan." His spirit collapsed around us and a black hole spun from the floor, widening as it grew in strength, sucking at me, trying to pull me into its depths.

Jenson wrapped his arms around me and tugged from behind. My feet shooting out from under me, I slipped from Jenson's grasp. He clutched my hand as my body was lifted horizontal above the spinning hole. A hand gripped my leg, dragging it lower.

"No!" hollered Jenson as he gripped my hand, his hands one by one climbing my arm with a firm grip. He tugged until little by little my body edged further from the deep, dark, spinning pit. I toppled backwards onto him.

Wasting no time, I grasped his hand and ran downstairs into the basement. The dark vortex spun in the center of the room. Jenson grasped my arm with one hand and the stair railing with the other as I pasted myself along the wall and reached downward towards the wooden box encircled in salt.

I touched the top of it, my fingers moving downward towards the latch, fumbling as they went. I knew my strong Jenson couldn't hold on forever and if I didn't unlock it soon we'd both be lost. My fingers touched the clasp and the vortex spun in our direction, sucking us further and my hand away from the clasp, brushing it against the floor and smearing the salt circle, tossing the vortex another direction further from us.

It was the break I needed. I squirmed my hand free of Jenson and scrambled to the box, unlatching it, lifting the lid and grasping the bag of stones and herbs. Standing upright, my body scooted closer to the vortex as its pull sucked me in.

"Scarlett!" Jenson's voice screamed in terror as he grasped for me, taking hold of my arm.

I lifted the bag above my head. "Let me go."

He released my hand, unwilling but trusting my intuition, and as I neared the spinning black hole dropped the bag into it. "You will join me, one day," resonated as the vortex snapped shut.

His physical body aborted, but his spirit never left the womb. They meshed, each containing separate memories. Timmy's bonded with the evil half, and Philmonia and her husband's abuse brought out the worst in the sweet half. The child filled with hatred and vengeance. It ate him up inside as his distaste grew. He stopped fighting and let the malevolent side take control. But what of Timmy and the evil twin's merged soul?

Epilogue

My fight wasn't over and people would know the truth. When Eilida came forward with her memories they shut the case on The Hurricane Killer, but it was far from over. She was the connection. The victim with a sixth sense, not as astute as my own, but present. It drove her to remembering what a two-year-old should never recall and a craving similar to my own to save the world from such malicious harm.

My DNA held indisputable proof that I was Evan's biological mother. It also held other secrets -- my brother's DNA entwined with mine. From birth, Evan was as much mine as Timmy's, and no doubt why they merged so seamlessly.

Penelope drew me up papers and I paid a visit to the O'Conners' lawyer, Mr. Fritz, who nearly had a heart attack. He'd known of my existence.

His actions were proof. Poppy Hills
and its full inheritance became solely
mine. I gave a small chunk to Tommy
for his assistance, because his
involvement made it happen, and a
larger chunk I put in trust for Erica, my
great niece, and final victim of The
Hurricane Killer.

Emily
Part 1
Denial

Chapter 1
Hay Fever

I watched the boys scamper over the gravel and stop at the end of the road. The bus would be here soon to pick them up and whisk them away to school. Erica leaned her head back as she sucked the last of the milk from her sippy cup.

Light filtered through the trees. The shrubs were in full bloom. Days like this always brought me back to my childhood in flashes of déjà vu. It wasn't so much something I saw in my mind's eye but a feeling of happiness, of everything right in the world.

I hiked Erica higher onto my hip as she was beginning to drop. At two years old she was getting too heavy for me to carry, but I did it anyways. It was the feeling of her warm, pudgy little body next to mine. We'd been through so much the months I was pregnant with her I had trouble letting her go now. She was also the youngest. One day they'd all be grown. I pushed those thoughts from my head. That was one day and today they were beautiful young children.

Spring also reminded me of hay fever. *Had I remembered to give Ethan his medicine?* I closed my eyes and ran through the morning's events and sighed relief when it came to me. Right after breakfast. He had the worst case of hay fever I'd ever seen and to make it through a school day in the spring he needed a dose, otherwise I'd have a call from the nurse.

Erica became so heavy I set her down and took her little hand. Together we walked inside the house. I sat on the sofa with my coffee. Erica climbed onto the couch next to me and grabbed a book from the small table beside her. She pushed the pages and pointed, curling her lips into words. "Fi," she smiled up at me with bright, inquisitive, blue eyes. Her tight blond curls needed a brush. "Fi" was her word for fish.

She flipped the next page and repeated the word. I reached for the book in her lap, *The Rainbow Fish,* and opened it to the first page. "Fi, fi, fi," she repeated as I read it.

I read her the story four times before I turned on the TV for her to watch Elmo. He was one of her favorites. "Momo" she called him. Her face lit up in glee and she danced around the room. This gave me time to clean up the breakfast mess in the kitchen.

The boys were getting better about putting their dishes in the sink but Erica had a few years before she could even reach it. Hard pieces of cereal and half a banana lay on the floor below her high chair. I watched my step and leaned over and grabbed the banana. After tossing it in the trash I swept up her mess.

The room grew dark. A single large cloud blotted out the sun but only for a moment as the light returned and spread across the floor. The phone rang, startling me from my thoughts. The caller ID displayed Eric's cell number. Without hesitation I grabbed it off the receiver.

Seldom did he call me. The last time was to tell me he'd been in an accident. Someone had rear-ended him. It wasn't fatal, but trepidation filled me up as I brought the receiver to my mouth. "Hi, honey".

Chapter 2

Mommy Time

rush of adrenaline pushed through my veins, followed by a sinking feeling in my gut. *Stop it Emily!* I chuckled at myself. If it was a true emergency and something bad happened to him he wouldn't be the one calling.

"Babe," excitement came through in his voice. Not the foreboding excitement but glee. "I just got a promotion!"

The sour feeling fell away and I was excited for him. "That's amazing!" He'd put in for the position but the competition was strong and we crossed our fingers he'd get it.

"Make yourself even more beautiful. I'll be home early and I'm taking the family to dinner tonight!"

It had been hard to shake the fear after the stalker. The mountains, fresh air, and trees helped. They offered serenity and a new start -- a blank slate-- but darkness had taken a resting seat inside me. Every so often it reared its head, but not today. This promotion meant Eric would get a sizable raise and we wouldn't have to pinch pennies so much.

I'd offered to go to work but he squashed it with the cost of daycare. We'd break even and it wasn't worth it. It wasn't that we were poor. The great price we got on the house was a big help but we had to buy a new car because Eric commuted further and the old clunker wouldn't make the drive for long. We paid more each month to get it paid off sooner but still owed several thousand.

I spread peanut butter over a slice of bread and squashed it over the strawberry jelly slice. It was one of Erica's favorite meals. I washed and refilled Erica's sippy cup then entered the living room. "Momo," she sang and danced. She tilted her head and stared at me. "Mommy, mommy, mommy." She grabbed onto my legs and held up her hands. My cue to pick her up.

"Are you hungry?"

She nodded as I lifted her into my arms and carried her into the kitchen. One of the features I loved best about the house. We had a scenic view of the mountain. This time of year, the trees and bushes were so dense I couldn't see my neighbors' homes. It felt as if we were in a world completely of our own.

Lost in the outside world, Erica brought me back to the reality when she chuckled at the squished piece of peanut butter and jelly sandwich she chucked on the floor. I wiped her face and changed her pants then put her down for a nap.

After cleaning the kitchen for the second time I ran a hot bath, poured a liberal amount of bubbles into it, then lit two fragrant candles. I peeked into Erica's room. Her little arms were wrapped around her pink blanket and her tiny chest rose and fell, confirming she was asleep.

I flipped the lights off in the bathroom and eased into the tub as my body adjusted to the temperature of the water. I pushed the button and allowed the jets to blast against my back and sides. The spa tub was my other favorite feature. With three children, I didn't use it as much as I'd like, but when I did I made it count.

I closed my eyes and allowed the bubbles and warmth to take me away. All the worries of daily life vanished and my mind thought of Eric. His soft lips against mine and the gentle caress of his hands over my breasts, tracing a line down my belly. His fingers travelling to my clit and fondling the knob. Desire coursed through me and my breathing became heavy. From the moment I met him I wanted him. It wasn't only my carnal desires and the leaps my libido went through while in his presence. It was all of him. His kindness, level-headedness, his sincerity and trustworthiness, and also his stubbornness and pride. It was everything about him. The whole package and I'd made the pledge to always be his.

I opened my eyes and gasped, bubbles spilled over the tub. I'd added too many bubbles and left the jets on as my mind escaped. I pushed the button off and sighed. I'd have to clean up the mess but wasn't shortening my bath over it. The water was still warm and enveloped me like a cocoon.

I lost track of time, place, and purpose until I heard Erica babble from her room. She would play in her crib for the next few minutes until she got loud, letting me know she wanted out. The scent of jasmine filled my nose and I sighed at leaving my warm, sudsy world. I pushed up and stepped out of the tub. Once I patted dry and smoothed lotion over my body I slipped into a comfortable sundress and dropped my towel onto the bubble mess around the tub.

Luckily the mess hadn't been as bad as it could have been. I tossed the towel into the washer and peeked into Erica's room. She giggled when she spotted my eyes then threw her pink blanket over hers, dropped it and hollered "Pee-boo." I chuckled and we continued the game for a few minutes until she spread her arms and said "Ou," indicating she was done and wanted out.

The doorbell rang. I wasn't expecting anyone and figured maybe it was my neighbor Eilida. We lived so far in the middle of nowhere a run to the store for eggs or sugar took thirty minutes so we'd often borrow from each other.

Erica tagged along beside me as I pulled the door open. A face I didn't recognize stared at me from the other side. His head as bald as a cue ball. His roundish face had a thick jaw and short forehead but his eyes... Something about them lingered at the edge of my brain. A small glint of recognition.

Chapter 3

Hanging

"**G**ood afternoon. I work for Nox Pharmaceuticals and we have free packages we're handing out. All it costs is allowing me to do a small demonstration." His lips turned upwards into a smile.

The thing about living in the country is we didn't have a homeowners association and got solicitors from time to time. Usually I didn't open the door. My mistake today. I hadn't even looked through the peep hole, expecting to see my neighbor.

I was ready to politely say "No, thank you" and shut the door, but I was curious. I'd never heard of any company selling drugs door to door.

That was odd. "I've never heard of drugs pedaled door to door?"

He smiled wider. "They're not prescription drugs in here." He held up a bag. "Allergy medications -- over the counter."

A little voice in my head reminded me of Ethan's allergies, maybe they had something that worked better than his current medication. The package they were handing out was free. It really wouldn't hurt anything to allow him in and I could always kick him out when he was done. There was no obligation to buy anything today. I relented. "My son has allergy problems. He's ten."

"Safe for children," he assured me.

"Alright, alright come in."

He didn't waste time showing me the products in his bag and giving me a sample kit that included a catalog. Sure enough, they did have allergy medication for children. I'd look into it further, maybe even ask the pediatrician before investing any money. I couldn't shake the strange feeling and glint of something in his eyes that reminded me of... something I couldn't remember. I shook the thought.

As he shuffled around his bag, straightening it out to zip it up, he praised the home, how beautiful it was then asked about our view. We didn't have company much. The occasional cook-out with friends and family but certainly not often enough. The scene from the deck was something I always enjoyed showing off so he hit a button and I decided it wouldn't do any harm. He'd been polite enough and hadn't tried to force a sale as so many others did.

Erica was busy with her toys that were covering the floor where she played. I brought him through the kitchen. I wrapped my hand around the door knob when he said, "Emily."

I'd introduced myself as Mrs. Turnwell and hadn't given him my first name. I was sure of that. *How did he know?* I slid my hand from the doorknob as his voice and my name echoed through my mind. *Had the stalker found me?* From the corner of my eye I spotted the rolling pin I'd left on the table this morning while putting the clean dishes away. I'd meant to put it away too but had forgotten it until now. I stepped backwards, figuring I could grab it, hit him over the head, grab Erica, and run to the neighbors. "Who are you?" I asked, doing my best to stay calm and not alert him.

He smiled, but not the friendly one he'd given me earlier. This time it was sadistic and black flashed across the blue of his eyes. It triggered a fear in me that I hid deep, deep inside. Terror I'd all but forgotten. Flashes of lightning and thunder, creaks in the hallway, and hiding in a dark spot filled with shadows.

"You remember, don't you?" His voice calm.

The perfect spring day became dark as recollection coiled in my brain. "I... I... don't know." It was bubbling in my head, rising to the surface of my consciousness.

"Sure you do." The flashes of black passed over his eyes like the clouds passed over the sun, obstructing its radiance. He moved closer to me and touched my arm, prickles chased up it and the overwhelming urge to vomit hit my stomach. My life rushed back to me. The darkness I'd all but forgotten. The evil that lurked in my earliest memories.

"I'm your brother. I spent years searching for you."

My brothers were kind, loving, protective. Not this man. He wasn't my brother. I didn't know who he was, but his words brought me horror. My gut clenched as I gripped the rolling pin. Bits and pieces of memory drifted across my mind; the police sirens screaming and a set of secure arms carrying me. My mind tried so hard, but I couldn't see a face. I swung the rolling pin at his head. He ducked and lunged forward, pushing me onto the table.

My head stung as it crashed against the thick wood. The rolling pin clattered to the floor.

"Mommy, mommy," came Erica's tiny voice and the pitter patter of her tiny feet.

My baby! I pushed against his bulk to free myself and save my child, but any effort was futile. His chest firmly pressed against mine. I was squashed between him and the table; neither would give.

"Go to your room!" His voice captured a memory that evaporated when a prick stung my neck. Blackness coated the world and my mind sunk into the past, searching for the clues.

Chapter 4

Oh Brothers!

My brother Ray slid his skateboard onto the driveway and coasted to a stop a couple feet from where I sat with my dolls, a ragged ball cap on his head. "Want a popsicle, Em?" he said, lifting his skate board effortlessly with one hand and propping it beside the house.

I nodded. "I want a red one." Cherry was always my favorite.

He ruffled my hair and took my hand as we entered the house. The foyer was a pale yellow, reminding me of warm spring days. Taking off his ball cap he set it on the foyer table and I followed him through the family room into the kitchen where I scrambled onto one of the spinning barstools.

He grabbed a box of popsicles out of the freezer and pulled out a red one, unwrapped it, and handed it to me.

"Thank you," I said and brought the cherry sweetness to my mouth.

Thumps pounded into the kitchen as Mike entered. He didn't do anything quietly. "Where's mine?" he asked, eying me licking on a popsicle.

Ray let out a breath. "You're ten. I don't need to get one for you. Do it yourself." He took a seat next to me and spun me around.

The room swirled around me and I barely saw Mike's eyes deflate as I spun to a stop.

"You always do stuff for her."

"She's four, Mike, get over it." He spun me again.

"Fine," Mike said and reluctantly stalked to the freezer.

The creak of the front door and my mother's voice sailed through the air, "We're home and could use some help, boys."

My chair spun to a stop and I hopped off. In dismay, Mike set his popsicle on the counter on the wrapper. "No one's going to make you put yours down," he said in an angry sing-song voice as he glared at me.

I ignored him and ran into the family room, grabbing hold of my father's leg with my vacant arm. "I love you, Daddy!"

Mike scowled as he walked past me; shivers ran over my spine. It wasn't that Mike ever hurt me. At times he was even my favorite brother as we played *Lego* and *Lincoln Logs* together. He even played *Strawberry Shortcake* with me when no one was watching.

I let go of my father's leg and bounded outside to join my brothers. "Leave something for me," I called, wanting to help.

"You're too small and you have popsicle all over your hands," said Mike as he tugged at a large brown suitcase.

"Who do you think you are *Stretch Armstrong*?" Ray chuckled as he glanced at Mike. "That bag is too big for you. I'll get it."

Ray went to grab the handle but Mike pulled hard enough he and the bag tumbled backwards. He managed to catch his balance and didn't hit the ground.

"Suit yourself," Ray shrugged and grabbed the smaller bag.

"What about me?" I questioned, meeting Ray's eyes and stuffing the popsicle stick into the front pocket of my shorts.

He rummaged in the back of the car for a minute. "You can get this." He handed me a manila envelope.

Happily, I grabbed it and skipped back into the house, tossed the stick in the trash, the envelope on the table, and bounded down the hall to my room.

When I got to my room I remembered I left my dolls in the kitchen. Filled with cheer I skipped down the hall and stopped when I heard my parents and Ray talking.

"He's getting worse. He's totally jealous of her," Ray said.

"He's ten and was the baby for several years. He's still adjusting," my mom said, her voice thoughtful.

475

"It's been over a year and he's not getting better."

My father cleared his throat. "Family is family. She's a little girl and needed us. We were the best match and she fits so well into the family."

She: were they talking about me? I knew I was adopted and I understood that meant I had another family but something happened to them. A couple years later I learned they'd died. I peered around the corner as if watching them would give me the answers. They stood in a semi-circle facing each other.

My mother, in her warm soothing voice, said, "I enjoy having a girl around the house. Being the only one for so long, it's refreshing." She paused for a moment. "Your brother just needs a little more time. Pay him a little more attention. You'll see."

"Yeah, OK. How's Daren?"

"He's settling in. We helped him unpack, paid his meal card and the rest of his tuition for the semester. I tell you, the price of a college education is an arm and a leg and then some," sighed my father.

Ray shuffled his feet like he did when he had something to say he knew Mom and Dad wouldn't agree with. "Don't worry about me. I'm not going to college. I'm going to intern with IBM and get a job with them."

My mother swished her mouth in annoyance. "That is very competitive. You think they'll want you without a college degree?"

Ray nodded. "You watch!" He turned on his heel and headed towards the hallway.

I scurried back to my room. I hadn't done anything wrong, but sure felt like I did.

Later that night in my room, the shadows danced in the corners. I pulled the covers over my face and scrunched my eyes. The footfalls moved through the hallway and the swirling vortex of sadness and pain swallowed me as I snugged into a ball.

The Evan's Girls Series is based on the children left behind after serial killer Evan O'Conner murdered their families. Each story is about one of his living victims – too young to identify him as a murderer. Too young to even remember their families. They are catapulted into lives that aren't forgiving and some find along the way that they have supernatural gifts.

Evan is a fictional character and serial killer found in The Ruthless Storm Trilogy.

Volume 1 - Eye of the Storm Eilida's Tragedy (Award winning title)

Volume 2 – The Calm Before the Storm Evan's Sins

Volume 3 – In the Midst of the Storm Tommy's Deception

These books can be found in paperback, ebook and audio. If you enjoy the Evan's Girl series the author suggests you read the trilogy too.

Prologue

Narrator

Above Eilida's head, the clouds streaked the sky in deep indigo and fuchsias as the sun began to set. In the distance they rumbled in disagreement, slinging squallish threats across the heavens. A mishmash of thoughts coursed through her brain. She thought of work and her boss, how he behaved as a dictator, in a way which was similar to Hitler or Napoleon. He was a small framed man and such as with other men his size, he threw his weight around, leaving her to ponder why all undersized men she knew conducted themselves in that fashion.

Most evenings, Eilida went for walks down the gravel road leading to and from her house. She paused for a moment to smell the honeysuckle growing wild along the roadside. Her mind bantered a concert of short dictators whose worlds unraveled a millennia ago. The wind rushed through the treetops whipping hair across her eyes, momentarily blindfolding her. She smoothed the strands of hair away from her face and looked to the sky. Eilida's train of thoughts shifted from short dictators, replaced by the pending storm cell of doom racing towards her. She

479

contemplated whether or not she had enough time to shower and meet her best friend and roommate, Sage, for their usual Friday night treat, Gino's for live music, beer, and sloppy pizza. Quickening her pace, she hurried home.

Eilida marched around the corner following the gravel road leading to her house. She was about five feet three inches with dark brown hair and a small frame. Her eyes were such a deep and dark blue they appeared black. Sage was a few inches taller with succulent long legs, strawberry blond hair which framed her delicate features, and built like a runway model.

At that very moment, a noise caught her attention. On instinct, she followed the disturbance with her eyes tilting her head towards the direction from which it came. She paused and listened for an instant before continuing her walk, half expecting a fox to be peering coyly through the shrubs or a squirrel or rabbit bounding through the brush. Living high up in the woods, she had grown used to creepy noises which most times were forest creatures. Her home loomed within feet of her; the door knob only a hand's width away.

Once more, she turned her head and focused her attention on the house across the street. For a fraction of a moment, she lingered before continuing inside. She closed and locked the door behind her sure that she was safe from unwanted peril. Gingerly sweeping the curtains aside, she peered through them where she observed the outline of someone walking through her neighbor's living room. She assumed it was nothing more than Mr. Turnwell and dismissed the shadowy figure. Upstairs, she took a shower allowing the warm water to wash off the rest of the stress from her day.

A collection of thoughts about her neighbor's home blasted through her brain. She couldn't place what was off, however, she knew something was different. A steady stream of consciousness cruised through her brain, looking for that one element which wasn't in its place. The cars were parked out front in their usual spots. The plants and lawn were manicured to perfection which she had always thought strange. High up in the mountains most people left their yards to the elements with the exception of keeping their grass mowed and planting bulbs in the spring but not the Turnwell's. Their yard looked like something from a home and garden magazine. Woods surrounded their abode on three sides, the fourth side a gravel road. Who would ever notice their house, except for Eilida, Sage, and the ultra-weird neighbors at the road's end?

Her meditation briefly switched focus to the ultra weirdos. She found them strange, and seriously lacking social skills. They never chirped a hello, or a half-cocked smile, and not once engaged in neighbor-like conversation. They spent an extensive amount of time yelling at each other, *damn stupid bitch-whore*, and her famous comeback *shit for balls asshole*. On occasion they threatened one another or other random creatures, and possessions in their back yard. Other days or nights their patch of Earth sounded like a war zone. The amount of bullets flying from their weapons were highly illegal; nevertheless this never stopped them and with their weirdness, Eilida was not about to say a word because she valued her life and feared they may shoot her and bury her remains deep in the woods where she would never be found. Or worse, leave her to the wolves!

Eilida stepped out of the shower and towel-patted her body, wrapping up her long, dark, wild mane which gave her the appearance of a naked swami. Using a hand towel, she wiped condensation off the mirror and leaned in to apply moisturizer to her face, richly lathering her body in lotion. As she lowered her head to swath her legs in creaminess a shadow passed behind her, although she never noticed as her mind was still focused on the Turnwell's and their perfect yard. She couldn't place her finger on it, but something was amiss, as it yanked and twisted at her guts. She thought the Turnwell's were the epitome of a happy family. They had three small children, two boys ages ten and seven, and a girl not old enough yet for school. They were cordial people, always ready to lend a helping hand. Out in the woods, she knew it was good to have neighbors like them, although she always thought they seemed more like suburban people. They claimed city life was too stressful; too many negative influences were around tempting their young down the wrong paths.

'We want to raise our children in a small town, where everybody knows everybody,' were Mrs. Turnwell's words. 'The woods are peaceful, like heaven in our own backyard,' was Mr. Turnwell's reasoning. Eilida had no children, but understood their sentiment as the children within the community couldn't get into much trouble because everybody knew everybody and many were related in some way.

Eilida finished polishing her hair and face, got dressed and grabbed for her purse. She habitually left her handbag in an exact location and when her hand came up empty, she panicked for a second, until her eyes zeroed in on the familiar fabric bag forming a lump on the sofa. Without giving thought to her purse's strange location, she tossed it over her shoulder as she headed out the door. Her mind was far more occupied with whether or not she would be able to get into town before the storm, as the darkening night sky was moving in at warp speed.

The night sky appeared starless, and thunder continued a forceful battle cry. Her deep sapphire eyes scanned the churning menace above her as she opened her car door. Mid movement her body froze like a deer scanning the forest for predators. Her eyes cemented on the Turnwells' residence. Inside her head the puzzle pieces began to fit, one matching up to the next, until her quandary over the house across the street finally came together. After a few split seconds, she quietly closed her car door with the keys still in her hand, and crept across the street. All the lights were off in the house but one, glowing dimly in the back.

Silently, she stole across the street, but instead of going to the front door, she put her ear up to the wall and listened. From somewhere buried inside her a primordial instinct welled up, which frightened her more than the storm brewing overhead. With her body close to the Turnwells' house and her chest facing out, she advanced to the back. Trembling sobs alternated with short, shallow breaths told her ears that a small child was wailing inside. Her eyes caught sight of a dim light shining from the door which had been left open a crack. As she slid along the wall of the house. The back deck steps unfolded in front of her. She cocked her head, glancing towards the window and slowly progressed up the steps without a creak, something like a cat stalking its prey. As she reached the final step, she melted along the wall until her head became flush against the door frame. Taking a deep and silent breath; her guts inside wrenching and twisting, she peered inside through the cracked door, gasping at the scene before her eyes. Eilida tore down the steps at warp speed, descending the tree stuffed mountain, while tears cascaded violently down her cheeks.

Thoughts raged through her brain, churning and contorting. Her legs charged down the mountain as if on auto-pilot. The horrific scene inside the house played like a broken record in her head. Tree branches tore at her clothes and scratched at her flesh as she dashed down the ridge. She barely felt them stinging as her mind was too consumed by the vivid spectacle she had witnessed inside the Turnwells' home. Bleeding gashes covered her arms, face, and legs. Gnarled tree branches grew arms, jutting into the path before her eyes. The rain began to pour across her forehead, leaving flowing rivulets washing away her tears and blood. Chunks of hair plastered against her face.

The solid earth had become bombarded with water rushing hard under her feet, causing her to slip in its wetness. Eilida reached her hand out for something to grab hold of but the trees curled in their disfigured appendages while her feet slipped further beneath; digging into the wet savage ground. Desperate mud covered hands penetrated the sludge groping for a large tree root. Her feet sank further into the ooze until they hit a large rock, sending Eilida flying, like an unwanted toy, down the ridge. Tree trunks and small rocks got their licks in bouncing her to and fro. The inertia of her body halted by a large boulder nestled beside the river, leaving her petite frame motionless against the flooding rains. A mess of blood curled and flowed from her head, leaving tributaries along her cheek. Shreds of fabric that used to be clothing clung to her bloody skin as the shadowy moonlight bathed her immobile and unconscious body.

www.ingramcontent.com/pod-product-compliance
Lightning Source LLC
Chambersburg PA
CBHW051204120726
47905CB00004B/975